CHOSEN OF GODS

Wolves of Autumn book one

CHOSEN of GODS

Nico Silver

WHITE RAVEN PRESS

Second Edition, 2024.
ISBN: 978-1-998212-29-3
This book was previously published as by Nicole Silver.

White Raven Press
North Cowichan, British Columbia, Canada

Cover design and digital alterations by Nik Sylvan
Model stock © Neo-Stock via www.neo-stock.com
Animal stock © Denis Pepin via Dreamstime.com
Background stock (moon) © Dary423 via Dreamstime.com
Background stock (forest) © Shukaylova Zinaida via Shutterstock.com
Fog brushes © Krist A via brusheezy.com
Title typefaces: Eva Antiqua Heavy by Spiece Graphics, and Snell Roundhand by Linotype

Content warning: This book contains material that is not suitable for all audiences. It is recommended for readers 18+. Some content that may be triggering for readers includes explicit sex, violence, and sexual violence.

For the old one-eyed bastard himself.

Chapter One

A WEREWOLF WALKS into an art gallery. Sounds like the set up for a real groaner of a joke, no? Well, there's groaning, all right, but not much of a joke.

I'm supposed to be re-hanging the gallery, but instead I'm trying to decide how to frame the latest painting I took on consignment when a guy walks in with a portfolio under his arm, and I have to work *really* hard not to stare.

Because I gotta tell you, this dude is worth looking at. Tall, seriously built, strong jaw, killer cheekbones, and dark hair that should look unkempt but instead looks like he just rolled out of bed after giving you the fuck of your life. Every movement is relaxed but efficient, sending his muscles sliding under his skin and my libido soaring.

He looks at me and smiles, and fuck me, he's got a dimple in his cheek. And deep brown eyes I could stare into all day.

"Hello!" I say, putting on my helpful gallery owner voice. *Do not drool, Raine*, I tell myself.

"Hey," he says. "I'm told you're the best framing shop in town." His voice is deep and smoky, like really, really expensive whiskey, and makes me shiver like whiskey does, too. I mean, I don't actually, physically shiver, but I feel that voice from the top of my head and the tips of my toes right to my crotch.

"We do our best," I say, walking over to the design table and patting its top. "Let's see what you've brought me."

"Okay, but don't laugh," he says, but he's grinning, and shit, he's got *two* dimples. He opens the portfolio and pulls out a canvas board, lays it on the table, bottom towards me. Automatically, I spin it around, so the bottom faces him to make it easier for him to choose a frame. I'm used to looking at art upside-down. And then I *do* look at it.

And I barely manage not to laugh. "I never laugh at anyone's art," I say. I think I manage to get it out with a straight face and an even voice.

"At least not to their face," he says, which is of course exactly what I was thinking, and I can hear the amusement in his voice. I glance up, and his eyes are crinkling at the corners.

Fuck. I love a guy who smiles with his eyes as much as his mouth. And speaking of mouths, this guy's got a wide one, built for grinning. And kissing. And other things.

So the painting he's deposited on my design table is a wolf. A howling wolf against a full moon. Painted with an airbrush. It's one of the tackiest things I've ever seen. It *might* be tackier if it was painted on black velvet.

"So," I say. "Any thoughts on how you want to frame this? Black? Bright colors? Fancy? Plain?"

"Completely over the fucking top," he says. Then, "Sorry. I spend too much time on construction sites."

Okay, construction worker. Not exactly intellectual or artistic. But a good honest job. Pays well. Not that I'm interested in anything long-term. Or even medium-term. I like to take home strays, give them something good to eat, and send them on their way. I sneak a look at his hands, and they're clean. No dirt under the fingernails is a good sign. Or maybe it's a sign he's got someone to keep them clean *for*. His hands are also calloused and muscular. Clever-looking, if a bit hairy-knuckled.

"No shit," I say, and he laughs. "I went to art school and dated a chef. I can handle swearing." I lean on the table and contemplate the painting. "If you want over the top, I'd start with a linen liner. No. Black silk. And an ornate gilded frame. But maybe silver rather than gold, because of all the cool tones in the painting."

"I like the sound of that." I look at his face again and he still looks like he's trying to hold back laughter.

"Is it for a gift, or for yourself?" I say, reaching for a sample of the fanciest silver-gilt frame we carry, and grabbing a wide silk-covered liner and arranging them on one corner of the painting.

"It's for a joke," he says.

I raise my eyebrows. "Custom framing is expensive," I say. "Might be a bit pricey for a joke."

"It's been a while since I had something framed, but I have an idea," he says. "And when my girlfriend sees this, the look on her face is going to be worth whatever it costs."

"Ah, gift for the girlfriend." Damn. I try not to let my disappointment show. But they do say all the hot ones are taken. Or is that all the good ones are taken, and the hot ones are assholes? I always get those mixed up.

"She thinks I have terrible taste in art," he says. "That I actually, unironically love the airbrush howling wolf shit."

"But you don't." This guy seems nice, too. Even if he was single, he probably wouldn't act like a dog, which is kind of what you need when you want to take a guy home for a good lay and nothing more.

"I think it's amusing. Crap, but amusing. I got a buddy who pinstripes and airbrushes cars to paint this for me. He's going to hang it in his shop once the joke's over."

Then he glances up at movement outside the window. "Hang on," he says. "I parked in a fifteen and a spot out front just opened up. I'll be right back."

I watch him walk to the door, and holy hell, that ass! Firm and muscular and his jeans fit so perfectly I can imagine what his butt looks like naked. I fan myself with the stack of work orders.

My colleague Katie pops her head out of the back room. I wondered how long it would take for her to react to the sexy as fuck male voice and make an appearance. She whistles, low and long, after the door closes. "Tell me he has a brother," she says.

"He has a girlfriend, but I'll report back on the sibling situation."

"Excellent," she says, and vanishes again.

I look back to the window and an absolutely pristine Chevy C-10 pickup, blue with white roof, gotta be a 1970, pulls up at the curb. I can feel the rumble of the big engine more than I can hear it. And smokin' hot airbrush wolf dude gets out and heads back into the store. Even his fucking ride is hot.

"So, you found a nice woman who'll put up with your idea of a great joke, hunh, cowboy?" I say, and immediately bite my tongue. It's a good thing I'm half-owner of this place, or I'd have been fired a long time ago for being cheeky. Thirty-seven and still as mouthy as when I was seventeen.

But he smiles and his face goes soft, by which I can tell he's completely in love with her, whomever the lucky woman is. Okay, for real no chance with this morsel. Damn.

"She's a saint," he says. "And a goddess." Then he opens the portfolio and pulls out another piece. As the sun through the window hits it from behind, I recognize the watermark on the paper. Top quality, and very expensive, watercolor paper. "This is what I'm really going to hang on the wall, after she sees the wolf."

He hesitates, then puts the paper on the table, over the hideous airbrushed piece. He handles it by the edges, like he knows his way around art on paper. So okay, maybe I misjudged him. Big, muscley construction guy doesn't necessarily mean unrefined, right?

I lean over and look at the paper, and then I have to turn it to face me so I can *really* look at it.

"Wow," I say. It's a watercolor, rich, but restrained. Whoever did this knows how to handle a brush, knows when to add a hint of darker outline to bring out a shape, and when to let the white of the paper do the work. "Let me guess," I say. "Your girlfriend?" It's a stunning portrait of a woman with a fox. She's fucking gorgeous but shown in a way that looks like she's unaware of being observed. Her river of black hair – painted without even a touch of black paint – swirls around the paper, and her eyes are the same amber as those of the fox.

"Yeah," he says. I glance up and I swear he's blushing under his day or two's worth of facial scruff.

"This might sound weird, seeing as it's a painting of your girlfriend, but who's the artist? I'd love to get a print. Maybe carry their work in the gallery."

"Oh," he says. "It's mine."

"Your work?"

"Yeah."

"Fuck me," I say (see, mouthy). "You're really good."

He's staring at the painting, but he looks up at me, surprise in his wide – fucking gorgeous – brown eyes. "Thanks," he says.

"You ever want to have a show, let me know. We're always looking for new artists."

"I mostly draw comics," he says.

"No shit."

He shrugs. "I was thinking about putting them up online, maybe crowdfund to print a paperback."

So we do a design for the beautiful watercolor – just as extravagant as the wolf, but it looks elegant instead of overdone – and when I give him the quote he doesn't even flinch, and this is one of the highest-priced jobs I've done in a while.

I write his name and number on the work order. "Magne Thorvaldson. Very Scandinavian."

"Norwegian," he says. "My dad and my brothers were born in Norway."

"You have brothers?" I can't help the note of interest that creeps into my voice. In fact, I might even encourage it.

"I'd offer to introduce you," he says, "but they're both assholes."

"Don't all brothers say that about each other?"

He shrugs.

"Older or younger?" I ask and a smirk tugs up one corner of his mouth.

"Older," he says. "But really, total dogs, both of them."

"I like dogs." I look him right in the eye as I say it, and one of his eyebrows quirks up. And "older" is the right answer, because he looks thirty, maybe thirty-five, which is on the young side for my current tastes.

"Who's a dog?" That's Katie again. I'm surprised she stayed out back as long as she did, with Mr Sexy Voice out here. As usual, she's dressed to the hilt in the perfect retro outfit: fifties-style red-dyed hair, makeup, dress, shoes, and all. Even her pointy bra is period appropriate. I don't miss the appreciative look Magne gives her, but I also don't miss that there's not a trace of lust in it.

Katie makes me feel underdressed in my comfy linen trousers and flowy top, with my dark hair gathered into a simple bun at the nape of my neck. She turns heads everywhere, and to tell the truth, we bonded over drinks and tales of past conquests before we ever realized we both loved art and dreamed of opening a gallery. We even sometimes make bets on who gets a particular tasty specimen of manhood into bed first. We enable each other, is what I'm saying, which is great for our friendship, but maybe not so good for the condition of the hearts of the kinder men we've collected.

Unlucky for her, another customer comes in before she gets her answer, and she has to go be helpful instead of flirting with Mr Tall, Dark, and Taken.

"Your brothers like art, too?" I ask.

"Not that I'm aware of."

"Are they as… tall as you?" I say, 'cause he's gotta be well over six feet and my five-foot-four ass has to look way up to meet his eyes. Not that I've ever shied away from climbing a tall man.

"Thors is taller," he says. "Bjarni is… not."

"Taller?" I say, looking him up and down. It hardly seems possible.

"Taller."

"And how tall is not?"

"Only five eleven."

"That's not so short."

"Not according to Bjarni, whose baby brother bests him by five inches."

"And how much taller is taller?"

"Six ten." He seems very amused by my questioning, and leans one hip against the counter, like he figures I'm going to keep him there a while.

"Holy fuck."

"He's also very… burly."

"Is that a euphemism for fat? 'Cause that's not a deal breaker." I mean, if he's half as good looking as this specimen, I don't care. I'm an equal-opportunity slut.

"No, it's a euphemism for muscles on top of muscles."

"More than you?"

His mouth twitches and a dimple appears then vanishes. "More. But really, my brothers are assholes."

"Irredeemable assholes?"

"There might be hope for Thors. Bjarni's been a dick for a very long time, and I don't think he plans to change. I'm pretty sure he *likes* being an asshole."

"So can I get his number?"

"Bjarni?"

"The other one. Thors?"

"Thorstein," he says, and frowns. Something soft and pained crosses his face and is gone. "He's had some pretty bad mental health issues." Regret, that's what I'm seeing.

"Still," I say. "Not necessarily a dealbreaker. What kind of issues? And does he look anything like you?" I'm trying not to come right out and tell this guy he's hot right to his face. Maybe he already knows. But he strikes me as a guy who's comfortable in his body, in his own skin, who likes his physical self but really isn't concerned with what other people think. And that's just extra hot, you know?

"There's a family resemblance," Magne says. "Thors is taller, bigger, blonder, and has no interest in much other than taking over the family farm from my parents."

"Farmboy, hey?" I say. "I like animals."

"Bjarni is shorter, not quite as blond, and has similar ambitions, except for the part that's actually hard work."

I shrug. "I wasn't thinking of proposing marriage. But honestly, this Bjarni sounds like Katie's type. She likes assholes." I point my chin to where my colleague is showing an older lady the selection of signed reproductions we just started carrying. And it's true. You fuck an asshole, you don't have to worry about him hanging around too long after.

"And you like dogs," he says, his lips curving. Understanding has crossed his face, that I'm only interested in a good time. Then he shrugs and pulls out his phone. "I'll text them, but I can't guarantee a response. We don't get along."

He doesn't hide the screen as he types, and I see the message before he sends it.

Hey asshole. Excellent Framing on Station Street has a couple of very lovely women who are for some inexplicable reason interested in meeting my brothers. Try not to be a dick.

Texts in full sentences. With big words. And checks to make sure everything is spelled correctly before sending. A bit weird, but okay.

His phone buzzes and he glances at the screen and then turns it so I can see better.

fuck u shitstain, it says. I'm pretty sure I can guess which brother sent it.

"Thanks for trying," I say as I ring up his deposit.

"Bjarni's too curious for his own good," he says. "He'll be here. And Thors might just come along to keep an eye on him."

I hand him my card and give him a wink as he leaves. I can't resist saying, "If you ever decide to leave your gorgeous girlfriend, look me up."

"Not gonna happen," he says, and his grin has a lot of teeth in it. "But I appreciate the sentiment."

I hope he's right and his brothers do show, because if I can't have that one, I want one like him.

Chapter Two

A FEW DAYS LATER, and I'm chatting up a silver-fox type with serious DILF energy when the door chimes and Katie emerges from the back, so I don't have to leave off flirting.

I almost ditch the fox immediately when I notice what's walked through my door, but I manage to sell him a small original painting and see him on his way politely before making my way over to Katie and Magne's two brothers.

'Cause fucking hell, there's no way they could be anyone else. Katie's leaning in close to talk to the shorter one, who still towers over her five-feet-in-heels stature. He looks an awful lot like his younger brother, right down to the dimples, but he's got a swaggery way of standing that shouts cocky. As I thought, just Katie's type.

The oldest brother, the huge one – and Magne was not exaggerating his size – hangs back. His hands are stuffed in the front pockets of his jeans like he's afraid to touch anything and he keeps his eyes down like he might break something just by looking at it.

"Come on Thorstein," his brother says. "Don't be rude. I have it on good authority our little bro's already charmed the pants off these lovely ladies."

"For fuck's sake Bjarni," the tall one growls. "Have some goddamn tact." His voice might be even deeper than Magne's and even more rumbly. I swear it vibrates my lady parts and I suddenly feel damp.

Bjarni looks right at me, like he knows what I'm thinking, and smirks. I ignore him as I hold my hand out to Thorstein. "I'm Raine," I say.

He looks at my hand – startled or nervous – and finally takes it in his. His grip is surprisingly gentle and the fair skin of his cheeks, freckled but not tanned by the summer sun – shows a flush of pink. He doesn't have dimples that I can see, but a grown man blushing has an appeal all its own.

"Thorstein," he says. "I'm sorry. I didn't know that's why Bjarni wanted to come here. I actually thought he might be finally taking an interest in something cultural."

I give him a grin and a wink. "Well, he's taken an interest in something, anyway."

He glances at Bjarni, who leans close to Katie. He probably sees his brother coming on way too strong to an attractive woman. I see Katie reeling in a hottie, hook, line, and sinker. It's actually an advantage, to her way of thinking, that he's only interested in fucking her. Because that's all she wants from him. It's so much easier without feelings involved.

I link my arm with Thorstein's and lead him farther into the gallery. "Well, I might as well give you the tour while they drool all over each other."

He looks down at me – way down – in surprise. "She doesn't mind?"

I lean close and say conspiratorially, "Katie's a big fucking slut. And I say that with deep affection. She knows what she wants, and she usually gets it."

"Oh," he says. Not a big talker, but that's okay; I talk enough for two people. Maybe three.

I take him around the gallery, showing him my favorite pieces, and he seems to relax a bit, even to move more easily. He's got the same grace Magne has, completely in control of his body, efficient and easy. Once he's let go of the self-consciousness that makes him stoop a little, like he's trying to make himself smaller, to disappear. When he first came in he was as nervous and awkward as a teenager after a growth spurt.

Shy men are sexy, but I think Thorstein's got some serious social anxiety and I feel myself wanting very badly to make him more at ease.

And the more he realizes he's not expected to say anything to my running commentary, the more he relaxes, until I stop to show him a large-scale painting of farm animals.

"This artist does a lot of custom animal portraits," I say. "And she's got a wry sense of humor."

He bends to read the label. "The Gang's All Here," he reads, then steps back to contemplate the piece. I watch his face. It's a skillfully-painted realistic piece of a truly odd assortment of animals, including a highland cow, a llama, and an ostrich, wearing black leather biker jackets and standing around a manger full of hay. He snorts, and smiles, a grin growing on his lips.

"Thank you," he says, when we finally make it back to the front of the gallery and I stop talking. "I don't know a lot about art, but that was… very enjoyable." I think I can just detect an accent in his voice, traces in the way he pronounces some words, and I remember Magne saying his brothers were born in Norway. It makes me want to listen to him talk more. With that voice he could read me the dictionary all day and I'd be happy. Shit, he could probably make me come just by talking.

"Anytime you want to hear me yammering about painting, feel free to stop by." I snag one of my business cards on the way past the till, scribble my cell number on the back and hand it to him. "And maybe we can get some coffee sometime."

"Yeah," says Bjarni, suddenly appearing next to his brother. I didn't even hear him coming, and the floors of this old building creak more than an old man's knees. "You can double-date with me and Katie." Bjarni smacks his brother on the shoulder and Thorstein grimaces in distaste.

As they leave the gallery, Thorstein slides my business card into the back pocket of his jeans. And of course I notice the ass filling out said jeans. Jesus fuck on a popsicle stick, that is one fine butt.

"Guess who's getting laid tomorrow!" says Katie once they're gone.

As if I had any doubt. "Heartbreaker," I say.

"That's the advantage of the selfish ones," she says. "They have no hearts to break."

I laugh. She has a point. The problem for me is, I'm pretty sure Thorstein *does* have a heart, and while I've enjoyed a good heartbreaking now and then, I really don't think I want to break his. Of course, he might not even text me, in which case I have nothing to worry about save an empty bed.

Also of course, my phone vibrates in my pocket just as I'm thinking those dismal thoughts. Text from one Thorstein Thorvaldson. Of course, I knew that was probably his last name, since that's the name Magne gave me for his framing order. But fuck, did his parents like the name "Thor." Maybe they're Norse pagans. I mean long hair with braids in would fit the type, no?

Coffee tmrw eve? it says. I wonder how long I should leave him hanging before I answer. I'm seriously starting to think I'm losing my heartless bitch cred because I don't even wait five minutes.

What time & where?

He's slower to answer. Second thoughts? But no. *8 @ river cafe?*

I want to text, "Fuck yeah," but settle for a thumbs up. Then I delete that before I send and type, *see you then.*

He sends back a thumbs up.

When I get to the cafe, Thorstein is waiting, pointedly ignoring his brother and Katie sitting obnoxiously close together at an outdoor table. We get our coffees to go and I wiggle my fingers at Katie as I pass and she waggles her tongue in response. Bjarni has his face buried in her neck and doesn't even see us.

I'm usually pretty careful about who I go places alone with, unlike Katie who'll go home with a guy immediately if he's hot enough, and Magne's comment about his brother's mental issues niggles at the back of my brain. But there are still lots of people strolling, and it's summer, so it's not even dark yet.

We walk without talking and Thorstein is tense, like he's worried he's going to have to come up with something to say. Like he's afraid he'll open his mouth to speak, and nothing will come out. And I totally get it. I have social anxiety, too, though you'd probably never guess it now.

There was a time when I'd be standing there with someone, trying to make conversation, and I'd get so nervous I'd just freeze. Inside, my brain would be screaming at me to say something, anything. Like even something really stupid would be better than saying nothing. But even knowing that, no words would come out. So I'm pretty sure I know what he's feeling.

Of course, for me, I found out pretty quickly that guys don't care about you talking if you've got your hand down their pants or your tongue in their mouth. Hell, even if you just look good and never touch them, they don't notice you not talking. And somehow that freed me up. A lot. And I've hardly shut up since. I mean, there are times when it all comes back, like big social gatherings and high-stress meetings. Or talking on the phone. And that's why I prefer texting.

Anyway, I walk quietly tonight, watching the people we pass by, and just trying not to seem expectant, like I'm just enjoying Thorstein's company with no need for words. I think it's the fact that it's actually completely true that makes it work. He gradually loses the tension that was making him awkward and then he's just a big, gorgeous man strolling next to me instead of a tight-strung bundle of anxiety.

I could get used to this, that's for damn sure.

We pause on the dock to watch the Wonder Island ferry unload and take on more passengers. Thorstein stares out across the water towards the huge, brightly-lit Ferris wheel and leans on the railing.

He's cute when he's nervous, but in this relaxed state, like he's forgotten he's not alone and is as comfortable in his own skin as I've seen few people be, he's so fucking sexy I could scream.

I watch him, how the light breeze picks at strands of his long hair, so blond it looks silver in the fading daylight. It's down to his shoulders and interspersed with thin braids, like a Viking. His beard is short, closely trimmed, and looks good on him. I mean, not all guys can pull off a beard. His eyes are blue, with a touch of green, instead of dark like Magne's. They're like clear glass or a semi-precious stone. And yeah, that's a big fucking cliché, but I calls 'em like I sees 'em.

He's very masculine, all hard surfaces, and right now I wish I knew him better so I could touch him.

"I fucking hate that place," he says, and I'm startled by the vehemence in his voice.

"I admit it's pretty tacky," I say. "Not so sure I'd go as far as hate, though."

He glances at me, like he really *had* forgotten I was here. "It took… something important from me."

Okay, that's cryptic, but whatever. I can deal with cryptic. I'm starting to think I might like to spend time – a lot of time – unravelling this guy's mysteries. And fuck if that's not a change from my usual use 'em and lose 'em strategy. Me and Katie are alike that way – bonding over conquests, remember? I must be getting old.

But there's just something compelling about Thorstein, and maybe something a little broken. When Magne mentioned mental health, was he just talking about Thorstein's social anxiety, or is it something more? 'Cause I haven't seen anything too concerning yet. Or anything that would cause me think he's an asshole.

I lean against the rail next to him, move close enough that our arms touch, and I can feel the heat of him through two layers of cotton sleeve. He looks down at me and I see something in his expression – longing, maybe – and damn I wish I was bold enough to kiss him.

And why aren't I? Pretty much every guy I ever went on a date with had his tongue in my mouth by now, and usually at my instigation.

He looks out over the water again, and the setting sun catches him, making him look younger, and then as it shifts, older. He looks like he could be anything from thirty-five to fifty. I mean, that's a range I'm entirely comfortable with, but I *am* curious. But I can't ask, not yet. I don't want to do anything to make him anxious again.

He doesn't lean away from my arm pressing against his, which is a good sign. In fact, he glances back at me again, and looks at me for a long time before smiling.

I smile back.

"Why did you ask me out?" he finally says. That's not a question I was expecting.

I want to blurt out, "Do you *own* a mirror?" but I bite back the urge. Instead, I say, "I enjoyed talking to you at the gallery."

He looks away. "I'm not much of a conversationalist."

"I did say 'talking *to* you'."

He looks back at me, startled, but I smile, and his smile slowly grows in return. And *there's* a dimple. Oh god, it looks even better on him than either of his brothers. "Thank you," he says, softly. "I'm not at ease around people. It's nice…" He hesitates, flexes his fingers on the railing. His hands are large and muscular, calloused. I want to know what they feel like touching me.

"It's nice to meet someone I can feel comfortable with," he says.

And fuck, that just makes me want to kiss him even more. Instead, I lean my head against his arm. "I'm glad you feel comfortable with me."

We spend a long time just standing that way, and by the time we head back the way we came, it's full dark and there are fewer people around. But it's okay. Thorstein makes me feel safe. Who's going to fuck with a heavily-muscled six-foot-ten Viking?

Three whip-thin white guys in dark hoodies with knives, as it turns out.

"Hey, Fabio," says one. "Let's see what you got in your pockets."

Fabio? Really? Does anyone under forty even know who that is anymore? And why is it always white guys in hoodies jumping people in the street? I mean, I'm pale enough and not-rez-enough I can pass for white, except when folks are looking for a "Native" girl to put their imaginary ideas on, but here in Riverbend the drug dealers, the muggers, the slash-and-grab thieves, always seem to be skinny white guys in hoodies. Usually carrying backpacks and riding Frankensteined bicycles and carrying parts of other bikes with them.

Thorstein pulls me behind him, puts himself between me and them. And growls. Like he doesn't say anything at all, just growls. And it's fucking scary, but the skinny dudes are too dumb or too high to notice.

"Come on Pocahontas," says one of the other guys, trying to circle Thors to see me better. Why is it always Pocahontas? Like don't they know any other Indigenous famous people? "Spread your legs for me and maybe I won't rob you. I won't even hurt you."

"Leave her alone," Thorstein says, his voice so deep in his chest it seems to echo. And I swear he looks bigger than he did a moment ago, scarier, and I'm only seeing him from behind.

He doesn't seem to be afraid, but I can see a dark stain of sweat between his shoulder blades, see the tension quivering in his muscles, and I wonder. Sometimes the big guys are the biggest scaredy cats of all.

One guy tries circling around the other way, then the first flicks his arm out casually, and I can't see what's happening, but I hear Thorstein's sharp inhale and the skinny guy's laughter.

"Empty your pockets, meathead, or I'll keep cutting you till you cry like a baby."

And that's when everything *really* goes to shit.

Another of the guys says, "I'll deal with him," and darts towards Thorstein with his knife and then he's flung backwards, crashing to the street, and Thorstein seems to have hardly moved. And the guy screams, and runs, and the other two follow.

And then Thorstein turns around and he's… how do I say this without sounding bugfuck crazy? He's a monster. All big teeth and wolf muzzle and his hands don't look right – does he have claws? He looks like he's in pain, and it's not just physical pain. There's a different sort of agony in his eyes. Then they catch the light of a streetlamp and flare orange.

"Run," he says. "Please, Raine, go."

And I stupidly stand there, staring. Fuck of a way to find out monsters are real, by watching your date, who you were starting to like in a way you haven't liked any guy since, well, ever, turn into a … whatever the hell he is.

"Run," he says again, and this time it comes out as a roar, and my feet finally obey even if my brain is lagging behind, and I flee. And naturally I violate every shred of common sense, every yelled warning at the movie screen, and head into the woods along the river instead of running for the city and lights and people. *Human* people.

Chapter Three

IT'S HARD ENOUGH to run in the woods during the day – and I should know, since I grew up in the River District and spent a large part of my childhood running in the woods to evade my cousins. Running in the woods at night is pretty much impossible. But I give it a good try and almost make it to the riverbank before something I didn't even hear coming hits me from behind and I'm flat on the ground with a hot weight on top of me. All hard muscles and body hair and deep, deep growling.

He holds me pinned down on my belly and I don't even try to move. And absurdly, what I'm thinking is that I'd like to do something very unpleasant to those three asswipes who turned my shy, sexy date into a drooling monster.

Then the weight lifts and I scramble to roll over. He looms above me, arms braced on either side of me, shaggy head hanging so his hair brushes my neck. I can't see his face.

His shirt is gone and I see how his shoulder muscles strain, not to hold him up, but like he's fighting against something. Like he's fighting himself.

"Thors?" I say.

He lifts his head slightly, but not quite enough for me to see his face.

"Only my baby brother ever called me Thors," he says. His voice sounds forced, painful, and it's more than half growl.

"You mean Magne?"

He snarls and I cringe. His breath comes out in gasps.

"He said you were having mental health issues," I say. I know if I move, he can catch me again, easily, but I've talked my way out of more than one bad situation. I bite my lip, then slowly lift my arms, put a hand on each side of Thorstein's face. I can feel the new shape of it, a muzzle almost, with teeth too big, too sharp.

He's a fucking werewolf. Well, at least I know what I'm dealing with. "No," he says, but he doesn't try to shake off my hands.

I lift his head and he lets me, until I can see his face. I brush his hair out of the way, and I can't help but notice the fineness of the strands, how soft they are under my fingers. I see the b-movie werewolf muzzle, but his blue-green eyes are just as clear as always, but tormented.

"I've been a werewolf since I was sixteen," he says, words slurred around his big teeth.

"But that's not a problem?"

He snorts. I think it might be a laugh. Good sign. Maybe. I stroke one side of his face and he closes his eyes. His breathing is not loud, but it doesn't sound right. It's shallow and gasping, hectic.

"Do you know what a *berserkr* is?" he says.

"That's like Viking warriors. They thought they could turn into wolves or bears when they went to battle."

"They were screaming madmen," he says. "It's worse when you're a werewolf, as it turns out. And worse yet when the moon is full."

Is the moon full tonight? I was too busy checking out my date's ass to look at the sky.

"That's what you are? A berserker?"

He doesn't answer. When he opens his eyes, I don't see Thorstein, I see madness and it's terrifying. But, and call me crazy if you like, it also makes me understand him better. Empathize.

"You're afraid you're going to hurt me."

He blinks, and I see recognition again, I see Thorstein again. "I *will* hurt you," he says, and then for a moment he seems to be gone once more, leaving only something primal and hungry behind.

"Thors," I say, softly, and stroke his face again. He leans into my touch. "You're not going to hurt me." I can't know this, of course. Fuck, I've only met the man twice. But I have to believe it to be true. I *want* to believe it.

"I always do," he says. "Being a wolf should be wonderful, joyous. Hunting with your family, sharing food and warmth. Running under the moon or in the darkness of the woods."

"That sounds lovely."

"Not for me," he says. "Not for me!" And he roars the words like he roared "Run!" and I scramble backwards away from him until I hit a tree and then he's over me again, arms on each side of me, snarling in my face, inches from my nose. And I should be terrified.

"I'm so sorry, Thors," I say.

"I almost killed my brother when I was like this. I *loved* him, and I almost killed him. He should have died, but he was stronger than anyone thought."

"But you didn't kill him," I say. "He just thinks you're an asshole."

That startles him into looking at me. And fuck if I can't see the sizzling hot man behind his eyes. I touch his face again.

"I don't want to hurt you," he says.

I trace the shape of his eyebrow, his cheekbone, follow the line of his muzzle. He closes his eyes, breathes in short, sharp breaths, panting, but not from exertion.

"You're not going to hurt me," I whisper, like if I say it enough times, it will be true. I run my finger along his jaw, trace his lips where they stretch over his teeth.

He moans softly.

"Thors," I say.

"Raine." His voice is almost normal, his huge teeth retracted, not all the way, but enough to make him look a little more human.

"Look at me," I say.

He opens his eyes. "I'm a monster," he says.

I slide both hands into his hair, around his neck, and pull myself up closer to him. His eyes widen in surprise, and then I kiss him.

Kissing a werewolf is not very much like kissing a human guy. Except it is, in all the important ways. His teeth get in the way, his mouth is too big, his lips stretched too thin, but somehow it doesn't matter.

When I relax my arms and lower myself back to the ground, he stares at me.

"Don't," he says softly.

"Why not?" I run my hands over his shoulders, feel the wolf-hair I hadn't noticed before, and wonder how it would feel against my naked skin.

He shivers. "I'm a monster."

"Maybe I like monsters." Hell, flirting and subtle touching has gotten me out of sketchy situations before.

He looks startled again.

I trail my fingers over his chest – oh fuck, those pecs! I want to run my tongue where my fingers are exploring, especially the fine tracery of scars that covers his skin, but I don't dare. His belly is firm and sculpted and … nope, he's not wearing his jeans anymore. I grab his perfect ass and try to pull him closer.

"Raine…" His face is tormented. "I'm barely in control. If you… I can't."

I don't know if getting him aroused will make the situation better or worse, but I've stopped caring. I slide my hand down to his crotch, and oh look, he's already aroused. I curl my fingers around him, stroke him, and he holds very still.

"Oh gods," he says, and I absently note the plural. "Please don't."

I touch his face with my other hand, make him look into my eyes. "Tell me to stop, and I'll stop. No questions."

He doesn't say anything, just pants, loud and harsh.

"Do you want me to stop?"

"No." His voice is so quiet I can hardly hear him.

"Do you want me?" *My* voice has gone rough, and it's not from fear. Not anymore.

"Yes, Raine, I want you."

"Say it again."

"I want you." He says it like it hurts, but he dips his head and kisses me so hard my head presses into tree bark, dirt forest floor, and I don't care.

"I want you, Thorstein."

He groans, shifts his weight over me, and I realize his legs have gained an extra joint or changed proportions or something somewhere along the line, that lets him crouch over me. I pull him closer.

"If I lose control, I'll hurt you, or worse. I *am* a monster," he says.

"Then I'm a monster fucker," I say, and kiss him again.

He pulls away, but it's not to protest again, it's to bury his face in my neck, to shift his weight again so he can touch me with one hand, stroke my skin under my t-shirt. He tries to pull it out of the way, and it tears, and I'm glad I'm not wearing a bra.

His mouth is hot on my skin, his tongue burning against my nipple, my belly. He hikes up my skirt, pulls my underwear off in strips of fabric, and buries his head between my legs. My moans when I climax are at least as loud as his roar was, and I'm glad now that I ran the wrong way, stupidly into the woods.

He crawls back up my body to loom over me again and his eyes are burning. I reach down, find his hardness, make him groan.

Then I reach my other hand for the waistband of my skirt where I have a hidden pocket, fumble the button open, and get out a condom. Like, shit, I'm about to bone a monster, but I'm not *stupid*.

When I open the package, he looks at me, brow furrowed, and holds up one hand – which is tipped in a set of impressive claws.

"I don't think I can manage that," he says.

I just smile, reach down, and roll it onto him. And then I wrap my legs around him and pull him to me, into me. And I don't know if werewolf dicks are shaped differently – I mean it didn't feel different in my hand – but he feels so good inside me I think I might come again.

He grunts and thrusts, gasps and does it again, and again. He's not gentle, but I don't want gentle. I want him to fuck me. His yell when he finishes is almost a howl and it sends shivers up and down my skin.

Then he goes still, stares at me, touches my face with a claw that retracts and leaves an ordinary human fingernail, an ordinary human finger. He pulls me close, but I wriggle and say, "I'm not done yet."

He lifts his face from where he nestled it against my shoulder and says, "Again?"

"Again." And I guide his hand down my body. And I learn that his fingers are just as good at bringing me to orgasm as his tongue. After, he curls around me, spoons me, and nuzzles my hair.

"Why?" he says.

"Why what?"

He doesn't answer.

"Because you're hot," I say. "And you're sweet. And I like you."

"I'm –"

"If you say you're a monster one more time, I'm going to bop you on the nose with a rolled up newspaper."

"I'm not a stray dog to be disciplined. I'm a *berserkr*."

"Isn't there anything you can do? Anyone who can help?"

He kisses my neck. "You can, apparently."

"You know what I mean."

"Maybe. There might be someone."

"So we'll go see this person."

"We?"

"You didn't think I was going to ghost you after the best sex of – in a long time." Best not to inflate his ego too much.

"My brother Bjarni seems to be under the impression that both you and your colleague are…"

"Man-eaters?"

He laughs. "In a manner of speaking."

"That's the old me," I say.

"I'm not an easy man to be with," he murmurs into my shoulder.

"You're not an easy man to get naked, either."

He snorts. "I promise next time will be easier."

"I don't mind the work," I say. "It was worth it."

"I suppose you'll be wanting to meet my family, next." He's teasing, but there's something wary in his voice.

"Are they so bad?"

"My dad is. Bjarni takes after him, except Bjarni's a shit and a goofball."

"He a racist, your dad?" I might be half white, but it's the other half some people object to. And they're the ones, naturally, who think I look the most Indigenous. Though they'd say "Indian," probably.

"Racist, sexist, homophobic." He sighs, rolls over on his back, and I sit up to better enjoy the view. Holy fucking hell, he's beautiful. There's a stainless steel ring through his left nipple that I somehow didn't notice earlier, and it's *very* hard not to reach out to tug on it now. His right nipple is bisected with a scar. That I do touch.

"How'd you get this?" I ask.

"Got in a fight with a bull," he says, lips twitching.

"You picked a fight with a bull?"

His smile grows. "*He* picked the fight. I just finished it. Unfortunately, not until after he'd caught the tip of one horn in my piercing and ripped it out."

"Ow," I say. He laughs.

Then I notice the scars on the insides of his wrists. I mean, his whole body is pretty much covered in thin, pale scars that I can see now that they're not covered in clothing. If I had to guess, I'd assume they had something to do with being a werewolf. Magne had scars like that, too, on his arms. But the ones on Thorstein's wrists, those are thick and ragged, not healed well.

I brush his closest wrist with the tips of my fingers, and he turns both arms so I can't see the scars.

"What happened?" I say, keeping my voice soft.

He won't look at me, for long enough that I almost ask again, but then he meets my eyes, and I can see raw sorrow. "I told you I almost killed him," he says, his voice even softer than mine. "My brother Magne." He relaxes back into the loam of the forest floor and closes his eyes. He rubs the inside of one wrist with his other hand.

"I… when he was little, he was the only one who could get near me when I was like that. When the *berserkergang*, the frenzy, was on me. But somehow Dad… He found a way around that, a way to make me hurt Magne.

"Mostly I don't remember anything when it happens. But I… woke up, I guess. After. And I saw what I had done. And I ran. I didn't stop until I hit the river. And I…" He switches hands, rubbing the other wrist. I want to touch him, to comfort him, but I make myself sit still and wait.

"I thought he was dead. And I didn't want to live anymore."

"You tried to kill yourself."

"The symbiont – the thing that lives in my bloodstream and makes me a werewolf – it wouldn't let me die. It healed me, over and over." He sits up, holds his arms wrist up in his lap and stares down at the scars. "Bjarni found me. I was too weak from blood loss or I'd have run again. If I'd had more time, maybe I could have finished it. Ended my useless life."

He's growling now, voice so full of self-hatred I almost get up and walk away. He's more broken that I suspected and I'm not sure I can deal with that. But I don't leave. I lean against him.

"Your life isn't useless," I say. "I'm glad you lived."

"My life isn't my own," he says. "Dad didn't even tell me that Magne wasn't dead. Even after he came home. Magne's mother told me."

"You don't have the same mother?"

He shakes his head. "She's younger than me. Colleen. Magne's mom. But she's been more of a mother than my birth mother was. *She* died when I was ten, so I guess she didn't get much of a chance."

"It sounds to me like you're not responsible for trying to kill your brother."

"I fucking gutted him," he growls, hunching away from me. "His fucking intestines were spilling out." He's shaking, from grief or anger or hatred; I can't tell. I put my arms around him.

"You may have been the tool," I say. "But your father did that."

He relaxes against me again, defeated. "He's definitely the reason Magne left."

"His abuse or his attempted murder?"

"Dad's reasoning is that he was trying to make Magne stronger. It was a punishment. I told you he's homophobic."

"Magne's not gay though. Is he bi?"

"No, he's just decent. He refuses to be what Dad wants him to be."

"What about you?"

"I *can't* be what Dad wants me to be. I can't be the next pack leader if I can't control the *berserkr*."

"That's not what I meant."

He closes his eyes, opens them again. "I try not to be," he says. "I don't always succeed. Magne… He made me want to be a better person. To be a better role model for my baby brother. I fucked that up big time."

"It's not too late."

"It might be."

The next week, I actually *am* rehanging the gallery when Magne comes in to pick up his art. He pays the balance, complements me on the quality of the work, then leans casually on the counter. He makes casual look natural.

"So did you meet my brothers?"

"You were right, Bjarni is an asshole. Katie chewed him up and spit him out, and I'm not sure he knew what hit him."

"He probably thought he was the one doing the chewing and spitting."

"No doubt."

He laughs and turns to go.

"You have two brothers," I say.

"I guess I assumed Thors would do the smart thing and stay home."

"The smart thing?" I raise an eyebrow and he laughs. "He's okay," I say. I think he reads some of what I'm not saying in my face, and he smirks.

"Just be careful," he says. "He's… unstable."

I nod and he walks away, and right as he's opening the door I say, "You didn't tell me he was a werewolf."

He turns and it's his turn to raise an eyebrow. "He told you?"

"It was an accident."

"You didn't run screaming?"

"Well," I say. "There was screaming."

He grins and both dimples appear. "Hunh," he says, and I can tell from his expression that he probably knows exactly what I'm referring to. And I don't think he's used to being struck speechless.

Then I say, quietly, "He misses you."

He doesn't answer. He just pushes open the door and leaves. But just as the door closes behind him, I think I hear him say, "Me too."

Chapter Four

STOP ME IF YOU'VE HEARD this one: A werewolf walks into an art gallery. Okay, I've used that one before, and recently, but hey, it's a good one. And anyway, this time it's a different werewolf. A very large werewolf.

Not that you'd know he was anything other than human – six foot ten, bulging with muscle, and ridiculously blond – just by looking at him. But I've seen him under other circumstances, bad circumstances, big teeth, claws, and all.

I don't realize he's come in at first. I hear the door chime, of course, but it's Katie's turn to watch the front of the gallery, and I'm in the work room, sorting through the art for an upcoming show, cutting mats and glass and fitting everything together.

He moves quietly for such a large man, partly because he's a werewolf, but also because he doesn't like to make noise, to draw attention to himself. And it's hard *not* to draw attention when you look like a Viking giant.

"Hey," he says, in his soft, deep, rumbly voice.

I look up, and he's just poked his head thorough the work room door.

"Hey, yourself." I can't help the smile that comes over my face. He smiles back and, in a few heartbeats, we're grinning stupidly at each other.

Fuck, but he's fine to look at.

"Come in," I say.

"Sorry to stop in so close to closing," he says, and I have to glance at my watch to see it is, indeed, almost five. "I was just going to the bookstore, and thought I'd say hi." He pauses, looks down at his feet.

"No worries," I say. "Want to see what I'm working on?"

He looks back up at me, a touch of pink on the ridge of each cheekbone, by which I know he's embarrassed. Probably because he can't make words come out.

I hold out my hand, wave it in a beckoning motion, and he edges farther into the room, past the massive CNC mat cutter that hulks along one wall. It's crowded in here, packed with framing supplies and art that won't fit on the gallery walls until we sell something, and he's huge. Even I feel awkward back here sometimes, and I'm only five four and on the skinny side.

I haven't seen him since our coffee date and near mugging last month. The date on which I found out the startling way that he's a werewolf. The date on which I also found out that him turning into a giant hairy monster with huge teeth and claws isn't a dealbreaker for me.

We *have* texted back and forth quite a bit – turns out he's actually really good with words when he doesn't have to say them out loud – so I know he's still interested. It turns out, though, that helping run his family farm is a lot of work and takes a lot of time. So, we still haven't managed a second date.

Also, I'm *supposed* to be one the Heartbreak Harridans, co-owners of Excellent Framing, destroyers of hot men's hearts. But I've barely even *looked* at any hot guys since that very strange date with Thorstein.

Katie is convinced I'm coming down with a terrible illness that will ruin me as a slut forever. I'm not sure she's wrong.

And speak of the devil, my co-owner herself, tiny fierce sexpot Katie Hemmingway, pops into the work room just then, and squeezes past Thorstein, entirely shameless about the fact that it means pressing her boobs against him.

Once past, she looks him up and down and smirks. "Back for more, eh?" she says.

Thorstein blushes. "Um," he says. "Just came to say hi."

"Sure," says Katie and turns away. She's not very interested in a man she can't seduce. "I cashed out and shut down up front," she tells me. "And now I'm off to meet that delicious silver fox you declined to pursue the other day."

"Got condoms?" I say, carefully *not* looking at Thorstein, who has suddenly found the painting on top of the worktable extremely interesting.

"You know I do," Katie says. She grabs her purse and her jacket and squeezes past Thorstein again, even though he's moved aside, and she doesn't actually have to press so close. She does like to torment hot guys. Or any guys, really.

I watch Thors as she passes. He's keeping his eyes on the painting, but I don't think he's really seeing it. He must have been working outside a lot lately, because he's got more freckles on his fair skin than last time I saw him, and some of the pink might be sunburn instead of blush.

His fine, pale hair has a few more braids than before and it looks like he hasn't trimmed his beard in a week or two. He looks up as Katie swings out of the room, shutting the door behind her, and his blue-green eyes widen slightly as he realizes I'm watching him.

"Lock up on your way out," I call after Katie.

"Already on it," she calls back. Then I hear the door chime. Thorstein cocks his head like he's listening, then relaxes a little, so I guess he heard the lock click to behind her.

"How've you been?" I ask, then regret saying something that requires an answer.

"Okay," he says. "Busy." He looks at his hands. "You?"

"Good." I step around the table, and gesture at the painting he's not really seeing. "You like it?"

"Mmm," he says.

I can feel his warmth, this close. Werewolves run hot, apparently. I keep my shoulder against his arm. "When are you going to take me on another date?" Okay, maybe he doesn't want another date, but why else is he here?

I turn to look at him and he's watching me. He looks away when I meet his eyes, so I touch his cheek and he looks back at me.

"Do you *want* to go on another date?" I ask. I mean, I think I've been pretty clear in our text exchanges. That I was interested, anyway.

"Yes." The word comes out in a rush of air. He relaxes a little more.

I slide my hand into his hair. I forgot how crazy fine and soft it is.

When he turns to face me, I back away, just a half step, and he follows. I keep going, only a half step ahead so he knows I want him to follow, until we've edged around the table to a spot where he won't feel so crowded. I have to say, it's a bit heady to get such a large, sexy man to do what I want, even if it's as simple as following me a few feet.

When I stop, he keeps moving until he's as close as he can get without actually touching me.

The skin of his face feels hot under my palm.

"It's been so busy," he says. "On the farm. I haven't been able to get away. But I wanted to see you." His voice is so deep and soft I swear I feel it rumble right through me.

I curve my lips into a smile. He never says much about what he *wants*, like he's not supposed to want anything. Like he hasn't been allowed to.

"I'm glad you came by." I let my hand slide down his face to his neck, past his collarbone, and finally rest it on his chest. His muscles are tense under my fingers.

I step towards him, close that last little bit of space.

For a moment, we just look at each other, then he bends down to brush his lips against mine. He barely touches me, like he's afraid I'll pull away, like he's asking permission, except he leans his body against mine, puts his hands on my hips to pull me against him. And holy fuck, I'd forgotten how *good* he feels, how confident he is with his physicality, even through his anxiety about speaking.

I push up onto my toes so I can press my mouth against his, and all at once he relaxes, moves a hand to the small of my back, and kisses me harder, parting my lips and sliding his tongue against mine.

By the time we pull apart, I've got both hands in his hair, and I'm trying to figure out how to press closer.

"Raine," he says, my name soft in his deep, smoky voice. I feel that voice shiver through me. This man could read me the dictionary and I'd die happy. He kisses me again, almost desperately, and I feel his teeth.

Then, suddenly, he shifts his weight, moves his hands on my waist, and I'm lifted up to sit on the worktable. He edges my knees apart with his hips and stands between my legs, pulling me close.

When he pulls his mouth away, he tilts his head so his forehead rests against mine.

"Sorry," he says.

"For kissing me until I can't catch my breath?" I say. "I don't think you need to apologize for that."

He snorts a little laugh. "For being so pushy," he says. "For not making time to take you out for dinner. For – "

I put my fingers against his lips. "You're here now."

"Do you want…" He hesitates.

"Another date? Yes."

He glances at me, then away.

"You?" I say. "Yes, again."

That gets me a smile.

"What do *you* want?" I say. "Magne told me you want to take over your family farm one day, but you must want other things."

"I want –" He makes a frustrated motion, looks away, staring at the wall hung with racks of frames. He starts to step away from the table, but I wrap my legs around him so he can't. I want to take him home and fuck his brains out.

"Do you want to come back to my place?" I say.

"Fuck, yes," he says, resting his forehead on mine again. "But I can't. Dad's expecting me back soon to help bring the cows in, and I have the vet coming first thing in the morning."

Right. His dad. His father, his employer, his jailer. And though he'd never admit it, probably, his abuser.

"Have you…" Now it's my turn to hesitate. I know mental health can be a big issue for some guys – an issue to be ignored, mostly. But fuck it, he needs help. So he can have the life he wants and not be stuck forever as his father's henchman. "Have you talked to whoever it was you were going to ask for help?"

"No." His voice is soft, but the word is hard.

"You need – "

"I know. I will."

"Hey," I say, putting my hands on his face again, making him meet my plain brown eyes with his clear blue-green gaze.

"Sorry," he says.

"Stop saying you're sorry," I say, not changing my tone. "You have nothing to be sorry for." I press my hands harder against his face as he tries to look away. There's something raw in the way he looks at me, something he wants that he feels he can't ask for.

Then he's kissing me again, insistent, taking, not asking. I pull him closer, slide my hands down his arms, find the hem of his shirt and touch his bare skin.

He growls, an almost inaudible rumble in his chest, and I trace the shape of his sculpted muscles, feel the crisp hair on his abs, his chest. He pulls back and I say, "Don't stop kissing me," so he returns his lips to mine.

When I dig my fingers into the muscles of his back, he slides his hands down my legs, pushes my skirt up, then suddenly lifts me to pull the fabric right up to my waist.

Then he moves his mouth to my neck, kisses me below the ear, in that exact spot guaranteed to make me shiver.

I pop the button on his jeans, and he hesitates, but only a moment, because I pull the zipper down, slide my hands inside, and free his hard length from his clothes.

This time the rumble in his throat is a moan.

"Raine," he says. "Are you sure?" Like this is our first time, like we haven't already had loud obnoxious sex on the forest floor.

"Fuck yes," I say. I take one hand away from stroking him to find the little pocket in the waistband of my skirt – and I realize this is the same skirt I was wearing on our last (and so far, only) date.

I pull out a condom, unwrap it, and unroll it onto him while he watches.

"Fuck," he says softly.

"Yes," I say. "Let's." I usually try to keep work and sex separate, except flirting of course, and I've never actually fucked any of my dates in the gallery, but Thorstein, apparently, has me making a number of changes to how I used to do things. And goddamn, I'm pretty sure I'd fuck him anywhere he wanted.

And I'm suddenly lifted again, this time to yank my underwear down.

He moves from between my legs just long enough for me to free one leg and then he's there again, pulling me to him. I get him aimed properly, and he slides into me, slowly, carefully, like he's afraid of hurting me.

I tighten my legs around him, pull him in, scoot my butt closer to the edge of the table to get him deeper inside me.

"Thorstein?" I say.

He pulls his head away from my neck to look at me. "Mm?"

"You feel really fucking good."

He smiles and shows both dimple and teeth. "You too." He finds a slow, delicious rhythm, moving in and out of me, taking complete control of the way we slide together.

I lean back, way back, elbows on the table, so I can watch his face.

He looks at where we're joined, watches himself as he fucks me, and I watch him watching. One side of his mouth quirks up a little and he lifts his thumb to his mouth, slides in it, and withdraws it glistening with saliva. Then he rests his hand against my hip and slides his wet thumb between my legs, finds my center and circles, teasing.

I have to close my eyes as the pleasure builds, and when I open them again, he's watching my face.

"This okay?" he says.

"Hell, yes." And then I can't make words anymore and only moans come out as my orgasm builds and breaks, and I wrap my legs tighter around him, pull him in harder and faster until he's the one moaning.

When he goes still, I realize I've closed my eyes again. When I open them, he's got both hands braced on the table next to my hips, his long pale hair hanging over his face.

I push myself to sit up, careful to keep my legs around him, to keep him inside a little longer. I put my arms around his torso and feel the muscled bulk of him.

I could get used to this. Not fucking on the worktable, but being with Thorstein in general. Do I want to get used to this? I haven't wanted anything long term since I was a teenager full of stories of true love. I prefer – I *used to* prefer – to do what Katie does: get one or two nights of great sex and then move on. But for some reason I can't explain, I don't want to move on from Thorstein.

"I want to help you," I say and he raises his head to look at me, startled. "Whatever it takes. You need to be free." And when I say it out loud, I realize it's true. One date, two fucks, and a few of weeks of text messages, and it's starting to feel like my life would be incomplete without this man in it. And the thought terrifies me.

"I want to live my own life," he says. Then I feel him start to go soft inside me and his eyes widen, and I almost laugh.

"Behind you," I say. "There's a box of tissues on the shelf."

He twists, grabs the box, and turns away to clean himself up. He hands me the box and tosses his wad of tissue in the garbage. When we're more or less reassembled, he turns back to me and gathers me against him.

"Tell me what other things you want," I say.

"I do want the farm," he says. "But not if it means I have to keep being my dad's enforcer. I can't… I need…"

"To be yourself."

"I'm not even sure who that is anymore." He rests his head on top of mine. "I haven't wanted anything for myself since…"

I shift so I can lean my head on his chest without dislodging his. If I look at him, he might stop talking.

He strokes my hair. "Since Magne left. Maybe even before that. Since I –." He sighs. "I didn't care anymore. I drove my little brother away from the family, from the pack, and it didn't seem to matter what happened to me anymore. A werewolf needs a pack, and I'm the reason he was alone."

"You didn't drive him away," I say, trying to keep the anger out of my voice, because I'm not angry at *him*. "Your father did."

"Mm."

"I admit, I don't know all the details, but from what you've told me, the only one to blame – for everything – is your dad."

He sighs, deep, like something's released from his chest. "When I said I knew someone who might be able to help… it was Magne."

The little brother he almost killed. Who thinks he's an asshole and wants nothing to do with him. *That* Magne.

"He's having a show here soon," I say. "The painter we had lined up pulled out at the last minute and I bullied Magne into agreeing to take his place."

Thorstein leans back enough to look at me.

"Is he?" When I meet his eyes, he's smiling. There's pain behind it, too, but he looks unbelievably proud. "Good."

"He's really good," I say. "Will you come to the opening?"

"He won't want me there," he says. "But I wouldn't miss it for the world."

Chapter Five

Do you want to see it? Magne's work?"

"Now?"

"You were staring at one of his paintings, earlier." I try not to laugh, because I'm still not sure how sensitive he is to that kind of thing.

"What?"

"When Katie squeezed her boobs past you earlier."

He steps away, but leaves one hand touching my back, like he wants to make sure I'm still there. He looks at the other half of the table, where a stack of art waits for mats and framing – the half of the table we were *not* just fucking on.

"That one?" he says. On top of the stack is a watercolor landscape. It's not my favorite of Magne's pieces, but I know it will sell.

"All of those," I say.

"Shit," he says, and moves around the table for a better look, peering closely at the bottom right corner to find the signature, then stepping back to look at the whole again. "It's a lot different from the comic book stuff and fantasy knights he used to draw."

I lift away the top painting and set it aside. "There's some of that, too," I say. I like using shows as a way to educate people about art as well as generate profit to keep the gallery running.

The next piece in the stack is smaller, an ink drawing on illustration board, colored with subtle watercolor washes, though the subject matter is anything but subtle. I watch Thorstein's face as he glances at it, then looks more carefully.

He looks like he wants to say something, but for a long time he just stares, face almost completely blank. Then he pulls out his phone, pokes the screen, and turns it towards me. The image on the lock screen is almost a twin to the one on my framing table, but cruder, like it was done by a kid. A kid who would grow up to become the man who drew the piece Thorstein is staring at.

"Fuck me," I say. "How old was he when he did that?"

"Ten, I think." He stuffs the phone back into his pocket but keeps looking at the drawing. There's a little smile growing, pulling up one side of his mouth, crinkling the corners of his eyes.

"He made the mistake of showing Dad a drawing he did."

"Oh no." I feel dread building in my stomach, even though I know the story he's telling happened years ago. Decades.

"Dad smacked him for it, told him he was wasting his time on stupid shit when he should be doing his chores. Like Magne ever missed doing a chore his whole fucking life." Thorstein's hands clench on the edge of the table. The story might have been decades ago, but he still feels it as though it just happened.

"What did Magne do?"

"He watched while Dad threw his whole sketchbook in the fireplace. Didn't even cry. When Dad left, I pulled the pages out, but there wasn't much left."

He relaxes again, leaning on the table and just looking at the drawing. It's not what I usually hang in the gallery – most of our regulars would think a comic-book-style werewolf was beneath their impeccable taste, but I wanted to include it for two reasons. One, to draw in an audience who might not normally feel welcome in a gallery. And two, to teach the snooty art-buying public that many artists have considerable breadth – of skill and of interest.

Thorstein touches the corner of the board gently. "I had to drive into Great Valley the next day. I don't even remember what for. But I passed a big art supply store. I stopped in and asked them to give me everything my kid brother would need to figure out what kind of art he wanted to make.

"The bill was astronomical, but the look on Magne's face when I handed him a big bag of art supplies and told him to make sure Dad didn't catch him again… it was worth every fucking cent."

When he looks up at me finally, he's grinning.

Absurdly, I want to tell him I love him, because what's filling up my heart and threatening to spill over can't be anything other than love. But obviously, this is too new, and I don't know if I even want something long term, so I just grin back.

"You did a good thing," I say.

"The first thing he drew in his new sketchbook was that werewolf," Thorstein says. "He gave it to me on my birthday that year. When Dad was out checking the fences."

Then his phone chimes and the smile vanishes. He checks the message.

"I have to get back," he says. "Apparently, one of the cows got herself stuck and she won't cooperate with Dad's rescue attempts."

I just nod. I hate seeing how the joy drains out of him whenever he has to go back to the farm.

"When's the opening?" he says as he heads for the door.

"Saturday next week," I say. "It's short notice, but…"

"I'll be there," he says, suddenly stopping and kissing me hard on the lips. "Dinner after?"

"An actual date?" I say, letting a teasing note creep into my voice.

"One of many," he says, turning for the door. "I hope."

"You bet your ass," I say, clicking open the lock so he can leave. Then I glance at my watch. "You still have time to make it to the bookstore."

"Shit," he says.

"He won't know you were five minutes later because you stopped to buy a book, or because traffic was heavy heading out of town."

"On a Tuesday?" he says.

"How often does he come to town?"

"As seldom as possible."

"See."

He smiles and kisses me again and hurries off towards the bookstore.

When I'm pretty sure he'll have finished at the bookstore and headed home, I leave the gallery and lock up behind me.

And fuck yeah, it's underhanded, but I want to know what a giant Viking werewolf reads for fun, but I *don't* want to make him feel interrogated by asking. Maybe later when he's more comfortable with me we can bond over reading.

The bookstore is always open later than anything else on Station Street because, according to a friend who works there, they do a lot of business among local shop owners and employees stopping by after work.

I'm pretty sure a considerable amount of that business is me. Which makes it interesting that I've never run into Thorstein there before. I mean, he's not exactly easy to miss. But maybe he usually goes there in the morning.

And shit, I hope he's not a *morning* person.

Lucky for me, my friend Elias is running the shop this evening and he hardly bats an eye when I ask what the big blond guy bought.

"You know I'm not supposed to divulge that information, right?" he says, tossing his dreads back over one shoulder.

"You know you're not a therapist, right?" I shoot back.

He smiles, teeth very white in his pretty, dark face. "Helping avid readers is not all that different from being a shrink," he says. "Or a counsellor."

I can't really argue with that. We readers are an emotional lot, and books are our therapy.

"So what does he read?" I say, leaning on the counter. "I'm not going to spill the information to the masses."

Elias leans on the other side of the counter. "And why, Miss Heartbreaker, do you want to know?"

He's allowed to call me that, because he's an honorary member of the Heartbreak Harridans, and has probably broken at least as many men's hearts as I have. Maybe even as many as Katie.

"I might," I say quietly, making him lean closer to hear, "And I emphasize *might*, be dating him."

He leans away in mock indignation. "*Dating?* Girl, you're supposed to be laying and leaving, not getting attached."

"Yeah, well, I did say *might*."

He sighs. "No, I can see it now. You really *like* him. And not just for his spectacular ass." He turns and pokes a few keys on his computer. "It's because he's shy, isn't it? You never could resist a mysterious hunk."

"I don't know why," I say. "He's just really *nice*."

"Nice bod, you mean," he says, chuckling. He types a bit more. "Thorvaldson, wasn't it?"

"Yeah."

"Magne, Bjarni, or Thorstein?"

"Bjarni *reads*?" I say. And fine, I don't really know the middle Thorvaldson brother, but he did *not* seem like a reader.

Elias laughs. "If I recall correctly, he likes thrillers. Spy shit. Tom Clancy and the like. The more formulaic, the better." He looks up at the ceiling. "And Magne… he's the dark one. Fuck, I'd like to –."

I reach over and smack his arm. "If you already know which brother is which, why did you ask? And why all the typing on that computer?"

"Because I wanted to see if *you* knew."

"I should hope I know his name," I say. "I already –." And then I realize what I'm about to say and snap my mouth shut.

"Already what, my sister in sex crime? Fucked his delicious brains out?"

"Shh," I say, but there's only one other person in the store, and she's as far away from us as one can get and still be inside.

"Have you?" he says. "Spill, or I won't tell you what you want to know."

"Fine," I say. "Yes. Twice."

"He was that good you went back for more?"

"Elias…"

He laughs, then looks back at the ceiling, resuming his contemplative pose. "Tall, dark, and very straight…"

"Magne," I say.

"Yes. *He* reads pretty much everything. Loves graphic novels and big fat fantasy novels the best, though."

"And Thorstein?" As interesting as it is to hear what interests the other brothers, there's only one I really want to know about.

"Ah, the object of your lust likes attractive editions of classic literature, non-fiction on a very wide array of subjects, and ye olde science fiction."

"Like Jules Verne?"

"Jules Verne, Mary Shelley, etcetera, etcetera."

"Hunh," I say.

"Not what you expected?" He's not even pretending to look at his computer anymore, or to pensively stare into space. "How about this? He also buys a lot, and I do mean a lot, of paranormal romance."

I stare at him.

"He says," Elias says, flashing me his cheekiest grin, "That they're for his sister, but I have my doubts. I thought maybe he was gay, but as he failed to respond to my considerable charms –" another grin here, "– and he did succumb to yours, I'm going to go with very, very straight, but secretly a marshmallow who likes happily-ever-afters."

He leans back over the counter. "And you will *not*," he says, pointing at my face, "reveal that I told you any of this, on pain of me never speaking to you again."

"I won't say a word." I lean on the counter, thinking. I mean, it's not implausible that the paranormal romance books are for his sister. Maybe she doesn't like leaving the farm much.

"If they *are* for him," Elias adds, "He's reading a lot of the same stuff you are."

I look back at him. "No shit."

"No shit. He likes books where smart, sassy women meet big, scary monsters."

"And the monsters get the happily ever after."

"Or happy for now," Elias says. "Yes."

Now that is interesting. And it sure as fuck makes a good topic to bond over. So long as I can get him talking about books without revealing that I spied on him at the bookstore.

"What did he buy today?" I say.

Elias points at a display next to the till. One of my favorite authors of super steamy fantasy romance.

"Wait, that's out?" I grab a copy and stroke the pretty cover – silver designs, moons and stars and leaves, twine around a couple embracing in front of a fairytale castle in moonlight. "Gimme," I say.

"You must be very busy, or very easily distracted, if you missed *that* coming out," he says. "When you didn't pre-order, I thought you were cheating on me with another bookseller."

"Never." I pull out my debit card to pay for the book. "I *have* been busy. We had an artist cancel and I had to scramble to find a replacement."

"That would do it," he says, tucking my receipt into the cover of the book.

"You should come," I say, pulling an announcement card out of my bag and sliding it across the counter.

"Oh yeah?" he says. Elias isn't big on contemporary art – not enough male nudes – but he tries to be supportive.

"There's one piece in particular I think you'll like."

"Oh yeah?" he says again.

"You know tall, dark, and youngest Thorvaldson brother?"

"Graphic novels and epic fantasy? He's an artist?"

"He is. A very good one." I stare until he narrows his eyes at me.

"And?" he says.

I scoop my book and my receipt off the counter.

"He drew a very striking self-portrait," I say.

He scowls at me. "Don't tease."

"Nude," I say.

He grabs an invoice off the counter and fans himself vigorously. "Damn."

"Saturday next week, at noon," I say.

"I will be there," he says.

"On your best behavior. The artist will be in attendance."

"Fine."

"No undressing him with your eyes."

"Spoilsport," he says. "Though if this self-portrait is *that* good, I won't have to."

"At least not when he's looking." That gets me another cheeky grin and

I leave the bookstore feeling cheerful, and not even minding that I now have to go back to the gallery and work late so we have a hope of getting all the art framed and on the walls for a next Saturday opening.

By eight, I've made good progress and decide I can knock off for the night. I'm hungry and I have a new book waiting.

Magne's art is looking amazing in the framing we chose and I'm pretty sure the show is going to do well.

As I'm about to head up front to lock up and go home, my phone vibrates in my pocket.

i want to buy the werewolf, the text says. I smile. I was wondering how long it would take for him to decide.

one condition, I text back.

?? he replies.

If you still have the other one, lend it to me for the show.

1 on my phone?

Yes. Want to hang with new one.

2 sho ppl artists improve?

yep. I smile wider. *will frame to match. you keep frame after.*

not 4 sale, he says.

I know. Will label private collection.

ok

I head back to the front desk. I'm going to have to order a frame right now, and hope it's not backordered. Then I realize I don't know how big it is.

I pull out my phone again. *What size is it?* I text. *Have to order frame.*

There's a long pause. I pull up our supplier's website and type in the frame code. It's one of my favorite moldings, so I don't even have to look it up.

9x12 pper he finally writes back. *need xact #s?*

Can adjust mat if need be. Thx. My thumb hovers over the heart emoji, but finally I send the text without it.

He texts back a thumbs up, then *when do u need?*

Weds next week? I say. The frame won't have come in till then, so there's no point in getting it sooner.

Mght hv 2 send w bjarni

Can't get away? I try to smother my disappointment. Maybe we already have a date in a week and a half, but I wouldn't say no to banging him on the work table again. Not that I'm going to *tell* him that.

will try. hv mare 2 foal soon

You have horses? There's something else we can bond over. And the idea of trying to find things in common with a guy, especially one I've already slept with, is so foreign it makes me nervous. And excited. Hopeful.

mostly belgians, he says. *mare is friesian*

My family breeds quarter horses, I text back.

wait. There's a long pause. I don't know if he means wait, he's in the middle of something, or wait, what?

Then, *ur that chevalier?*

Knightsbridge Quarter Horses, I text. *That's us.* Then I add, *Well, my parents.*

shit

Is that bad? I'm teasing, of course. Horse people know my family. My dad has the best Quarter Horses in Autumn County. Maybe even the country. Prize-winning, but also sought after as working horses.

fuck no, that's amazing

Want to meet my parents?

There's a long pause, but the three little dots pulse on my screen, so I know he's formulating whatever he's going to say next.

I already wanted to meet your parents. Whoever they were, the message says. He's switched to complete sentences, which means something, I just haven't figured out what. The dots keep pulsing. *Now I do even more.* More dots. *But*

No dots follow.

But what? I type.

Do they know my dad? he finally types. *He's on the wait list for one of their horses.*

Don't know, I say.

Hope not.

Doesn't matter, I type. *You're not him.*

I stare at my phone, trying to think of the right thing to say. But I'm saved from having to.

Good night, Raine, he sends. *See you Saturday next.* There's a short pause. *Sooner, if I can manage.*

Night, Thors, I send back. *Looking forward to Saturday.*

Me too.

Chapter Six

THE WEEK GOES far more quickly than it should, and Thorstein doesn't manage to drop off the werewolf drawing. Fortunately, Katie is out getting coffee when Bjarni stops by, so I don't have to watch them pretend the other doesn't exist.

He plops the envelope on my desk, smirks at me, and says, "Thorstein asked me to drop this off. Must be something special, because he threatened to kill me if I opened it or damaged it."

"Thanks," I say, hoping he doesn't decide to loiter. "I appreciate it."

"I'm pretty sure he wasn't kidding, either. So, what is it?"

"Just a piece of art I'm borrowing for an upcoming show." I don't know if Bjarni has seen the press release about Magne's show in the paper or online, and I'm not going to be the one to tell him.

"Thorstein owns art?" He leans his hip on my desk, and I try not to obviously clench my teeth. "Like nude art? Of you? 'Cause why else would he be so serious about me not seeing it?"

I look him dead in the eye, and it's disconcerting how much his features look like Magne's, how the set of his jaw and his pale eyes look like Thorstein's. I'm really glad his hair is different from both his brothers, that the blue of his eyes lacks the hint of green, or else I'd be kind of freaked out.

"No, not nudes," I say. "And not me."

"I bet you look fantastic naked," he says, leering.

I really just want him to leave, but I refuse to be intimidated by a sexist pig, even if he does look like a combination of a man I like and a man I… also like. A lot.

"I do," I say, keeping my eyes on his. "I look better than fantastic naked, and you –" I poke him in the collarbone, and he takes a step back, "– will never see me that way."

He laughs. "Too bad. If Thorstein can make you stick around for more, I bet I could have you begging."

I pick up the envelope, walk around my desk and over to the door, and hold it open. "Thank you for dropping this off, but please get the fuck out of my gallery."

"I was just messing with you," he says, giving me what I think is supposed to be an apologetic grin.

"Would you like me to tell Katie you stopped by?"

The grin vanishes. Interesting. Either he very badly doesn't want to run into her, or he *does* want to see her, but thinks she doesn't want to see him. I'd bet on the second one, which gains my colleague a whole lot of points for damaging the heart of a man who was supposed to be heartless.

"Nah, that's okay," he says, and steps out the door. "And maybe don't tell Thorstein those things I said." The grin creeps back a little, and so do his fucking dimples.

"If you don't want your brother to kick your ass for being a dick, maybe try not being a dick in the first place." And I shut the door in his face.

In the back room, I slide the drawing out of the envelope and look at it. It's done on decent-quality paper with good ink, colored with not-inexpensive pencil crayon. I mean, a good artist can make good art with supplies of any quality, but anyone who tells you that better tools don't make a difference has obviously never tried out a really good brush compared to a crappy one.

The drawing is on the crude side, but damn good for a ten-year-old. There are a few creases and tears around the edges, but it's obviously been kept somewhere safe. A piece of tape on the back shows where maybe it had been in an off-the-shelf frame, which would explain why it's relatively undamaged.

I dig through the stack of frames from this week's delivery to find the one I ordered for this drawing – after a few late nights, this is the last piece for the show that needs finishing. Then I just have to print tags and hang the show.

Once the drawing is matted and framed, I put it next to the newer piece, and it's then I notice something so obvious I can't believe I didn't see it before. Thorstein almost certainly did.

The werewolf in both pictures is half-transformed, caught between man and wolf, baring wolf teeth and drooling saliva, muscles bulging and clothing torn. The hair that hangs over his face is threaded with thin braids and colored pale yellow. Not quite white-blond, but still very fair. In one image, the wolf's eyes are visible enough to show a bit of color. Blue-green.

The posture – better-captured in the newer image but apparent in both – is tortured. In the older piece, it looks like the creature is in physical pain. In the newer, it shows as much mental anguish as anything else.

What I missed, is that they are both drawings of Thorstein. He's trapped in the throes of… what did he call it?… *berserkrgang*. The Viking warrior's berserker fit. I pull out my phone to call up the list of titles for Magne's show, scroll through until I find it. "Chosen of Odin." Of course. I've been doing a bit of reading online, mostly when I have customers in the gallery who don't want help, and according to many sources, berserker warriors were not only dedicated to the service of Odin, but were chosen as young men by the god himself.

There's no artist's statement to go with these pieces – and Magne doesn't know yet that I've borrowed the older one – so I find a good quote from Wikipedia to use instead, something that makes a b-movie werewolf seem like a perfectly reasonable choice of subject for an up-and-coming fine artist.

The old piece I decide to title simply "Werewolf," and add the note "Juvenilia, ink and colored pencil on paper." I resist calling it "Portrait of the Artist's Brother as a Young Werewolf," even though I really want to. I don't think either Magne or Thorstein would appreciate my sense of humor.

On the day of the opening Katie is calm and cool as an early winter, while I feel sweaty and manic. I *know* this show is going to go well, but I'm still nervous.

Or maybe it's just because Thorstein is going to be there and we're going on a date, and when the hell have I ever been nervous about a date? Not since I was a teenager. A *young* teenager. And this won't even be our first date. For fuck's sake, I've seen him completely naked and sprawled on the forest floor. I've seen scars I'm pretty sure he doesn't let most people see.

Magne looks magnificent, of course. He's actually outgoing and friendly, unlike his brother, and looks fine as hell in black jeans and a snug-fitting black t-shirt with "Artist" printed on the front in bold white letters. A sports jacket in deep green sets off his eyes and gives a slightly professional veneer to his laid-back look.

Next to him, his girlfriend Su looks proud as all fuck, but like she'd much rather hide in a corner until this whole thing is over. She keeps giving nervous glances to the portrait of her that forms the centerpiece of one of the walls, but if she's worried it'll upstage her, she needn't be. She's elegant and gorgeous in a short black skirt and rusty silk top, her hair in a braid of impossible length down her back.

I try really hard not to stare at how she and Magne interact. Like, they don't seem to need to be close together to know exactly what the other is feeling, and when they *are* close together, there's a kind of energy between them that I swear is almost visible. Every movement and glance is casual and unstudied, but at the same time full of caring. Like, a soft touch from Magne's hand on the small of Su's back serves to let her know someone is trying to squeeze past, or the barest tap of her finger on his sleeve tells him an older lady he hasn't noticed wants to ask him a question about one of the paintings. And it's like each of those little touches also says "I love you" without saying anything at all.

And fuck, that sounds like I'm getting all new-agey and granola, but it's true, I swear. And I *want* that. Not with Magne, obviously. It's even more apparent that even if I wanted him, I could never have him. It's blindingly obvious from the way he looks at Su. But I won't even contemplate who I might build such a relationship with. Not yet.

Even though there are way more people here than I expected, and little red dots to indicate sales are going up on labels as fast as Katie can peel them off the sticker sheet, Magne looks totally unaffected by it all, like he's just having a few friends over for drinks and snacks.

Then the door chimes, like it has been all afternoon, but this time, Magne looks up when he hears it. I look up, too, and Thorstein is filling the doorway. Literally.

"Oh my god," someone says in a loud whisper – one of our more outrageous older woman regulars, I think. "There are *two* of them."

Magne doesn't look away from the door, but replies to the woman, "Actually, there are three of us, but you should be glad Bjarni didn't come." Then he winks at her, excuses himself politely to the older gentleman from one of the local arts groups who has been yammering at him for the past ten minutes, and begins threading his way through the crowd.

Thorstein doesn't move from the doorway. He's backlit by the afternoon sun and it makes him look even bigger than usual. And it hides his expression so I can't tell what he might be thinking.

I realize I'm staring like a wild animal caught in the lights on an oncoming train when Katie pokes my arm. "If your blondie feels about his little brother the way Bjarni does, you might want to intercept."

"Yeah," I say. "Right." And I begin to make my way towards the door. I have no hope of actually intercepting anything, since the crowd parts for Magne, but for me everyone seems to want to get in my way and talk to me.

When I do make it to the door, the brothers are just staring at each other. Magne, though he's half a foot shorter, doesn't seem the least bit intimidated by Thorstein. In fact, as I watch, Thors slides his gaze away from his brother.

"It's nice of you to come," Su says, appearing suddenly at Magne's side.

Thorstein snaps his gaze up from the floor to look at her.

"Assuming you're not here to attack him again." She glares at Thorstein from narrowed eyes, apparently also unbothered by the fact that he towers over her.

"What?" he says, softly.

"I was there, that night," she says.

"I didn't see you." Thorstein sounds confused.

I have no idea what night she's talking about. As far as I know, Thorstein only attacked Magne once, when they were much younger, and Su couldn't have been there then.

"No, you didn't," she says. "The wolves stopped me, or you would have."

Something passes over Thorstein's face. A mix of awe and trepidation, maybe.

"I wasn't…" he says.

"I know," says Su, her voice softer. "I don't blame you." Something in her emphasis on the word "you" says she does blame *someone*, for whatever it is they're referring to.

Thorstein nods slightly and flicks his eyes back to Magne.

"I've never blamed you," Magne says, though his posture doesn't relax. "We're good, as long as Dad isn't with you. Or Bjarni."

"I'm here alone," Thorstein says.

"You owe me for what you did to my truck," Magne says, and I still have no idea what they're talking about.

"I know." Thorstein's voice is soft and full of regret. "I owe you for a lot of things."

Magne shakes his head. "Why are you here, Thors?"

"I invited him." I finally scrape together the presence of mind to step forward, to try to defuse the situation.

Thorstein glances at me, smiles just a tiny smile, then looks around the room, at the art of the walls, the people milling around sipping wine and eating fancy crackers and paying good prices for work from a new artist.

"You didn't think I'd miss your first art show, did you, Monster?"

Oh my god and fuck me stupid, Thorstein has cute pet name for Magne.

Magne snorts. "You haven't called me that in –." He stops himself from whatever he was going to say next. An actual number of years? Not for the first time, I wonder how old the brothers are. Do werewolves age differently from humans? Is that something I'm going to have to contend with some day? Do I like Thorstein enough for that?

Thorstein's smile grows, tentatively. "Congratulations, Mags. It might not be worth much anymore, but I'm proud of you." Then he steps past his brother, bends to brush a kiss on my cheek, and continues into the gallery.

Magne turns to watch him move cautiously around the viewers to look at the art. Then he looks at Su, glances at me. "It means more than he can fucking know." Then he moves away, around to the other side of the room from his brother, to talk to all the visitors eager to know more about this hot new artist – and I do use "hot" in more ways than one.

"You care about him," Su says. I hadn't realized she was still there.

"Magne? Of course. We're friends, I think."

She snorts and smiles. "Of course you are. But I meant Thorstein."

I turn to look where she is, and he's there, hands in pockets, gravely studying one of the paintings.

"Yeah," I say. "I wish I could figure out how much."

"Does it matter? I can see he cares for you."

"I'm not the loyal type, usually," I say. "I like to keep my entanglements as short as possible." I look at her and she's got a look in her eye. "Unless they're spectacular in bed," I add. "Even then I let them hang around a few weeks at most."

"No desire to settle down?" she asks, "Or do you not believe in love?"

"Not true love," I say. "Not like in novels. I fucking love those books, you know? Give me a spicy romance, and I'm happy. But real life? Nope."

"And yet," she says.

"Yeah," I say. "And yet."

"Magne says he's…" She hesitates.

"Broken?" I say. "Unpredictable? Mentally unstable? I know."

"And is he?"

"Maybe. Probably. He needs help. But he's also…" I don't know how to finish that sentence.

"Sometimes the worst mistake we can make is thinking we can fix a broken man," she says, and the sorrow in her voice makes me pretty sure she's speaking from experience.

"Not Magne?" I say.

"No," she smiles. "Definitely not Magne. There was someone before him." She shakes her head. "It hurts, not being able to help."

"He *wants* help, though," I say. "Not from me. I don't think I *can* help, except be there." So here I am, confessing to a woman I hardly know, to things I can't even admit to myself.

"Well, then," she says. "The path might not be easy, but I'd say the choice is. Be there for him, and if he gets the help he needs, see where things go then."

"But what if I…"

"Get bored?"

"No. I mean, maybe. I don't want to hurt him."

"He's a big, strong boy. He'll be fine. Besides, I don't think just being there will hurt him."

"I mean after. What if he wants more? What if I decide I don't?"

She shrugs. "A few months ago, I couldn't figure out if I loved Magne, or if I missed my ex and Mags was the closest person being kind to me."

I look at her, study her calm, beautiful face and see there are uncertainties hidden in her eyes. Not about Magne I don't think, but about herself. Her eyes scan the room and when they stop, I don't have to look to know she's looking at my featured artist. A little smile tugs up the corners of her mouth.

"I stopped thinking about how hurt I was, and realized all I wanted was to stop *his* hurting."

I guess I look at her funny and when her gaze turns back to me, she says, "He got dumped right around the same time I did."

"Seriously?" I say. "What woman in her right mind would dump *him*?"

"I know, right?" She tucks a stray bit of hair behind one ear and sighs. "I realized that what it meant, me wanting *him* to be happy even more than I wanted myself to be, was that I loved him." She starts away, then pauses to look at me again. "Lucky for me, he felt the same." She looks around, spots Thorstein, then looks back at me. "I really don't think you need to worry about *that* at least."

"Wait," I say, following her as she makes her way from the door back towards the drinks table, where she snags two glasses of wine and hands me one.

"Are you saying Thorstein is…" And how do I finish *that* sentence?

"At the very least," she says, "He cares about you." She sips the wine, makes an appreciative face – I let Katie pick the wine because I know next to nothing in that department. "But going by the way he keeps glancing at you with puppy dog eyes –" She stops to laugh when I look around, to see Thorstein carefully studying another painting. "He's completely smitten."

"Oh," I say. "Shit."

"He is kind of huge," she says. "But he seems sweet. *I* say you should just go for it."

"Hell, me too," says Katie, reaching around me to snag herself a glass of wine.

"*You,*" I say. "Traitor."

Katie laughs. "I will fuck enough men and break enough fragile hearts for the both of us."

"You'll have *my* help," says Elias, reaching around my other side for a glass.

"And the ranks of the Heartbreak Harridans are once again reduced to two," says Katie. "Unless *you* want to enlist." She fixes Su with her contacts-enhanced green gaze.

"Thanks, but I'll pass," Su says. "But I wish you the best of luck." She raises her glass, then takes a second glass and goes off to find her hot boyfriend in the crowd. Not that he's any harder to spot than Thorstein.

"Katie," I say. "Explain."

"You obviously dig him," she says.

"And he's obviously a good enough lay that you want more," says Elias.

"So," Katie sips from her glass and looks at me from under her eyelashes. "Follow this thing and see where it goes."

"If nothing else," says Elias, "It'll be a new experience."

This time, when I glance over at Thorstein, he *is* looking at me, though nothing in his eyes says puppy dog. Instead, it promises heat and wakeful nights of the best kind. And maybe Su is right. Maybe there is something deeper there.

I smile at him, and he smiles back immediately. Okay, maybe I *could* get used to that.

Chapter Seven

CHEZ LOUISE IS A BIT more upscale a restaurant than I was expecting, and I really need to stop assuming a farm boy can't have good – or expensive – taste.

Fortunately, the little black dress and hand-woven shawl in soft tones of blue and green I chose for the opening is perfectly adequate for this place. And Thorstein, aside from his height and bright hair, blends in just fine in his charcoal gray trousers, button-down shirt in deep blue, and black wool jacket. Everything fits him so perfectly it must have been tailored, and when I complement him on how he looks he says, "I clean up okay," and smiles.

I stand on tiptoe to whisper in his ear, "I like you dirty, too," and he snorts so loud the people seated nearest the door look up.

It feels very good to walk into that place on the arm of the most attractive man there. The maître d' doesn't even ask for a name; he just leads us to a table and asks if we want to see the wine list.

"I heard the waitlist for a reservation here is months long," I say, looking around at the understated, very tasteful, decor.

Thorstein smiles, like he's keeping a delicious secret. "It is," he says.

"You made a reservation months ago?" I joke. "You hadn't even met me then." Then something terrible occurs to me. "Were you going to bring someone else here?"

His smile grows. "I made the reservation last week," he says. "I know the owner." He glances towards the door to the kitchen and nods at someone there. "And the executive chef."

It's not often these days I'm at a loss for words, and this man has managed it more than once.

"Thorstein," says a voice with an accent I can't place, and I look up to see a large man in chef's whites standing next to our table.

Thorstein stands and they grasp forearms – I'm beginning to think werewolves don't shake hands, though maybe the chef isn't a werewolf.

"Sven," Thorstein says. "How was that lamb I sent you?"

"Mouth-watering, as you will discover if you take my advice and order it tonight."

"I'll do that," Thorstein says. "I'd like you to meet my…" He hesitates. "Raine Chevalier."

"Very pleased," says the chef. "It's good to see you getting out, Thorvaldson." He smacks Thorstein on the shoulder. "You look happy."

"I am."

Sven the chef departs, and Thorstein settles himself back in his chair. He sees the look on my face and grins shyly.

"What?" he says.

"You know the owner and the chef at the poshest restaurant in Riverbend?"

"They buy from us," he says. "Meat, produce, dairy." He looks down at the table. "Bjarni's actually the one who handles the accounts and does most of the deliveries, but they like me better."

"Better than Bjarni? Imagine," I say, and that earns me a laugh. I touch his hand, then withdraw quickly as a waiter brings the wine list. Thorstein tries to hand it to me, but I push it back at him.

"I know dick all about wine," I say. "I'm more of a cider drinker at home."

"I know you don't like Bjarni," Thorstein says, a smirk making his lips twitch, "But he makes a really good cider from the apples on the farm." I raise my eyebrows. "And I really only know local wine." But he scans the list.

"All I know is, if we're having lamb, we should get red."

"A bottle of the Sharp-Shin Cabernet Sauvignon," Thorstein says to the waiter, who's been hovering nearby. I recognize the name of a vineyard in the River District, not too far from my parent's ranch.

When the waiter leaves, Thorstein reaches out for my hand, twining his fingers through mine. "I hope this date is less… eventful than the last one," he says.

"I don't know," I say. "The last one turned out pretty good in the end."

He snorts, but a smile curls his lips, and a hint of blush touches his cheekbones. "I guess it did."

"Can you stay tonight?" I ask. "After dinner?"

He nods. "I made sure there was nothing that needed doing that Dad or Bjarni can't handle. I'm yours for as long as you want me."

I almost blurt out something stupid, like, "So for the rest of my life, then," because, whatever I decided at the opening, I still don't know if I want an actual, ongoing relationship. So I say, "Drinks at my place after, then."

"Mm," he says, and I feel it rumble in his chest.

The lamb is amazing, of course, and we split a decadent chocolate dessert, and I'm so full by the time we leave the restaurant my dress feels tight.

"I think I might need a nap after that," I say. He takes my hand, and we walk slowly, ambling back towards the gallery.

When my shawl is caught in a gust of wind and blows off one shoulder, he catches it, and wraps it carefully back around me. He looks at it closely, fingers the weave. "Is this hand-woven?" he says.

"It is," I say. "I bought it from a vendor at the summer market." I study his face, wondering if he's just trying to find something to talk about, or if he has an interest in weaving.

"Was it Rachel Weston?" he asks, and I blink in surprise.

"Yeah," I say. "You know her?"

"We've met once or twice," he says. "But I know her work." He looks at my face, then away. "She buys wool from me. I think I even know what sheep that came off of."

I stop dead on the sidewalk, and he turns to regard me. "Are you telling me you can tell where wool yarn came from, right down to the sheep?"

He laughs. "I can if I spun and dyed it myself."

I stare at him for a few more heartbeats, then tuck my arm through his and we continue walking. "You are full of surprises," I say.

"Is that good or bad?'

"Very, very good."

After a few more steps, he says, "I used indigo for the blue, and over-dyed it with marigold for the green."

"Is there anything you don't know how to do?" I step slightly sideways so our hips bump together and he pretends to look thoughtful.

"I can't make baskets," he says. "Yet." A couple more steps. "I'm shit with anything electrical or computer driven. And while I *can* cook, baking eludes me except for the simplest quick breads and cookies."

"And how are you still single?" I say, then realize maybe that's not such a great question for a man with severe social anxiety who's been controlled and abused by his father his whole life.

But he's saved from having to answer when we reach his car. It's a mid-90s BMW in deep blue and I have to stop and stare at it. I may come from a horse-breeding family, but I can appreciate all varieties of horsepower. Plus, having a brother into cars means I know a lot more than I might have otherwise.

"Isn't your farm organic, regenerative, horse-plowed, super granola?" I say.

He laughs. "I don't think I'd call Bjarni or even Dad 'granola', but yes."

"But you drive an M5?"

"It's a nice car," he says, watching me circle the vehicle, amusement dancing in his eyes.

"It's a fucking amazing car," I say. "98?"

He nods.

"V8?"

"The S62, yes."

"Manual?"

"Who the fuck would buy an automatic 5 Series?" he says.

"Tell me it's the six speed," I say.

"It's the six speed."

"Can I drive it?" I feel my most wicked grin spread across my face, and he answers it with one of his own, and his laugh seems to release the last of the tension he was holding in. He pulls me into his arms as I complete my circuit around his sexy car.

"Any time you like," he says.

"Oh, fuck, please don't tell me it's your dad's," I say, the horrible thought creeping over me.

He laughs again, a soft rumble I can feel in my ribs. "My dad prefers rusty domestic pickups he can beat the shit out of, not cars that sit in the garage six months of the year."

"Damn," I say. "What do you drive the other six months?"

"Toyota Land Cruiser."

That's two out of three Thorvaldson brothers with hot rides, though their tastes in cars are very different. "It's hardly far enough to my place to waste the gas starting this gorgeous machine."

"We can go for a drive, if you'd rather." His voice is low and growly, and I think there's something else *he'd* rather do.

"We can go for a drive later," I say. "Right now, I want you to take me home."

For a moment, doubt flickers in his eyes, and I realize that statement could be taken in the sense of, "I don't want to be on this date anymore," rather than the, "I can't wait to get your clothes off," that I meant it as. So I wrap my arms around his neck, pull his head down to my level, and press a kiss to his lips.

There's no hesitation at all when he returns the kiss, parts my lips with his, and slides his tongue into my mouth. He pulls away and says softly, "Best get you home, then."

The flush that spreads across my skin from between my legs is distracting enough that I hardly notice the car's interior and the ride to my building is mercifully brief. I barely even notice the quick and efficient parallel park he executes because I'm too busy staring at his neck and the way the muscles and tendons stand out as he turns his head.

Inside my apartment, I pin him against the door, grab his hair with both hands, and kiss him again. I want his mouth on mine, his hands on my skin, so badly I can hardly think.

At first, his response is as needy as mine, his tongue probing, his lips hard against mine, his teeth bumping against mine. Then he eases off, slides one hand into my hair, and his mouth softens, turns gentle.

"Hey," he says, softly.

"Mm." I don't want to talk, just touch.

"We have all night," he says. "Unless you get tired of me before then."

"I'll never get tired of you," I mumble, still trying to kiss him. Then I realize what I've just said and pull back.

He touches my face with his fingertips, strokes my cheek, then tilts my chin up so I have to look at him.

"I'll never get tired of you," he says.

Oh shit. What have I started? But I'm not going to suddenly deny it. And anyway, what if it's true? He's already lasted longer than ninety-nine percent of the men I've gone home with. And I can't say "brought home" because I never bring guys back to my apartment. This is my safe space, my sanctuary.

And I've brought Thorstein here and didn't even hesitate over it.

"Raine?" he says, and I realized I've spaced out.

"Mm hmm?"

He strokes my cheekbone again. "I didn't get a chance to talk to Magne at the opening. About…"

I lean back so his face is in better focus. "That probably wasn't the best time or place to bring it up, anyway," I say.

"No, maybe not." His rests his forehead against mine. His other hand is on my hip, his thumb stroking just above my hipbone, sending heat radiating all over me.

"Can we go by his place?" I say. "I've been there. When I chose the art for his show."

"I know where he lives," he says, something regretful in his voice.

So I say, "What did he mean when he said you owed him for his truck."

He sighs. "Dad sent us – me and Bjarni – to bring Magne home. He was out. And I… Bjarni goaded me into scratching his truck." He holds up the hand that was stroking my cheekbone and suddenly there are huge claws on the ends of his fingers and his big hand shifts until it resembles nothing so much as a giant paw.

I breathe in sharply. I mean, I know he's a werewolf. I've *seen* it. Seen him. More than *seen* him. But it's easy to forget, for the human brain to just blur over things it's too inconvenient to remember.

"Sorry," he says. "I won't do that again."

"No," I say. "*I'm* sorry. I know it's part of you. The werewolf."

"It *is* me."

"I know." I take his hand in mine and kiss his palm. "You just startled me is all. I guess I started to forget." I trace the creases on his hand with my tongue, and he makes a soft noise in his throat. "I don't ever want you to feel you have to hide it from me. Hide *yourself* from me," I say, looking into his eyes as I say it. Then, feeling daring, I tell him, "I don't just want Thorstein the man. I want all of you."

"Gods, Raine," he says, voice more breath than words. "I can't tell you what that means to me." He closes his eyes. "It's going to take Magne hours to get the scratches out, to repaint the whole side of his truck."

"It's a wonder he didn't punch you in the face," I say. "You shouldn't treat a fine vintage ride like that. No matter how goaded you are."

"I know," he says and sighs. "It was a lousy thing to do. He probably *should* punch me in the face."

I rest my head on his chest and just enjoy being close to him for a moment, wondering where the urgency went.

"So do we go see him?" I say.

"Not at home," he says. "Last time he saw me… Dad tried…"

"He tried to make you kill him again?" Was that what Su was referring to at the gallery?

"He wanted to bring Magne home, to face the judgment of the Elders. Magne wouldn't come, so Dad told me to take care of him."

"By which he meant…?"

"Kill him, yes."

"But you didn't."

"No… I… whatever Dad did before, to get me to attack Magne, he did it again. But it didn't work. Or it wore off. And I just… I slammed into him , knocked him off his feet. But I didn't use teeth or claws. And…

someone showed up to intervene before Dad made me try again."

"What the hell did he do that your father thought he needed to die for?"

"I told you he's homophobic?" he says. "Most of the Elders agree. Or they're too afraid of him to disagree. So by our laws… our pack, not all packs, being gay is as bad as… as being a wife-beater or a pedophile."

"But Magne's not –."

"No, but he was helping people escape, to leave our pack and go to places where they actually live in the twenty-first century."

"He was running an underground railroad?"

"For queer werewolves. Yes."

"Fuck me. I like your brother more and more."

"Magne was always the best of us."

"So if you go to his place, he's going to think you're there for the same reason?"

"Likely, yes."

"So where do we go talk to him?"

"Wonder Island, I guess. According to Dad, he's under their protection now and beyond our pack's jurisdiction."

"Wonder Island? The carnival? I think I'm missing something."

He shrugs. "You and me both. But apparently, it's not just circus freaks that hang out there, but … beings beyond our understanding."

"Even weirder than werewolves?"

"It's complicated. I keep forgetting you're human and all this is new to you."

"One of these days, you're going to have to explain it to me."

"I will."

"So tomorrow we go to Wonder Island."

"Tomorrow?"

"You said I could have you as long as I wanted, and tomorrow I want to go to Wonder Island to talk to Magne."

"That wasn't really what I had in mind when I said that," he says, the deep rumble back in his voice.

"Our first date," I say. "You said Wonder Island took something from you."

"First Dad drove Magne away," he says. "And then Wonder Island took what was left. It made him… Something more than a werewolf."

"Like what?"

"I don't know."

"Okay," I say. "That's for tomorrow." I pull his mouth down to mine again. His eyes have gone distant, and I want him close. His kiss is almost absent, but when I tug his shirt tails out from his trousers and slide my hands onto his bare skin, I feel him begin to pay attention.

For a few minutes we stand against the door, hands sliding over each other, and then he pulls back. I don't want him to pull back, but he laughs softly and touches my lips with his fingertips.

"I assume you have a bedroom?" he says, the gentle laugh bleeding into his words. "With a bed in it?"

I raise my eyebrows at him. "Mr Thorvaldson, are you trying to get me into bed?"

"Yes," he says. "I am. I thought perhaps I could demonstrate that I actually do know how to use a bed properly and am not limited to forest floors and large tables."

Holy shit, he's making a sex joke.

"I see," I say. "I suppose I'd better show you where it is, then." Yeah, okay, I haven't got a witty comeback, but there's so much heat between my damn legs I can't think straight.

"Also," he says, "I've never actually seen you naked."

"I suppose you haven't," I say, and I take two big steps back from him. He lets me go reluctantly, his hands sliding across my hips as I step free. He leans back against the door, watching me.

I reach behind me, slide down the zipper on my dress, and let it fall down my body to the floor.

He nostrils flare and his eyes widen, but he doesn't move.

For a moment, I stand there in my lacy date underwear and matching bra, and stare back at him. "Quid pro quo," I say, and he grins.

He slides off his jacket, hangs it from the doorknob, and finishes untucking his shirt. Then he undoes the buttons, one at a time, agonizingly slowly, and slides the shirt off his shoulders.

A smile quirks the corners of his mouth as my gaze leaves his to wander down his perfect muscled chest, to his perfect sculpted abs, and back again.

Then he hooks a finger in the waistband of his trousers and pops the button, slides down the zipper, and his pants slide down his legs to puddle around his ankles. And he steps free, peeling his socks off with his toes, and the muscles in his legs flex and oh. my. jesus. His thighs!

Now it's his turn to raise an eyebrow, so I reach behind myself again, and unhook my bra. This time, instead of standing still, I take a step backwards, then another. Then I slide the straps over my arms and let the black lacy garment fall to the floor. I take another step, and another, then stop to slide my matching underwear over my hips, let it fall, and step backwards out of it.

My apartment isn't huge, and I'm at the bedroom door when I stop.

Thorstein's breathing has gone ragged. He stares at me, then says, "Gods, you're so fucking beautiful."

"So are you," I say. "I assume, since you still have clothes on."

He glances down at himself, like he's forgotten what he's wearing, and his lips curve. "So I do," he says, and pulls the waistband of his boxers away from his belly, and slides them down, stepping away from his clothes and towards me.

He moves forward, slowly, like he's stalking me, and if I thought he was beautiful standing still… In movement, he's fucking divine.

Every muscle slides smoothly under his skin and no movement is wasted. His erection stands proud, bobbing slightly with his steps, and I try not to stare. Even his cock is beautiful, and that's not something I've ever thought about the male sex organ. Mostly they're a little ridiculous. Or a lot ridiculous. But his is magnificent. He's uncut, and so swollen his foreskin has pulled back, leaving the tip bare, already glistening with fluid.

"Fuck, Thors," I breathe. "Could you *be* any more perfect?"

Pink spreads across his cheekbones, adding to his already considerable sex appeal. I'm so wet it's a wonder I'm not dripping down my legs.

He stops in front of me, not touching, but I can feel the heat off his body. His nostrils flare.

"You smell so fucking good," he says, and I don't think he means my perfume.

Then he bends slightly and scoops me up in his arms and carries me the last few steps into the bedroom.

Chapter Eight

FOR A LONG MOMENT after he lays me on the bed, he just looks at me, eyes moving constantly, like he's trying to memorize me.

Finally, I say, "Come here, dammit," and he steps to the end of the bed, crawls up the mattress and over me like something predatory. He doesn't touch me until he can reach my mouth with his, and then he brushes his lips against mine so gently I can barely feel it.

"Are you trying to torture me?" I say, craning my neck to try to capture his mouth.

"Yes," he says, and brushes his lips over mine again, a little more firmly. He slides his tongue into my mouth and then pulls away before I'm ready to place a soft kiss below my ear, first on one side, then the other.

I want to reach up, to pull his head down to me, to stroke his bare skin, but something stops me. I want to see what he's going to do, I guess.

And what he does is place those soft little kisses all down my neck, across my collarbone, and down my chest, the whole time crouched over me on hands and knees, not touching me with any other part of his body.

I want to wrap my legs around him, pull him close, and fuck him. But I also want to feel this slow, torturous build of pleasure.

I can't help the moan that escapes my throat when his lips find my left nipple, softly kiss, then suck.

"No," I say helplessly when he lifts his face away.

"No, as in stop?" he says, motionless now.

"No, as in don't fucking stop ever," I say.

"Mm," he says, and moves his mouth to my right nipple.

I realize my hands are clenched in fists in the duvet, my hips arching upwards, and still he only touches me with his lips, his tongue, making his way down and over my rib cage, my belly, the top of each thigh.

He nudges my right thigh over with his nose, then my left, so my legs are spread open. He kisses the inside of one thigh, licks, nibbles gently with his teeth. Then he moves to the other.

I'm panting now, breath in short sharp gasps and I don't care if I sound ridiculous. I stop breathing entirely when his tongue slips between my folds, slides, presses, and finds my center. And then I moan. Loud.

Thorstein growls, just a soft rumble, and swear I can feel it in my clit. His tongue strokes again, and again, and the pleasure builds and builds and then I'm arching, thrusting, crying out. He presses his tongue against me as the orgasm throbs and my muscles pulse and finally I relax.

Then he crawls back up my body, still not touching me. I finally free my hands from the duvet and tangle them in his hair, strain my neck up to kiss him. I can taste myself in his mouth, smell myself in his beard, and it just makes me want him more.

When I tell him so, my voice is hoarse from the exercise I've just given it.

He searches my eyes with his. "I'm all yours," he says.

"Fuck me," I tell him. "Please. Now."

He nudges my legs farther apart with his knee, and then pauses.

I don't even need to ask why. "In the drawer," I say, and he leans over me, his hard muscular form pressing against me as he reaches, and finds a condom in my bedside table.

I take it from him, open it, and reach down to put it on him. Then I wrap one leg around the back of his thigh, pull him closer, slide my leg higher, and then he shifts position slightly and I feel his hardness poised, just touching me.

"Now," I say. "Please, Thors."

And he kisses me deep and hard, all teeth and tongue, and as he does, he slides into me, at first slowly, then harder, deeper. I wrap my other leg around him, tighten both legs to pull him in faster.

He buries his face in my neck, and I feel his growl as much as I hear it. And I feel another orgasm building. I don't know when – if ever – I've climaxed just from having a guy inside me, but it's about to happen this time.

Instead of moaning his name, I bite his shoulder as the waves of pleasure flood over me and for a moment I think I've done the wrong thing, but then he growls, "Fuck fuck fuck," deep in his throat and spasms once, and again, and goes still.

For a long moment we both just lie there, panting, then he raises his head and looks into my eyes. I push his hair out of his face – it's come partly loose from the elastic he had it held back with. There are little beads of sweat on his forehead and some of his hair sticks to it.

I smile and stretch under him, run my hands over his back, and kiss the end of his nose.

He smiles back and traces the side of my face with his fingertips. He looks like he wants to say something, but then he shakes his head in wonder.

"Holy fuck," he says.

"Holy fuck yourself," I say. "I don't think you need to convince me you know how to use a bed anymore." His smile gets wider, and that infernal sexy dimple shows. "But if you should ever feel you need more practice…"

He laughs. "I will always need more practice," he says. "Besides, I wouldn't want you to think I only know one trick."

"I think that was at least two tricks," I say. "Maybe even three."

"I know one or two more," he says. "And I'm always eager to learn."

"I'll keep that in mind," I say, then make a complaining noise when he gets up.

"Be right back," he says. "If you'll tell me where your bathroom is."

"It's the only other room with a door," I say.

I don't move while he's gone; I'm too sated. But when he comes back, I climb out of bed and head to the bathroom myself. And when I get back, he's under the covers in my bed, smiling uncertainly at me.

"I hope it's okay," he says. "I can go, if you'd rather."

I pull the blankets back and climb in next to him. "Let's just assume I want you here unless I explicitly say otherwise."

He makes a soft, happy noise in his throat and tucks me against him, curling his body around mine and nuzzling the back of my neck.

His hand on my arm is gentle, stroking softly, then finally resting on my hip.

"Are you going to fall asleep on me?" I say, but I start to yawn halfway through the sentence and have to laugh.

"I might not be human," he says, trying to stifle his own yawn, "But I will need a few minutes to recover for round two."

He tucks the blankets carefully around me and I'm pretty sure I fall asleep before he does.

I'm awakened in the morning by my phone buzzing on the bedside table. I don't even remember putting it there. Wasn't I naked when Thorstein carried me in here?

I just want to ignore it, but it's Katie, so I pick up.

"Why are you calling me at this ungodly hour?" I say, and then I realize I'm alone in bed.

"It's almost ten," Katie says.

"What?" I say.

"It *is* Sunday," she says, "So I guess that's forgivable."

"Why are you calling me? The gallery's closed today. Shouldn't you be sleeping off your latest conquest?"

"Cranky pants," she says. "Didn't Mr Huge, Blond, and Smokin' put out last night?"

"Never you mind," I say. "What do you want?"

I hear clanking from my kitchen and realize I should probably get up and help Thorstein find whatever he's looking for. The fact that it doesn't bother me that there's a guy in my kitchen rummaging is a strange new feeling.

"I just thought you'd like to know that I decided to come in this morning to tally up yesterday's sales."

"And?"

"Well, to start, the lady who bought the big sexy nude self-portrait was representing the Public Art Gallery of Great Valley, and the piece is going in their permanent collection of work by local artists."

"Seriously? Holy shit."

"Seriously."

"What else? How did we do? I know we made a good number of sales, but I was –"

"A bit distracted?"

I'm a bit distracted *now*, with the sounds coming out of my kitchen and the sudden memory of Thorstein's face as he plunged into me last night.

"Yeah, a little, so spill."

"First, tell me where Romeo took you on your date? The Big Steer Steakhouse?"

"Nope," I say.

"Mr Joe's?"

"Oh, please."

"Where?"

"Chez Louise."

"No fucking way."

"Yes fucking way."

"How?"

"He knows the owner," I say. "And the chef. Now tell me how sales went."

"Was the food good?"

"What do you think?"

"Sometimes those upscale places have high-priced, small-portioned, weird shit, you know?"

"This was not one of those places."

"So good food?"

"Excellent food."

"Hunh."

"Now it's your turn. Spill."

"We fucking sold out," she says.

I can't get words out for a minute, and I hear her chuckling. Finally, I manage, "Say that again?"

"Every piece in that show, except the two that weren't for sale, was purchased, paid for, and will be hanging in someone else's house a month from now."

"Holy fuck."

"So, you book that boy for another show next year, okay?"

"Yeah, I will. Holy shit."

I sit for a moment after hanging up, contemplating the unlikelihood of selling out an entire art show on opening night.

"Magne's going to shit himself," I say, and don't realize I've said it out loud until Thorstein's voice penetrates my morning brain fog.

"It's been a while since we lived in the same house," he says. "But I'm pretty sure he's toilet trained."

I stare at him for a bit, and then grin. "His show sold out last night."

His smile is so wide you'd think *he* was the one who just sold several years of work in one afternoon.

"That's amazing," he says, and hands me a mug of coffee. I sip automatically, and then look up at him.

"Honey and cream, right?" he says. He must have been paying attention on our last date. "I hope it's okay that I went through all your kitchen cupboards looking for stuff. I didn't want to wake you."

"Thank you," I say. "This is perfect, and I don't mind. Now if you'd gone through my underwear drawer, that would be a different matter."

"You have things in your underwear drawer besides underwear?"

"Don't you?"

He sits on the side of the bed, and I realize underwear is all he has on. He takes a long sip of coffee before answering.

"I need better hiding places than a drawer full of boxer shorts to hide anything from my father."

"He goes through your stuff?"

"I'm pretty sure he makes regular inspections of my entire house," he says.

"You have your own house? Is it on the farm?"

"You didn't think I still lived with my parents?"

I shrug. "The house at our place is huge. My sister and her husband live there with my parents. Their kids will grow up there. My brother has an apartment in Great Valley, but he lives at home half the time, too. Even *I* still have my room there, for when I stay on holidays."

"I guess that's pretty normal for farm families," he says. "I guess it was normal for most people, not that long ago."

"But not your family?"

"There are three houses and a cabin," he says. "It's a big farm. Hilde lives in the farmhouse with Dad and Colleen, until she finally makes her mind up about which of her suitors she's going to marry, assuming she chooses any of them." He sips his coffee again. "Bjarni and I each have our own house, and Granddad has his cabin. We were going to build another house for Magne, but he left as soon as he turned eighteen and got into university."

His mention of Magne's age when he left home reminds me of that thing I've been meaning to ask, but it never seemed the time.

"Can I ask you a weird question?" I say. I lean over and snag a t-shirt from the top of my laundry bin and pull it over my head.

"Always," he says.

"How old are you?"

"That's a weird question?" He stares down at his coffee cup. "Are you sure you want me to answer that?"

"I'm thirty-seven," I say. "But people usually think I'm younger."

"I would have guessed younger," he says. "By five years at least."

"You look…" I tilt my head, meet his eyes when he finally looks up. "Sometimes you look thirty-five. Sometimes you look fifty. I can't tell." His mouth quirks, and I'm not sure it's a smile. "But you're a werewolf," I say. "And I have no idea what that means as far as age goes. You could be a hundred for all I know."

His eyes shift away from mine, and he stares back into his coffee mug.

"Holy shit," I say. "Are you a hundred?" He doesn't answer. "I read paranormal romance and urban fantasy like a ravenous book whore," I say, and he glances up at that. "The idea of you being a hundred years old, or even two hundred, really doesn't bother me."

"What if I was three hundred?" he says, and I stare at him for a moment until I see the crinkle in the corners of his eyes. He's laughing. Or trying not to.

"Oh, fuck off," I say, and he lets the laugh out.

"I'm not three hundred," he says.

"So how old?"

"Are you *sure* you want to know?"

"Do you want to be with me?" I say. "Like together?"

"Like a couple?" he says, still gently teasing. "Like I can introduce you as my girlfriend instead of as 'my… um… Raine'?"

"Yes, like that," I say. "Because if I'm going to be your girlfriend, I should probably know how old you are."

He sighs. "Okay," he says. "In July, I'm turning one hundred and seven. Which, I should point out, is equivalent to about forty or forty-five in human terms."

"A hundred and seven," I say. "Fuck me."

"I'd like to," he says. "Again. As often as possible. But maybe you think I'm too old to get it up."

Sex jokes, again? There really is so much more to this man than I ever guessed that day we met. I want to learn all of it.

"How old is Magne?" I ask finally.

"You planning to date him next?" he says, grinning.

"As if I had the choice," I say, and he laughs.

"That's probably for him to say."

"Oh, come one, I'm your girlfriend now. It's expected that you'll tell me everything."

"Is it? I don't think I got the updated rule book."

I poke his arm.

"He's forty-two."

"That's it? What is that in human terms, then?"

"About thirty."

"Wait, it takes…" I try to do the math in my head. "Um."

"Sixty-five years."

"It takes sixty-five years to age the equivalent of ten or fifteen years?"

"Something like that."

"But it only takes forty-two years to age thirty?"

"Don't try to think about it too hard," he says. "Werewolf aging slows down over time."

"So, you could live forever?"

He shakes his head. "It's rare to live more than two hundred years. Three hundred at the outside. We gradually lose the ability to shift out of wolf form. The changes become permanent, and it gets harder to blend in. Eventually, most werewolves go moon-mad. They run into the woods and can't take care of themselves. Sometimes their families put them down before it comes to that."

"And by put down, you mean…?"

"Euthanize them."

"Kill them?"

"Yes." He says it sadly, like he wishes it was different.

"Killing is the solution to a lot of werewolf problems, isn't it?"

"It probably doesn't have to be," he says, his voice soft. "But yes, it is."

Chapter Nine

I WANT TO LINGER OVER COFFEE, over getting up, to get used to waking up with another person in my apartment. To waking up with another person at all.

And I want to pull Thorstein back into bed, to taste all of him the way he tasted me last night. But if we can't get him help, all of this dreaming about maybe being together long term will be meaningless.

"This has to work," he says as we leave my apartment. "There has to be a way."

"We'll keep looking until we find a way." I lock the door and turn to find him staring into space.

"What if there isn't one?" he says, softly. "What if Magne can't help and I'm trapped forever? Locked up every month until my father decides to unleash the monster I become on some other innocent person?"

He looks at me and his eyes are bleak. The happiness I saw there this morning when I asked him if we were together is gone and the hopelessness is back. I don't want to see it there. He's survived this for nearly a century, surely that's enough.

"We'll figure it out," I say.

He sighs, stuffs his hands in his pockets and says, "I'm afraid to even hope."

"No," I say. "Fuck that, Thorstein." He blinks at me in surprise.

"Even if Magne can't help," I continue, "Something *has* changed." He cocks his head but doesn't speak.

"You've decided to fight," I say. "You've decided that just enduring isn't enough." I step closer, put my hand on his chest. "That's not nothing."

He blinks again, nods slightly.

"And you're allowed to hope."

A tiny smile starts at the corner of his mouth.

"*And*," I say, prodding his left pectoral muscle with one finger, "You're not alone anymore."

"I can't ask you –."

I don't let him finish. "You *didn't* ask," I say. "I butted in. And now that I've figured out what I want, I'm not ready to give it up."

The smile grows. "And what do you want?" he says, just a hint of cheekiness in his voice.

"What I told you last night. *You*. All of you."

"Man and monster." A can feel the rumble of his voice in the palm of my hand.

"Man and monster." I can't reach his mouth, so I settle for kissing his bearded chin. "I don't know what that will mean for the future. I'm okay waiting to see how things go. But right now, I want you, and I don't want to wait for you to get permission from your family to take me on another date."

"You're so fierce," he says, and I think he's only half teasing. He bends down to kiss me. "Shall we go, then? Find out if there's any reason to hope?"

"There's *always* reason to hope," I say, poking his chest again. "If Magne can't offer any, we try something else."

"Something else like what?" he says, taking my hand and leading the way outside. "Witches?"

"Witches exists?" I say, resisting the urge to stop dead until he explains.

"You didn't think it was just werewolves?"

"I have no idea. I only learned werewolves exist two months ago."

"Werewolves, witches, and vampires are what we refer to as *other* kind."

"Vampires, too? Great."

"They rarely attack people," he says, as if that's comforting. And I suppose it is, a bit. He opens the car door for me, then goes around to the driver's side.

"*Others* are very concerned that we aren't exposed. Humans are encouraged to believe we're just legends." He starts the car, which is quieter than you'd expect for something with such a big engine. Quiet for any car, really.

"And I found out by accident."

"Bjarni was… not pleased. He threatened to tell Dad."

"You *told* him?"

He shakes his head. "He saw the state of my clothes when I met him later that night to drive back to the farm. He's not the sharpest knife in the drawer, but he's not stupid. And it's very hard to lie to anther werewolf."

"What did he say?'

"That Dad was going to kick the shit out of me. That he'd want to eliminate you to solve the problem. Then I reminded him that our mother was human."

"You and Bjarni have a different mother than Magne. I forgot. Did he love her? Your dad?"

"Very much. He was always unhappy that she chose not to become a werewolf." He sounds sad, but it's an old hurt.

"How old were you?" I say softly.

He pulls the car away from the curb and heads for the nearest road to the highway. Wonder Island is on the edge of town, but this time of day, it'll be quicker to go around the city than through the middle. Even then, it'll take half an hour to get there, and I wonder if I can keep him talking that long. Or maybe I should just let him drive in silence. It's not like I mind silence. But there are things I want to know, things I *need* to know, if we're going to be together.

And sweet holy Christ on a stick, I'm actually thinking about a *relationship*. I've agreed to be a *girlfriend*. I think that horrifies me more than that fact that I'm fucking a werewolf.

But it's exciting, too.

He concentrates on driving and at first I think he's not going to answer. But he just needs time, I guess.

"I was ten," he says. "When she died. She was already over forty when she had me, and nearly fifty when Bjarni was born. Even these days that's late for carrying a child."

"A hundred years ago, it could've been a death sentence," I say softly.

He nods, shifts gears smoothly. Fuck, he even *drives* sexy.

"When Bjarni was born, something went wrong. It took her months to get out of bed, and she never really recovered. She died the day after his third birthday."

"I'm so sorry," I say.

"Dad was crazy with grief. I think that's really when he started to… when everything went bad. He left me at ten fucking years old to raise my little brother." He glances over at me, then away. "It's a wonder we didn't end up feral."

"You weren't born here," I say, after a long pause.

"No. We still lived in Norway, in the middle of nowhere. We hunted and fished and trapped. Dad brought us here, brought the few who were in the pack back then here, when I was twenty-three, and we've been on our farm ever since."

He stares out the windshield for a while, then says, "Dad met Colleen a decade later. He didn't think he'd ever find love again after Mom died, but he did. Hilde was born when I was fifty-two. She's the princess. Spoiled, but sweet, so nobody minds."

I settle back in my seat, watching him instead of looking out at the city zipping by out the window.

"And then Magne was born," I say.

He smiles. "Dad didn't want any more kids," he says. "He got his heir and his spare and a girl to spoil." He shakes his head. "Of course, he was beginning to realize by then that I could never take his place. That I'd never have kids of my own to carry on the Thorvaldson name." He states it like a simple fact, but I see the sadness in the set of his face.

"You can't have kids?" I say. I mean, I'm not sure I even *want* kids — and I'm getting close to being too old, anyway. So, no kids is kind of a plus relationship-wise. But he might feel differently. And it's nice to be able to have the choice.

He shakes his head again. "I *won't* have kids. I won't risk passing on the *berserkrgang*. It's no way to live. Not in the world we have now."

I don't have an answer for that, so I put a hand on his arm and squeeze.

"So, I'm sorry if you want children," he says, staring ahead at the road. "That's something I can't give you."

"I've never really thought about having kids," I say. "It was such a relief when my sister got pregnant, because my parents stopped asking."

He looks at me like he's not sure he believes me, but he doesn't question what I've said.

"So, Dad was done producing offspring," he says. "But Colleen wasn't. She got pregnant and didn't tell him until it was too obvious to hide."

"Shit," I say.

"The day he figured it out was the only time I was ever afraid he'd hit her."

"Did he?"

"No. If he had I might have killed him."

"You love her," I say.

He glances at me, then away. "I didn't want a stepmother. Especially one younger than me. But she just ignored my shitty behavior and treated me like a son anyway. After Magne was born…" He sighs deeply.

"I was completely illiterate," he says, voice so quiet I have to strain to hear, and I was not expecting *that*. "Bjarni was always good with numbers, so he got sent to school so he could be the farm's bookkeeper, but Dad didn't see any point in education beyond the immediately practical. He figured he could teach me everything we needed."

"Shit," I say. It seems to be my word of the day.

"The only time I've ever seen Colleen really, truly angry was when she found out I couldn't read, could barely write my own name."

"She was mad at *you*?"

"At Dad. I didn't think it was a big deal, really. I thought I didn't need to read to run a farm." He snorts and shakes his head. "Then Magne came along, and everyone loved him. Even Dad. He was the cutest little shit. Won over the whole pack. And when he was four, maybe, he decided he didn't want to wait to go to school. He always wanted to learn everything right away. But it was years before he learned patience."

His voice is full of such love for his little brother. I try not to think about how they've been estranged for so many years.

"It was around that time that he marched up to me one day and demanded I read him his favorite picture book. *Make Way for Ducklings.* 'Read to me Thors,' he said, and tried to hand me the book."

I swear Thorstein's eyes are full of moisture, but he blinks and it's gone.

"I was almost seventy years old. Not old, in werewolf terms, but not exactly a kid, and I had to tell him, 'I'm sorry, Monster. I can't.' He didn't understand, at first. He thought I meant I didn't have time. But he's always been too smart for his own good." He looks over at me.

"Do you know what he said?"

I shake my head.

"He said, 'That's okay, Thors, I'll read it to you.' He couldn't actually read yet, I don't think, but he'd memorized the whole book from having it read to him so often. So he sat on my lap, and he turned the pages, and recited the whole story."

His knuckles go white on the steering wheel, then relax. His voice is just above a whisper when he says, "I was so fucking ashamed. I couldn't even read a picture book to my baby brother. It just about killed me to swallow my pride, but the next day I went to Colleen and asked her to teach me. She taught both of us, me and Magne, sitting at her kitchen table. Dad wasn't happy, but that was something she refused to back down on. All her children would be able to read and write, whether she birthed them herself or no. And that was that."

He looks at me again, then back at the road. We're pulling off the highway now, and he has to pay more attention to traffic. "So your boyfriend was once an illiterate oaf," he says. "And you can still back out if you want to. I won't think any less of you."

"*I* would think less of me," I say, and I guess I sound fierce again because he looks away from the road to my face. "You're not illiterate *anymore.* And I doubt you were ever an oaf."

He snorts.

"Besides," I say. "You read now. Lots of people don't read at all, even if they're literate."

"Mm," he says.

"So what do you like to read?" I poke his nearest biceps gently. "You already know I read trashy romances. Just the fantasy ones, though. Also, urban fantasy, and pretty much anything with a bit of magic. And horror."

"I like horror," he says. "Not slashers so much, but folk horror, supernatural horror, ghost stories."

"What else?"

"Old science fiction," he says. "You know, you don't have to put down your reading habits as trashy."

"No?" I say.

"No. Read what you like. That's another thing I learned from Magne. Read what you like and don't be embarrassed about it."

"Magne's pretty smart," I say.

He just smiles. "Lately I've been picking up nice editions of literary fiction."

"Like the classics, or recent stuff?"

"Classics, mostly. That's not so much to read for fun, though."

"Why read it if you don't enjoy it?"

"To learn," he says. "I'm trying to read more non-fiction, too." His nostrils flare and he lifts his chin slightly. "I'm trying to make up for the education I wasn't allowed to have."

That makes me smile. "Just don't push yourself so much you start to hate learning."

It's his turn to smile. "I don't think that's a danger."

And maybe it's that – that he's trying so hard to make himself better despite getting dealt a shitty hand in life – that makes me want to come clean. To be honest.

"So," I say. "I might have gone into the bookstore right after you did." I look at him out of the corners of my eyes now. He's watching the road for the turnoff to River Road.

"Did you?" he says, voice carefully neutral.

"Elias said you bought the new Calliope Hunt book."

"Magne got me hooked on fantasy novels," he says lightly.

"Calliope Hunt writes very *spicy* fantasy," I point out, then, "He also said you buy a lot of books for your sister."

"Yeah?" I think he's trying not to smile.

"But *he* thinks you read them yourself. That you're a big marshmallow who likes happy endings."

"I see."

"Are they for you? The paranormal romance books?"

He doesn't answer.

"Because some very smart person told me you should never be ashamed of what you like to read. That you should never dismiss your favorite genre as trashy."

He licks his lips, glances at me, shakes his head.

"I mean, if you do read PNR and UF, we can trade books. Or read the same book together, like our own mini book club."

He can't keep the smile off his face now, though it is more than a bit self-deprecating. "Yes, they're for me. Hilde's not a big reader."

"I *knew* it!" He looks a bit mortified at my reaction. "That's *awesome!*"

"Yeah?" he says.

"Yeah."

"Not weird?"

"Nope."

"I do like happy endings," he says. "I like it when the monster gets the girl." He glances at me again. "It gives me hope."

"Hope of what?" I say softly, declining to point out that he'd earlier said he was afraid to hope.

"Hope that maybe I can have a happy ending, too."

We drive the last few minutes quietly, each thinking our own thoughts. We're almost at the Wonder Island ferry parking lot, when Thorstein suddenly pulls into a diner and parks.

I look at him, eyebrows raised. "Second thoughts?" I say.

"Gotta piss," he says, then frowns. "Sorry. I need to stop swearing so much."

"I swear, too," I say. "And when you swear it makes me feel like I don't have to be careful with my language all the time, like I do at the gallery." I touch his hand where it rests on the gearshift. "It's nice."

He raises an eyebrow at me.

"And," I say. "You need to stop apologizing so much. It's like you're trying to apologize for your whole existence."

"Maybe I am," he says.

"Well, don't. I *like* that you exist. I like that you have a filthy mouth. I like that you could turn into a monster at any moment." I touch his face, turn him to face me. "I like how you touch me." He blushes, the faint pink coloring his cheekbones. "I like how you make me feel. And I *really* like sitting in this fucking amazing car while you drive."

"Thank you," he says.

"And that's another thing," I say, stroking his cheekbone with my thumb. "You don't always have to thank people for everything. You deserve good things as much as anyone else." I stop when his smile starts to look like a laugh.

"What?"

"I —" he starts, then shakes his head. "I only want to make sure I never take you for granted. I'll never take *this* for granted." He leans over and kisses me.

"I know," I say, when he sits back. "And I *do* appreciate it. But you know, sometimes we *should* be able to take things for granted. Like you can take it for granted that I've got your back. Always." Then I shut my mouth because I don't know what the hell I'm saying.

"Okay," he says. "I'll try not to apologize so much." He lets a smile curve his lips until his dimple shows. "And I'll try not to say thank you so much. But right now I really need to piss or we're both going to be mortified."

I follow him into the diner, figuring I should probably pee, too, and maybe get some fries or something, since we didn't eat breakfast and lunch is fast approaching. And I'm not keen on carnival food or carnival food prices.

Two women pass us and they both turn to look at Thorstein as he goes by.

"Damn, girl," says one, turning back to me.

I grin. "I know, hey?" I say.

The other woman grins back. "You need a ladder to climb that one," she says.

"I manage," I say.

When I catch up to Thorstein, he gives me a questioning look.

"They were just appreciating your… assets," I say.

"What?" he looks back in the direction the women have gone.

"You didn't notice? Women check you out all the time."

"They don't," he says, cheeks flushing a deeper pink. "Do they?"

"Fuck yeah," I say, then sweep past him to the washrooms.

Chapter Ten

I'VE BEEN TO WONDER ISLAND before, of course. Pretty much everyone who grew up in Riverbend or the surrounding area has. And it's got a timeless sort of feel, so it really doesn't seem all that different now that it did when I was sixteen.

Except back then it was just weird, campy fun. Rides and greasy, sugary food, and weird sideshows we pointed out to each other but didn't quite dare venture in to. Now, there's something different about it. Maybe it's because I've learned since then that there are creatures from horror movies that are real and not just folklore, but the whole place seems more… not sinister, exactly, but as if it's hiding something.

If Thorstein is right, it's hiding a *lot* of somethings. If he's right, then magic is real and it can be found here, beyond the facade of old-timey circus kitsch.

We barely get off the boat and the burly guy in the ticket booth leaves his post to stand in front of Thorstein.

"You're not welcome here," he says. He doesn't seem intimidated by the fact that Thorstein is taller, and more muscular, by a significant amount.

"I'm not here as my father's representative," Thorstein says, standing very still.

"Don't matter," the man says. "I have orders not to admit any of your lot."

"My lot?" says Thorstein, voice soft, but not a *kind* soft. There's a warning in it.

"Thorvaldsons," says the other man. "Or any of your pack."

"Most of my pack," says Thorstein, voice still soft, "are innocent of whatever it is my father has done to get himself banned." He flares his nostrils slightly. "And I'm sure you had good reason to have banned him."

"Orders are orders."

"Fine," says Thorstein. "I'll wait here. Please have someone inform Magne *Thorvaldson,*" and he emphasizes the surname, "that his brother is here to see him."

"And it's urgent," I say. The big ticket guy looks at me, then back at Thorstein. He looks uncertain.

A fluttering movement catches my eye and I look up to the roof of the ticket booth. There's a big crow perched there, and it's just settling its wings. It cocks its head, glaring at me from one beady eye. Then it turns its head the other way, looks at Thorstein, and caws.

The ticket guy looks up at the bird and grimaces. "Fucking crow," he says. Then the looks back at Thorstein.

"I know Magne is here," Thorstein says, patience in every syllable. "I saw his truck in the parking lot."

The crow flaps its wings again, caws again, but a different sound this time, and suddenly launches from its perch. It swoops over us, circles, and flies away.

I like crows, but having one *look* at me like that is borderline creepy.

The ticket guy frowns. "Fine. Wait here." Then he turns his back on us and goes back to his ticket booth.

Thorstein doesn't move. He looks perfectly content to stand exactly where he is, making other carnival goers part ranks to move around him. He looks comfortable, like he could stand there all day. I watch the ticket guy, and he doesn't seem to be doing much inside his booth once the other passengers have filed past and paid their fare.

"Is he actually going to call someone?" I say.

"He will," Thorstein says. "Or I'll stand here and glare at him all day."

"The terrifying glower of Thorstein Thorvaldson," I say, in a mock horror movie announcer voice, and he snorts.

"I'll break something if I have to," he says, louder, and I'm pretty sure the ticket guy hears, because he glares at us before going back to whatever it is he's pretending to do.

"Raine, hi," says a quiet feminine voice next to me, and I almost jump out of my skin.

I turn, and there's Magne's girlfriend Su, holding out her hand.

I shake, hesitantly. "Hi Su." Absurdly, I babble out, "The show sold out. And one of the pieces, the big charcoal drawing, was acquired by the Great Valley Public Art Gallery." I snap my mouth shut before she thinks I'm a complete loon.

She's smiling, though. "Magne's going to be so thrilled that his naked body will be enshrined in the public art gallery for the whole world to enjoy." She looks past me at Thorstein. "Why are you here?" It's a challenge, but not hostile. She seems more curious than anything else.

Thorstein regards her. He looks emotionless, but I can almost feel the tension in him. "I need to talk to Magne," he says.

"Why?" She repeats the challenge.

For a moment, I don't think he's going to answer. Then, he says, "I need help."

She looks at him gravely. "You do," she says. "But I don't know if he can give you the help you need."

"Or that he *will* give me help," Thorstein says.

She shakes her head, and her smile is sad. "I think he will, if he can. But that's not for me to say."

"No, it isn't." Again, I just about jump out of my skin, only this time the voice is deep and smoky, and an awful lot like Thorstein's.

Su laughs when I jump, and says, "You're going to have to get a lot more observant, if you're going to date a werewolf."

So that answers that question – she knows Thorstein is a werewolf, and so is Magne, obviously. She almost certainly knows a lot more than I do about this *other* business. I wonder what she knows about witches or vampires. I wonder if *she's* a werewolf.

"Magne," says Thorstein.

Magne nods and stands, arms crossed over his chest, just looking at his brother. Thorstein is taller, but somehow, here, he doesn't seem taller, like Magne's gained *presence*, or something.

"I need help," says Thorstein.

"Yes, you do." Magne still doesn't move, doesn't show any expression that will let me even guess what he's thinking. This Magne is a very different person from the cheerful young artist I had in my gallery yesterday. Except, he's really not different at all.

"I need *your* help." Thorstein makes a frustrated motion with his hand. "I don't know who else to ask," he says. "Don't make me beg."

Still, Magne just looks at him. I start to move forward, like maybe I can say something, but Su puts a hand on my arm, and I stop.

"Wait," she says softly. "I know it's hard to stand by, but this is something they need to do."

And how the fuck is she so calm, so knowing, so goddamn smart, and so much younger than me? Like, I have ten years on her at least. I guess she's spent her time more productively than I have.

"I'm not asking you to forgive me, Magne," Thorstein says, voice soft and sad. "Just help me."

"Why now?" Magne says. "You've had more than twenty years to ask for my help. Why now?"

Thorstein looks at his hands, then glances at me, and away, but Magne catches the quick look and a hint of a smile tugs at his mouth. It's so obvious now that they're brothers.

"I found something worth living for," Thorstein says. "Something that makes merely existing not enough anymore."

Magne sighs, then. "Thorstein, you don't need me to forgive you."

"I –"

Magne cuts him off. "I never blamed you. There's nothing for me to forgive."

"Magne, you were *afraid* of me."

"Of course I was fucking *afraid* of you. You ripped my guts out." He slants me a look. "That's literally, but the way. I have the scars to prove it." And he pulls up the front of his t-shirt – black with white letters that say "definitely NOT a werewolf" – to reveal three long jagged scars that cross his belly from the bottom of his ribcage and disappear under the waistband of his jeans.

Thorstein makes a noise in his throat, and Magne pulls his shirt back down.

"You don't blame him," I say. "But you tell everyone he's an asshole. You act like you hate him." I realize my voice has more than a hint of anger in it.

Magne shakes his head. "Not because of that. That, I blame entirely on the worthless waste of oxygen that sired us."

"I don't…" Thorstein trails off, obviously confused.

"I don't blame you for that, Thors, so there's no need for me to forgive you. What I do blame you for is refusing to talk to me after. You wouldn't even *look* at me, for fuck's sake."

"You were afraid of me, Mags. I thought… I thought you wouldn't want to have me around."

"You were my fucking hero," Magne says, and I think of the werewolf drawing by that ten-year-old boy who idolized his older brother. "I just wanted you to be proud of me. I went to fucking university so you'd be proud of me."

Thorstein suddenly steps forward, grabs Magne behind the neck with one hand and presses his forehead to his brother's. "Fucking hell, Monster, I was always proud of you."

Magne makes a move like he's going to pull away, but then he stops, and instead he puts his hand behind Thorstein's neck, and they stand that way for a long moment.

"I miss you, Monster," Thorstein finally says, so softly I almost don't hear it.

"Fuck, Bear. I miss you too. And if you need to hear it, then I forgive you."

"Thank you."

They step apart and Magne holds out his hand. Thors grips his forearm, and Magne grips back. As they start to let go, I see a frown cross Magne's face, and his other hand darts out, quick as a snake striking, to grab Thorstein's wrist. He pushes back the sleeve of his brother's shirt.

Thorstein tries to pull away, but Magne doesn't let go. For a moment that stretches on way too long, he stares at the ridges of scar tissue, and then he studies Thorstein's face.

"Why, Bear?" he says, gently.

"I thought you were dead."

"That night?" Magne's voice is so soft, like he's soothing a wild animal, and I swear I can see the little boy he once was, facing his monstrous brother without fear.

Thorstein nods. "The symbiont wouldn't let me die. It kept healing me, faster than I've ever healed before. Over and over. I might have eventually succeeded if Bjarni hadn't found me and dragged me home."

"What did Dad do?"

"He *didn't* tell me you were alive," Thorstein says. "Your mom did, eventually. When I confronted him, Dad said if I ever tried to… if I ever did it again, he'd kill you himself. That was his price for my cooperation."

Mage shakes his head. "He wouldn't have, though. He's not that monstrous. It took me a long time to realize it, but he never wanted me dead. He wanted me obedient." He lets go of Thorstein's wrist, pulls his sleeve down, and grips his brother's shoulder.

"He could've just told me he wanted me to be pack leader after him and saved us all a lot of trouble."

"You'd have agreed to be his heir?"

"Fuck no, but we'd all have figured that out a lot sooner."

"Fuck," says Thorstein.

"Yeah."

Su steps forward then and says, "So how do you think Magne can help?"

Thorstein looks at her, then at Magne. "I need to control the *berserkrgang*, so Dad can't control me."

"I don't know how to help you do that," Magne says. "Why would you think I could?"

"You could always calm me, when you were a kid. I thought maybe… maybe you could figure out how you did it."

"Even if I knew," Magne says, "And I really don't, that's not enough to put you in control. All I did was keep you from going nuts. I couldn't return you to yourself. Not while the moon was full and singing in your veins."

"I didn't know who else to ask." Thorstein's shoulders slump in defeat, and I can't fucking stand it. I take his hand in mine and squeeze.

"Hey," I say. "Don't give up now. We've only just started looking for a solution."

Magne takes a deep breath. "*I* can't help you, Thors, but I might know someone who can."

Thorstein looks up sharply at that.

"Who?"

"Let me ask first," Magne says. "But I have some conditions."

Thorstein nods. "Tell me."

"First, does Raine know how werewolf aging works?"

"I have an idea," I say. "And Raine is standing right here."

He smiles and his dimples show. Fucking Thorvaldson boys and their fucking dimples.

"Thors?" he says.

"Yes," says Thorstein. "I told her the basics. She knows my mother was human. She knows –"

"I know I'm going to get old and wrinkled before he does," I say. "I'll figure out how to deal with *that* once we've got Thorstein's life back."

Magne stares at me until Su pokes his arm, and then he nods. "There's something else you need to tell her," he says, turning back to Thorstein. "Do that and I'll see if I can get you help."

"Why can't you just get help now?" I say.

"He's right," Thorstein says.

Magne puts a finger under my chin and tilts my head up to make me look into his eyes. "Because I can see that he loves you," he says. "And you need to know exactly what it means to be loved by a werewolf. If you're not okay with that, there's not a whole lot of point in getting him his life back, because he's not going to want it."

"What?" I can't process what he's said beyond the idea that Thorstein loves me. He *can't*. Not this soon. But I think of the times he's started to say something that begins with "I," and has stopped himself.

"Is it so obvious?" Thorstein says, something a bit broken in his voice.

"It is to me, brother. I'm suffering the same affliction." That earns

Magne another poke in the arm from Su, this time much harder.

"An affliction, am I?" she says, but there's laughter in her eyes. I mean, it *is* pretty obvious how those two feel about each other. But Thorstein, loving me? I need to think, desperately, but there's no time.

"Now?" says Thorstein.

"Now," says Magne. "Su and I will go talk to our contact, if he's available. I'll come find you. In the meantime, feel free to enjoy the carnival." He motions to the ticket guy, who scowls, but tosses a thick roll of tickets like he's pitching a softball. Magne catches it and hands it to me. "Get something to eat, too. Unless he's changed –" he glances from me to Thors "– he's probably forgotten to eat this morning."

"We had fries," I say, then look at the ticket guy. "Could he hear us?"

"No," says Su. "He just knew what Magne was probably going to ask for."

Thorstein squeezes my hand and I almost pull mine away. I *so* need to think. I think he realizes something's wrong, because he lets go and takes a half-step away, like he wants to stay close, but knows I need space.

Magne and Su disappear into the crowd and Thorstein gestures towards the midway.

"Ride?" he says, almost timidly.

"Let's just walk," I say, and start moving without waiting to see if he'll follow.

"Raine," he says. "Are you mad at me?"

I whip around and he almost walks into me, puts his hands on my shoulders so he won't knock me over.

"No," I say. "But I would have liked to have had that bit of information from you, not from your brother."

"That I –?" He can't even say it out loud. "It was too soon," he says. "I didn't want to scare you off. And… I wasn't sure." He drops his hands from my shoulders, stuffs them in his pockets, and follows when I start to walk again.

"I was worried," he says. "That I was just… infatuated. Because you're the first woman in a long time who has looked at me like a person. Not like my father's son and presumed heir, and not like my father's thug."

"And is it?"

"Is what?"

"Infatuation." I don't know why the thought makes me angry. I was the one who originally wanted to just take him to bed and then forget he existed.

"No," he says, in that almost inaudible soft voice he has when something hurts to say. "Magne's right. I *do* love you."

He stops suddenly, grabs my arm so I have to stop too and turn to face him, and he pulls me to his chest, presses me against him and looks deep into my eyes. "I love you, Raine."

I can't answer. I don't think he expects me to, but he probably hopes. He kisses me then, just softly, no tongue, and steps back. "It's okay if you don't feel the same. I value your friendship more than anything."

"Oh, shut up, Thorvaldson," I say, and stomp away. I can't look back, but I hope he follows me. I don't want to get away from him, I just need space to think.

I reach a grassy area where there don't seem to be as many people, and I realize I've marched right past the midway and the sideshows to a space beyond the carnival. I probably shouldn't go any farther if I don't want to be removed by security.

I turn, and Thorstein is there. Not close, but not too far away. Like he's keeping an eye on me, keeping me safe, but trying to stay out of my way.

I walk back to him, feeling a bit more sane now that there aren't so many people around.

"What did Magne mean?" I say, before he can say anything. "That I need to know what it means to be loved by a werewolf?"

"I told you that it's a symbiotic organism that makes a werewolf what he is?"

"Yes."

"Not magic."

"Yes."

"There's another thing the symbiont does, sometimes."

"Besides the speed and strength and olfactory acumen?"

He almost laughs at that. "And the transformation and the healing. Yes."

"What else does it sometimes do?"

"It… When a werewolf finds love – real love, not infatuation, not a fling or a short-term relationship, but love that las the potential to last the wolf's very long lifetime – "

"Oh fuck, this isn't a fated mates thing, is it?" And I know he'll know exactly what I'm talking about, because he reads as much PNR as I do.

He does laugh this time but stops when I glare at him.

"No, not fated mates. There's nothing of fate in it. It's just, when a werewolf falls in love, real, lasting love, the symbiont can sort of… make it permanent."

"Meaning what?"

"When a werewolf falls in love, for real, he stays in love. Until either his loved one dies, or he does. Sometimes it lasts even *after* the loved one dies."

"There's no choice in it?"

He shrugs. "It's supposed to be possible to refuse. Especially if the object of his affection isn't a werewolf."

"So you could refuse it? Loving me?"

He laughs. "I love you, Raine. That's a thing that happened. But I *could* have refused the symbiont bond."

"You *could* have?'

"Yes."

"Past tense?"

"Yes."

"But you didn't?"

"I –" He looks out over the lawn, but he's probably not seeing anything that's in front of him. "I should have recognized it, when it happened," he says. "I… I gave in without realizing what I'd done."

"So now you love me forever?"

"Maybe not *forever*." He tries to keep the smile on his face, but it slips away.

"When were you going to tell me?"

"If you decided you didn't want to be with me, I wasn't."

"So, you'd just suffer?"

"I'm pretty good at suffering. I've had a century to perfect it." He takes a half-step forward, holds out his hand, and even with an empty field of grass behind me, I feel cornered.

"Jesus, fuck, Thorstein. Let me *think*," I growl, and then I stalk away, back towards the tents and the glitz. When I turn to look behind me, he's still standing there. He doesn't follow.

Chapter Eleven

I DON'T KNOW HOW LONG I walk around the carnival, glaring at everyone who gets in my way, but eventually I make my way back towards the ticket booth and the dock. I can see Thorstein there, sitting on a fence with his legs stretched out in front of him and crossed at the ankle.

He looks gorgeous, and he looks sad. As I watch, a pretty woman with dyed-red hair approaches him, asks a question, and he gestures towards the food stalls. She doesn't leave, but keeps talking, leaning closer and touching his arm.

I realize I've stopped moving when Su's voice says, "Wolfram will see you now, if you're ready."

I turn to look at her, and she's noticed what I'm looking at.

She smiles. "He's really not used to women flirting with him, is he?"

I look back at Thorstein. He's shaking his head and pointing and the woman does not seem inclined to keep walking. "He doesn't even realize that's what they're doing. I don't think he gets out much."

"No, I don't suppose he does." She pauses and looks at me again, studying my face. "Are you okay?"

"Am *I* okay?" It feels weird to make any part of this trip about myself, but I guess it's already become that, at least a bit. "I think I said exactly the wrong thing to him."

"He's a big boy," she says.

"But he's fragile," I whisper.

She sighs. "He is. But he's endured worse."

"I don't want him to have to *endure* anything."

"So tell him," she says.

I look at her one more time, then I walk slowly towards Thors. The look on his face when he sees me sends the woman who was trying to flirt with him on her way with an apologetic smile.

"Hey," I say.

"Hey." He starts to reach for my hand but stops mid-motion. Before he can drop his hand back to where it was resting on the fence, I take it in mine, and squeeze, and he laces our fingers together.

"I guess I'm the one who needs to apologize this time," I say.

He shakes his head. "It was a lot to drop on you all at once."

I step closer, suddenly hesitant, feeling my old friend social anxiety lurking in the back of my throat again. I swallow hard, force it gone, and put my palm against his cheek. He turns his head into it, just a little, and closes his eyes.

"I do care about you," I say. "I just… Really, I hardly know you."

"I know," he says. "It's okay."

"I *want* to know you better. And I think… I think I *could* love you. I think I *will*. I just need to let my brain process everything."

"It's enough," he says. "I can't ask for more than that."

"Dammit," I say, suddenly angry at myself. "I *want* to be with you, and I just don't know how to process that."

He opens his eyes again, so startlingly pale, like the rest of him. So open. His lips part, like he's going to say something, but I take another step closer, close enough to feel his body heat. And sitting, leaning on the fence, his head is at the same height as mine, so I don't even have to stretch to kiss him.

I make it long and slow, pressing hard, reaching deep with my tongue, trying to fit everything I feel into the kiss – all the desire, the confusion, everything. When I step back, he looks at me, touches my lips with his fingertips.

"They're waiting for us," I say. "Shall we go find out if this trip will give us a way forward, or if we have to start again?"

He nods, and stands, and he's so tall, so big, I feel tiny. He keeps his fingers tangled with mine and we walk side by side after Su, to see if Magne has been able to find us any help.

The room we end up in is on the second floor of the big concrete building that dominates the background of the Wonder Island carnival. There are comfortable chairs and sofas grouped around a coffee table, and on the table is a huge teapot and an equally large coffee urn, with cups and spoons and the various things people might like to put in their hot beverages.

The big plate of pastries reminds me that the roll of tickets Magne gave me, untouched in my pocket, was supposed to go partly towards getting Thorstein something to eat.

Some girlfriend I am, forgetting to feed him because I was busy being too freaked out about something nice he said.

Magne is waiting there for us, and so is a tall, intimidating woman with black hair and clear gray eyes. He introduces her as Thea but doesn't say why she's there.

"Wolfram's on his way," Magne says, and I guess I look confused, because he adds, "Wolfram Gottfried runs the Island."

The woman, Thea, snorts. "Wolfram —" and she pronounces it with a V sound at the beginning, "— *owns* Wonder Island. It would soon fall to ruin if left to him to *run* it."

Magne smiles, his mouth twitching up at the corners.

"Wolfram is here, so we might as well sit down," says another voice, male, low and deep with an unidentifiable accent something like German.

Thea and Magne step aside and a very short man, as muscular in his way as Thorstein is, offers a hand to shake. Like Thea – his sister? – he has black hair and gray eyes, and how the hell did I never notice this city held so many gorgeous, deep-voiced men?

Wolfram is a dwarf, maybe four feet tall, but nothing about him seems small, if that makes any sense. In the same way that Magne seems as *significant* as Thorstein here, despite his shorter height, Wolfram Gottfried seems to have even more presence. Objectively, he's close to three feet shorter than Thorstein, but he feels like he's much bigger. Grander. I don't know what the hell I'm even trying to say.

After shaking my hand and gripping forearms with Thorstein, he gestures for us to sit.

Magne looks at his brother, points to the pastries, and says, "Eat."

"I'm okay," Thorstein says.

"Have you eaten anything since you got here?" Magne says. "Eat something for fuck's sake."

I notice Wolfram smirk when Magne points at the pastries again, and the smaller man lifts the plate and moves it down the table so Thorstein can reach it without standing up.

"He may be in my employ," says Wolfram, "But I find it's easiest to just do as Magne says." His mouth twitches into a smile. "Especially when he's right."

"Thank you," Thorstein says, and finally reaches for a danish.

"Coffee?" says Magne and Su starts pouring cups and passing them around.

"So," says Wolfram, when we've each got a mug and something to eat. "Magne tells me you've decided to attempt to remove yourself from your father's influence."

Thorstein sits up straight, like he's answering a strict schoolteacher, and puts the half-eaten danish next to his coffee cup on the table.

"I –" He stops, like he doesn't know what to say, but I know it's more likely that his anxiety is strangling the words in his throat. I lean against his arm, trying to lend him what strength I can. "Yes," he finally says.

I expect to see judgement in Wolfram's eyes, disdain or contempt, like I used to see so often when I was younger and couldn't make words come out. But there's nothing like that there. Instead, I see kindness, and such deep patience.

"When did you know you were a *berserkr*?" Wolfram says.

"I was fourteen," says Thorstein. "One of our goats wouldn't go into the pen…"

"It made you angry?"

Thorstein nods. "I… I was always patient before. But this time…"

"What did you do?"

"I don't remember doing anything." Thorstein looks at his hands, like he always does when he can't face someone's eyes. "The next thing I remember is the goat was dead at my feet. I broke its neck, apparently."

"You were not a werewolf yet?'

"No. Not until I was sixteen."

"That's young, is it not?"

"Dad thought…"

"He believed it would help you control the *berserkrgang*?"

"Yes."

"But it did not?"

"It made it worse. I was okay most of the time, as long as I could avoid getting angry. But at the full moon…"

"You spend the whole three days around the full moon afflicted by the *berserkrgang*?"

"Yes."

"And how is your temper on other days? Not back then, but now?"

"I'm… I got very good at staying calm, at not allowing myself to be provoked."

"And?"

"It hardly ever comes over me now, except when the moon is full."

"And then you can't resist it."

Thorstein nods.

"He's done remarkably well, considering he's had no one to train him," Thea says.

"Indeed," says Wolfram. He turns back to Thorstein. "Have you had any episodes recently that were not due to the moon?"

"Only one," Thorstein says, glancing at me.

"We were mugged," I say. "Well, these three guys *tried* to mug us."

"And?"

"They ran screaming."

Wolfram regards me seriously. "Did Thorstein pursue them?"

I shake my head and look at Thorstein. "He followed me instead."

"Ah," Wolfram looks thoughtful. "That was when you learned Thorstein was a werewolf?"

"Yeah. It was a bit of a shock."

Wolfram chuckles. "Did you run from him?"

"At first."

"If he chased you, he would have caught you."

"He did."

"Were you afraid?"

"Terrified," I say, looking at Thorstein again. He's watching me, studying my face, and I can't read his expression. "At first."

"But then?"

I shrug. "Then I… I don't know. He was in wolf shape…" Thorstein shakes his head slightly.

"What?" I say.

"I was only half-changed," he says.

"That wasn't your whole werewolf form?" Okay, did *not* know that.

"When the *berserkrgang* comes, my symbiont tries to protect me, I think," he says. "But I get stuck halfway." He shakes his head more vigorously. "That's a torment all its own."

Wolfram looks back and forth between us, a slight frown forming between his brows. "Go on," he says to me.

"So, he was half-changed," I say. "But except for a few times when he seemed to just… blank out… he was still Thorstein. I just couldn't believe he would hurt me, even though he kept saying he was afraid he would."

"And then?"

"Then…" I feel the flush creeping up my neck and I'm glad my skin is dark enough it won't be too obvious. Thorstein's cheekbones are pink, and he looks at where my fingers are twined with his.

"Um… well… he changed back to human," I say. I look at Wolfram and dare him to challenge me with my gaze. So of course, he does.

"Just like that?" he says, eyebrows raised.

"Well, no," I say. "I guess I… kissed him. And…" I can't go on. I look at Thorstein for help, but he's still staring at our hands, blush creeping up his neck now.

Then Magne suddenly snorts and barks out a laugh. "You didn't," he says. Then, "Of course you did."

I glare at him. Everyone looks at him, and he's got a huge shit-eating grin on his face.

"What did I miss?" Wolfram says.

"Magne." Su groans and leans her head on his shoulder.

Thea leans back in her chair with a smirk. "Use your imagination little brother," she says, and Wolfram stares at her.

Then he blinks and says, "Oh. I see." He thinks for a moment, then says, "What was the moon phase?"

"First quarter," says Thorstein. "Just a crescent, nowhere near full."

"Hm. And how old were you before you developed your full wolf form? Under normal circumstances?"

"Fifty-seven," he says.

"Ha!" says Magne. "I knew I was younger than you."

"You had a head start," Thorstein says. "You were born a werewolf."

Magne's face goes solemn at that, and he frowns. "And now I'm not –"

"Not now," Su says gently. "You and Thorstein can have a big old brother-to-brother discussion of what it means to be a werewolf once we've solved the current problem."

Thorstein looks like he wants to pursue whatever Magne was going to say, but then Wolfram stands up, and everyone looks at him.

He steps around the table and stops in front of Thorstein, looks into his eyes, then grasps his face and tilts his head like he's trying to get a better angle, or more light.

When he steps back, he's frowning. "I'm surprised your father didn't send you for training as soon as he realized you were *berserkr*. He was very adamant to me that you had been chosen by Wotan himself to be a divine warrior."

"My mother died when I was ten," Thorstein says. "Dad was still grieving when it came on me. And if he'd had the presence of mind to send me away, he'd have had to raise his other son himself."

Wolfram glances at Magne, then shakes his head. "Of course, you have another brother."

Thorstein nods. "Bjarni was only seven when it came on me. Dad didn't know how to deal with children."

"So he locked you up?"

Thorstein nods.

"Every full moon for how long?"

"Ninety-three years."

Wolfram mutters something under his breath that sounds like German. I'd bet money it's a swear.

"Your father has a lot to answer for."

Thorstein just nods.

"Unfortunately, with you being *other*, it's not under my authority to help you directly."

Magne starts to get up, "But you said –"

Wolfram turns and looks at him, and Magne sinks back into his chair.

"And to be honest, I'm not sure I *can* help you."

Thorstein nods sharply. "I understand," but I can see the slight sag of his shoulders.

"No, I very much doubt you do." Wolfram sighs. "There are protocols for beings such as I to offer assistance to beings such as you. And involving a human makes it an even more… delicate endeavor." He goes back to his chair and sits, almost collapses into it.

"I *want* to help you, son," Wolfram says, and I blink at the word "son." I mean, he doesn't look any older than Thorstein. Then again, who knows what kind of creature he is.

"Fuck," says Magne.

Wolfram looks at him, weariness suddenly evident in every line of his body. "Do you see what we face every day, Magne? Do you begin to understand what a difficult thing it is I've asked of you?"

Magne nods, but says, "I won't turn him away. There must be something we can do."

Wolfram smiles. "And that attitude is *why* I asked you. Why I asked *you*." He rubs a hand across his face, then looks back at Thorstein.

"Magne tells me you never attacked him when he was young, even when you were fully under the sway of the *berserkrgang*."

"That's true."

"But when he was to be punished," Wolfram says, "Even though he was still a child, you *did* attack him."

"Yes." Thorstein's voice is soft.

"Do you have thoughts on why?"

Thorstein shakes his head.

"Nothing you remember that was different from previous times he locked you away?"

"No. Only –"

"Only what?"

"I suppose maybe the water he gave me tasted different. Stale."

"Of herbs?"

"I don't think so."

"Did he say any words to you?"

"I don't remember what happens when the *berserkrgang* is on me. I might be aware, somewhat, but after I remember very little. And I can't think of anything he might have said before that that was different."

"You knew you hurt him, though."

"I… came back to myself right after. Sometimes that happens on the last night of the moon. I recover early. I saw Magne fall, and then I ran, so I… so Dad couldn't make me attack him again."

"Wait," Su says, sitting up straight suddenly. "I might remember something."

Wolfram looks at her and waits.

"Magne," she says. "Remember that night in the woods? You went for a run, and your brothers were waiting for you. And your father. You fought them."

Magne nods and rubs at one of his shoulders absently.

"Then your father…"

"He injured you," Thorstein says. "I almost remember. He…"

"He disabled me," Magne says, growling.

"Right," says Su. "And just before…" She looks from Wolfram to me and back to Wolfram, who gives a tiny nod. "Right before the wolves showed up to chase them away, your dad tried to get Thorstein to attack you again."

"He *did* attack me."

"Yes, but he just knocked you over."

"I wasn't entirely gone," says Thorstein. "It was the third night again, I think."

"Right," Su says turning to Thorstein. "And your dad turned to you and said, 'take care of him,' and you attacked."

Beside me, Thorstein has gone very still. His hand tightens on mine so much it rubs the bones together and I try to free my fingers, but he won't let go. He can't let go.

"Thors?" I say. He doesn't look at me. His eyes have glazed over. "Magne?" I say, and my voice sounds small and afraid.

"*Scheisse,*" says Wolfram and suddenly he's there, hand on Thorstein's forehead, and Thorstein almost collapses into the sofa.

Thorstein looks at our joined hands. "Fuck, Raine, did I hurt you?"

"I'm okay. But you…"

"What happened?" He touches my face. "Did I…"

"Well," says Wolfram. "Now we know how your father controlled you, and how reckless he was to use such a common phrase." He smiles, but there's no mirth in it. It's like a werewolf's smile, all teeth and anger. "And now I have a very good reason to step in and help you."

Chapter Twelve

I DON'T UNDERSTAND," Thorstein says.

"Your father has lead your pack for a long time," Wolfram says, settling back into his chair. "He is not unintelligent, and obviously he is observant."

Magne and Thorstein both watch him carefully as he speaks, like they might miss a word or a nuance if they look away.

"Somewhere, somehow, he has learned a little bit of true magic. Bought it from an unethical sorcerer, maybe, or read it in a book he had no business looking at."

"True magic?" says Thorstein, disbelief in his voice. He sounds like I sounded when he told me vampires and witches exist.

"Fuck," says Magne.

"There are things, werewolf," says Thea, still leaning comfortably back in her chair and looking very amused at everything. "That are as far beyond you *otherkind* as *others* are beyond human."

Thorstein frowns. "I've never thought *others* were more than humans."

"And that is why you're a better man than most of your kind," Thea says.

"So, magic. It exists."

"In infinite variety," says Wolfram. "And whatever magic your father found, he used it to bind you, likely beginning when you were very young. He may never have intended to use it, thinking only that it would give him power if he needed it. And, I think, he discovered a need to be in control always, and developed a thirst for power over others.

"It is… tragic that he did decide to use it, to force his will on you. Especially when he chose to use it to punish his youngest child."

"Dad used magic on me."

"He refused to have you trained in any techniques that would allow you to control your own *berserkr* nature, and instead used magic – is *still using* magic – to effectively enslave you. Yes."

Thorstein rubs his free hand over his face. He looks calm, but through our joined hands I can feel him shaking, his muscles tense and trembling.

"You feel the *berserkrgang* trying to descend upon you now, don't you?" Wolfram says kindly.

"Yes," Thorstein says between clenched teeth.

"Because you are angry."

"Furious."

"You have good reason to be, son, but right now, you need to calm your anger. There are people here who love you, and you do *not* want to hurt them."

"No," Thorstein's voice has dropped to a whisper and his hand tightens on mine, but not the bone-crushing grip from before. He closes his eyes and breathes in deeply, slowly. Breathes out, just as deep and just as slowly. In. Out. In. Out. Until I feel the trembling stop and the muscles in his arm relax. He opens his eyes and Wolfram smiles.

"Remarkable," says Thea.

"Indeed," says Wolfram. "I would have said he was far too old to begin training in *seidhr*, but I think what he just accomplished shows he's capable."

"I agree," says Thea. "But I don't think you or I are the ones to do it."

"No," says Wolfram, then he faces Thorstein again. "Are you willing to commit to a path of training that will require a lifelong practice? That will take time every day for the rest of your life? Can you be present for monthly sessions without fail?"

"Yes."

"You cannot skip a month because you're too busy. And missing a day could set you back to the beginning."

"I understand."

"What would happen if he missed a day?" I ask. I think they've all forgotten I'm even here, that I may have heard things no ordinary human should. But Wolfram only looks at me, and lets a smile twitch his lips.

"He would have to begin again at the beginning, probably. It's different for everyone. This is as much about maintaining a commitment as it is about anything else."

Then he turns back to Thorstein. "Can you be here for the three days of this coming full moon? And every dark moon after that until your teacher is convinced you're safe to practice on your own?"

"I…" Thorstein hesitates. "Yes. I'll find a way."

Wolfram nods. "I will have to ask Syr if she's willing to train you."

"Oh, I think she will," says Thea. "She's never been one to back down from a challenge. And maybe I'll consent to letting her teach me those advanced techniques she's been after me about."

Wolfram laughs. "Using yourself as a bargaining chip?"

"I like this kid," she says. "Almost as much as his little brother. They're both so amusingly *decent*. And I always have a good time with Syr."

"In the meantime," says Wolfram, "I can remove the magic that makes you respond to your father's commands."

"What if there are other phrases?" asks Su.

"I know what to look for now," Wolfram says. He gets up and gestures to Thorstein. "Come with me, son. You –" he says when I get up to follow, "– stay here. I think you've had enough shocks to your belief system for one day."

And it's true, the longer this day goes on, the more surreal it feels, and I wonder how long it will be until my humble human brain kicks in with the self-preservation mechanisms and starts rationalizing everything I've learned.

Thorstein turns to me, frees his fingers from mine, and strokes my face. He doesn't say anything – the look on his face says enough – but he kisses me softly before turning to follow Wolfram out of the room and up another flight of stairs.

"It's a lot to take in," says Su.

"Just a little," I say.

"I used to be human," she says. "Or I thought I was. No awareness of magic, no knowledge that werewolves or anything else existed."

"What happened?"

"It's a long and not very pleasant story, but I lost my memories of who I was, and learned *what* I was all at once. And then I found out vampires exist when one almost killed me."

She leans on Magne, and he puts an arm around her. "And then she learned that werewolves exist when her hot downstairs neighbor wouldn't stop hitting on her." She laughs and jabs him in the ribs with her elbow.

"You *were* a dog," she says. "For a long time, I believed the only non-humans were the ones we call *others* or *otherkind*."

"You and me both," says Magne.

"Werewolves and vampires," I say. "And witches."

"Pretty much. And weres and vamps are both made what they are by a symbiotic organism. No magic at all."

"And witches?"

"Until recently, we thought they were essentially just humans with a genetic ability to manipulate probability and do some pretty impressive, but non-magical, mind tricks," says Magne.

"You know," he says to Su. "That book Granddad wrote is wrong. He classified everything that could change shape as some variation of symbiont *other*. But I bet a lot of them are *kin*." He smirks. "I wonder if I should tell him."

Su nods absently. "Essentially, we learned there's a lot more out there than *otherkind*. I mean, what I can do can't be explained by a symbiont, or a mind trick."

"You're…" I have no idea what she could be.

"A fox-woman," she says. "Among other things, I can turn into a fox."

"Like an actual fox?"

"Yes," she laughs. "Nothing like the way a werewolf changes at all."

"And Evgeny…" Magne pauses, looking at Su.

"Our friend Evgeny," she says, her voice subdued, "Was born a witch. An *other*. And he was made a vampire."

"Also an *other*," says Magne.

"But it's not supposed to be possible to be two kinds of *other* at once, and he is."

"And," says Magne, pausing to kiss the top of Su's head – there's something there, some history, that makes them both sad ."He's gained some additional magic since then. True magic."

"And not only that," says Su. "Some witches can develop true magic."

"And some humans can even inherit it, in small amounts."

"So *kin* or *folk* is how we refer to beings with true magic. Or the ones that aren't human, anyway." Su pushes back a bit of hair that's escaped her braid. "And sometimes it seems like every being out of folklore or myth could potentially be real."

"And…" Magne hesitates a moment then shrugs. "A lot of them live here, on Wonder Island."

"It's a sort of sanctuary," Su says. "And Wolfram doesn't like offering aid to outsiders because it threatens to expose the people he protects."

I sit down again. "Holy shit."

"Yeah, it's a lot," says Magne. "Sorry."

"We thought you should at least have *some* idea," says Su.

"We're really still just figuring it all out ourselves."

"So," I say. "What kind of… being is Wolfram, that he protects a whole magic island?"

"Ah," says Su.

"We're still working that out, too," says Magne.

I look at him, trying to pull out a thought that's niggling at my brain.

"Your dad banished you," I say. "And… forbid you from using his name?"

"Yeah."

"Thorstein thinks the younger werewolves would support you, if you refused the banishment. Even most of the older ones."

"Does he?" Magne's voice is soft, regretful.

"You don't want to go back?" I say.

He shakes his head. "I can't go back now."

"But you could. Thors says —"

"No, Raine, I really can't. I'm not…" He looks helplessly at Su, like maybe she can find words when he can't.

"This island isn't just a place of sanctuary," she says. "It has a magic of its own. And a kind of sentience. It chose to give Magne… Well, I suppose the Island saw it as giving him a gift."

"It didn't ask first," he says, half growl. "To see if I even *wanted* its so-called gift."

"I know, love," says Su.

Magne sighs, a deep in and out of breath. "When I was here recovering from the injuries my father inflicted on me most recently," he rubs his shoulder again, a spot on the big muscle behind his collarbone, and I realize it's the opposite side from where he was rubbing before. "These ones he actually got his own fucking hands dirty for." He drops his hands, stuffs them in his front pockets and for a moment looks exactly like a younger Thorstein. "The island took the opportunity to also 'cure' me of my werewolf symbiont, so the thing it gave me instead could take root more efficiently."

"So," I say, puzzling through what he's telling me. "You're… not a werewolf anymore?

He smiles, and it reminds me of Wolfram's smile from earlier, all teeth and no merriment. "I can still change like a werewolf, but it gets harder and harder. I think the changes the symbiont made to me are slowly reversing." He clenches his teeth and holds out one hand, and with a snapping of tendons and creaking of joints, his hand flexes and rearranges into a paw, complete with claws. The transformation back to a human hand is quicker and looks much less painful.

"It took away something that was part of me before I was even born," he says.

I hear a strangled noise from the doorway and Thorstein is there, staring at Magne.

"Oh, Monster," he says. "No." He steps into the room and pulls Magne into his arms, holding him tightly. I think it's as much for his own comfort as Magne's.

"Hey," Magne says, gently. "It's okay. I didn't get left with nothing."

Thorstein steps back, holds Magne at arms' length, and examines him.

"First, gaining that magic meant I could seek sanctuary here, where

Dad couldn't touch me."

"I am glad for that," Thorstein says.

"And, well," Magne looks at me, grins his two-dimple smile. "You might want to close your eyes for this Raine, if you've had enough magic for one day. Don't want to overload you, like Wolfram said." And then he's not there. Where he was standing is a huge – and I do mean fucking huge – timber wolf with brown and gray fur and deep brown eyes. Magne's eyes.

Thorstein takes a step back, gropes for my hand, and says, "Holy fuck."

"Magne?" I say.

"He probably should have given you a little more warning," says Su.

Then Magne is back again, grinning his fool head off. Okay. Hot boy turns into for real, actual, wolf. Damn.

"Holy fuck," says Thorstein again.

"It's not the same," says Magne. "But it goes a long way towards making up for losing my symbiont."

"Does that," I say, making a vague gesture towards Magne, "Affect the whole 'being loved by a werewolf' thing?"

Su smiles and shrugs.

"Not that I can tell," says Magne. "The symbiont may be gone, but the bond seems to be firmly intact." He does not seem to be the least bit unhappy about that fact. Instead, the way he looks at Su says he enjoys it, and so does she.

I look at Thorstein out of the corners of my eyes. He's staring in awe at his little brother, a smile tugging insistently at the corners of his lips.

"So I kind of belong here, now," Magne says. "We're just going to have to get Thorstein fixed so he can take over from Dad like he was supposed to."

"Don't say 'get Thorstein fixed'," Thorstein growls.

"Oh, right," Magne says. "You've just discovered what the dangly bits in your crotch are for," he says, then dodges out of the way as Thorstein lunges for him.

He almost makes it.

"Hey,'" he says, laughing, "Watch the hair," as Thorstein gets him in a headlock and proceeds to give him a thorough noogie.

"Your hair," says Thorstein, "Looks like you've never brushed it in your life. I seriously doubt this is going to make it look worse."

"Boys," says Wolfram, appearing in the hallway. "*Some* of us have jobs to do."

They're still laughing as they stand apart and it's so amazing to see Thorstein happy. I meet Su's eyes and she grins, so I grin back.

"Be here before midnight on the night before the full moon," says Wolfram. "If anything changes, I'll have Magne let you know."

Back in the parking lot, I take a detour to where I see a vintage blue C-10 pickup with a white top.

"Shit," I say. "You really did fuck it up good." The scratches, five parallel grooves along the length of the longbox, continuing onto the door, are deep, showing the silver of metal and looking like they almost penetrate right through in some spots.

"The *berserkrgang* makes me stronger," says Thorsein. "And more aggressive."

"Well," I say, leaning into him when he puts an arm around me. "We have a solution now."

He smiles. "Yes. A long and difficult solution that I'll have to keep working on my entire life."

I look up at him. "I don't get the impression that that part of it actually bothers you much."

He smiles wider. "It doesn't. I've heard of *seidhr*. It's like a … a Nordic shamanic practice. I'm actually looking forward to learning."

"Good," I say.

It's later than I thought it would be, now, and I know Thorstein really should get back to the farm soon. Driving me home instead of heading directly for the highway and the Bottomlands is going to take him out of his way. But I don't want to give him up yet. I've had him for a whole twenty-four hours now and I just want to keep going.

We drive in silence, each lost in our own thoughts, but it's a comfortable silence. I watch the city pass out the windows, and when it gets too dark, I turn and watch Thorstein.

"What?" he finally says.

"What what?"

"You're watching me."

"I like looking at you," I say. "You're extremely nice to look at."

"Is that so?"

"Do you not own a mirror?" I say, finally voicing something I've wanted to say since our first date.

"I don't spend a lot of time looking in it," he says. "I don't like what I see."

I know he's not referring to his looks, but to what lies under, the things he's done. "He's forgiven you," I say. "And he never blamed you in the first place."

"Maybe now seeing myself in the mirror won't be so bad."

When he pulls up in front of my building, he leaves the car running, so I reach over and shut off the ignition.

"Raine," he says, turning and facing me. "I have to get back to the farm. I *want* to stay, but…"

"I know," I say. "You have a pregnant mare and sheep to see to." I smile. "I just want you for a few more minutes."

I press the button to release my seat belt, and then the one for his. I reach for him, and he leans across the gearshift and kisses me. After a long, delicious snog, I say, "You better put the parking brake on."

He pulls the lever and eases his foot off the brake pedal. "Okay, why?"

"So you don't accidentally send the car rolling into the neighbor's Jeep," I say.

"And why would I do that?"

"Because I'm going to do this," I say, and I lean across the space between the seats and pop the button of his trousers with my teeth.

He inhales sharply. "You do know we're parked on the street in full view of anyone who walks by?" he says, but he doesn't stop me from pulling his zipper down and sliding my hand into his shorts.

"It's dark," I say. "And I live on a very quiet street." I shift my weight to get my mouth closer to his crotch without impaling myself on the gear shift, and fish him out of his pants, feeling him growing hard in my hand. "And if you don't have time to come upstairs," I say, flicking out my tongue to stroke his velvet skin. "Then I'm going to see to it that you come right here."

Then I slide my mouth over him and suck until he's fully hard.

"Fuck, Raine."

"Mmm," I say. I run my tongue over the underside of him, then wrap my fingers around the base of him and slide my mouth back over his length and stroke and suck until his breath goes ragged and I feel him trying to hold himself back from thrusting farther into my mouth.

Then I sit up and look at him. His eyes are half-closed, and his pupils dilated, his hands clenched on the steering wheel.

"Don't," he says softly. "Gods."

"Don't what?" I say. I stroke the flat of my hand on the underside of his hardness, then curl my fingers around him again.

"Don't stop," he says.

"Don't stop what?" I don't know why I have to tease him, but I can't resist.

"Don't stop, Raine, please."

I smile, and kiss his mouth, then I bend back down again and take him in, as much of him as I can without gagging. And I suck him and slide off of him and plunge over him again and again until he goes utterly still and spasms and my tastebuds are flooded with the salty bitter flavor of him.

Chapter Thirteen

I CHECK THE CALENDAR when I get inside and discover that the full moon is only a week and a half away. Right in the middle of the week.

Katie's going to kill me when I ask her to work for three days solo. But I don't think she'll say no; I'd do it for her. She's going to want to know why I'm asking, though, and I'm going to have to lie.

I don't *want* to lie, but I can't exactly tell her my boyfriend is a werewolf who goes crazy at the full moon and I have to take him to a meditation retreat to cure him.

So I settle for, *hunky BF surprised me w/a 3-day trip nxt wk. can you cover W-F?*

Then I quickly add *will cvr yr wkends rest of mo.* I might as well offer her something in return.

I hate you, she texts back. *Because u no i will.*

I reply with a pink heart and she sends back a middle finger.

luv u 2 I reply.

Then I make myself something to eat and settle down with a book.

I'm just heading to bed when I get another text.

thinking about you, he says.

Thinking what? I answer.

things i cant put in text

Sexy things?
yes.
Me too, I say. *Trying to 4get with new book.*
which book?

I send him a snapshot of the dust jacket. It's got the usual PNR-style cover with a tough-but-gorgeous woman groping a shirtless muscular man, with swirls of magic twining around them. It's pretty well written and I was almost lost in the story when Thorstein texted.

I get back a string of cry-laughing emojis, and then the photo of the same book on what looks like a hand-quilted comforter in shades of deep green and gray.

No shit, I text.
she reminds me of you a bit, he sends.
He reminds me of you, I reply. *But mouthier.*
a fake plant is more talkative than i am
True. Good thing I like large, quiet men with great hair.

There's a long pause, and then he sends, *I need to figure out how I'm getting to WI for full moon.*
We, I send back.
?

**We* need to figure out how *we* are getting there,* I say.

There's another pause, then a kissy face emoji.

"Goofball," I mutter. Not for the first time, I wish I had a car. There's no way I can ask Katie to borrow hers. Not when she thinks I'm being whisked away for a sexy mid-week getaway. And I can't use Thorstein's car because he might not be capable of driving, and I won't be able to get to the farm to pick him – and the car – up.

I can drive, I say, *but need vehicle.*

Another, longer pause follows. Then *1 of farm trucks needs wrk. Will take it in early next wk. Can u get to Harkett Motors Tues to pick up?*
When do they close?
5:30
Then yes. Will go after work.

So that takes care of that part. Now we just have to figure out how I'm actually going to get him from the basement to the truck. And how I'm going to drive the truck up to the house unnoticed in the first place.

After a few more texts back and forth, I settle into bed to read one more chapter. Which is, of course, famous last words. Who can actually read only one more chapter? Plus, I keep thinking about how Thorstein is reading the same book and wondering if he's lying in bed feeling way too hot after reading that steamy scene, too. So it's very late when I finally turn out the light, but at least I fall asleep quickly.

So a werewolf walks in… Yeah, fine, but I could just about use that line every day, these days.

This time, it's Magne, and he looks around himself, at his art filling the walls, every single tag save the two "not for sale"s bearing the coveted red dot that means "sold" in the gallery world.

He wanders over to the drawing he did for his brother when he was ten. "I didn't know he kept it," he says, running his hand through his hair. As usual, the finger comb does nothing to tame the messy strands, but he manages to look hot as hell anyway. Though these days I'm far too interested in his older brother to notice any details. Obviously.

"If the two of you had talked, you'd probably know a lot more things about him." I don't mean to sound accusing, and Magne's my friend, but I guess maybe I do.

He doesn't turn away from the drawing. "I tried," he says. "For years."

"And then you left." Okay, this time I don't try to hide the accusation. "You left him with –"

He turns around and grabs my arm so fast I'm shocked into silence. But he only squeezes my shoulder gently, then drops his hand.

"You don't think I haven't thought of that every day since?" he says.

I blink at him.

"If I stayed, it would have killed me. *Dad* would have killed me. I wasn't capable of being his obedient little clone. I just kept hoping…" He turns away in frustration, gently brushes the edge of the picture frame with his fingertips.

"I kept hoping he'd stick up for himself. I didn't know Dad used *magic* to keep him in line."

He looks at me again. "I came here to let you know, in case Thors didn't tell you…" He pauses, and I wait, not sure if he's expecting me to say something.

"Dad used more magic than we thought at first. It wasn't just that one phrase. He –" He shakes his head sharply. "He used a spell. We think he gave it to Thors in water. We think it made him… not care. It made him just accept that things would always be the way they were." He steps closer to me, puts a hand on each arm, gripping me tight and making me look into his eyes.

"When you…" He blushes. Shameless Magne Thorvaldson *blushes* and looks more like Thorstein that he should with his rounder face and wider mouth. He breathes in deep. "When you accepted him as a monster, when you… *wanted* him anyway, you broke that hold Dad had over him.

"You made Thors want to live again. To really *live*. There aren't enough thanks in the world for that." Then he hugs me, crushing me to his big chest and wrapping both arms around me. "Thank you," he says.

"Falling in love with me broke the spell," I say, feeling a bit dazed.

Magne lets go and turns back to contemplating the picture. "Man," he says. "I really sucked when I was ten." He laughs. Then he says, "And no, it wasn't falling in love with you. I don't think that happened on your first date."

"Fucking him," I say, flaring my nostrils and daring him to laugh at me.

He only smiles a lopsided smile that shows one dimple but not the other.

"No," he says. "I think it was just the idea that a beautiful woman could *like* him enough that turning into a drooling beast didn't drive her away. It made him want to find out if it was a fluke. And wanting something so badly broke the spell. I think."

He pretends to study the next painting on the wall, and says, "It's like one of those books he likes."

When I look sharply at him, his grin has grown. I can't tell from the angle I'm at, but I'd bet money his other dimple is visible now.

He looks at me out of the corners of his eyes. "You know, where the monster finds love at the end."

I stare at him. "You know what kind of books he likes?" I finally say.

"We shop at the same bookstore," he says. "We have the same last name. Of course I know."

"Does Bjarni?"

"I doubt it. Bjarni's good with numbers and organizing. He's pretty stupid otherwise."

"He shops there. He has the same last name."

"Not very often. And he doesn't pay attention to anything other than himself."

"You don't like him very much."

"What's to like?" But he smiles. "He's not so bad when it comes down to it. As long as I don't have to see too much of him."

I stare at him a moment longer, watch the grin grow, and finally say, "Don't you ever make fun of Thorstein for what he likes to read." I'm surprised at the vehemence in my voice.

"Why would I?" he says, and I remember it was Magne who told Thorstein not to be embarrassed of the books he liked in the first place. Then Magne looks away again. "I'm proud of him, you know?"

"Because he used to be illiterate?"

He meets my eyes. "He told you?"

I just nod.

"You know, I thought it was the best fucking thing in the world, learning to read with my big brother." He looks back at his ten-year-old self's drawing, touches the frame again. "It was so hard sometimes, watching him struggle. But he never gave up. Paying attention to what he's been reading all these years was one way I could still feel like that kid sitting at the kitchen table, sounding out words with his hero."

"Thanks, Magne," I say, suddenly finding it hard to swallow.

"What for?"

"Being as much a hero for him as he was for you."

He cocks his head and frowns at me.

"You were," I say. "But you didn't have to come all the way across town to let me know about the extra shitty magic your dad used."

"Wolfram thinks he got it all, but he can't be sure. Dad could have had other kinds of magic that's less detectable, so be careful."

Then he digs in his pocket. "But I actually came here to give you this." And he pulls out a battered old dead bolt key and holds it up.

"The key to your dad's house?"

He shakes his head. "They never lock the door. This is the key to my dad's *basement*."

I take the key from him and examine it. I mean, it's a pretty ordinary key, brass and scratched, worn from years of use.

"How?" I say.

"Did he tell you I used to sneak down to see him?"

I nod.

"Before the farm was shifted over to organic and regenerative, we used tractors instead of horses, and Bjarni used to lose tractor keys all the fucking time. So Dad bought a used key-cutter at auction. I taught myself to use it and cut my own key, so I didn't have to risk getting caught stealing Dad's." He flicks the key in my hand, and it makes a bright "ping." "I wasn't sure I even still had it."

"I'm glad you did."

"Me, too," he says. "But you still have to get him out of there."

"Can you help?"

He shakes his head. "I'm banished. The dogs will have been trained to watch for me. Or rather to *smell* for me. I wouldn't be able to get anywhere near the house without them making an unholy racket."

"They won't react to me?"

"The rest of the pack is in and out all the time. If the dogs aren't trained specifically to your scent, they shouldn't bother with you."

"You're sure?" I don't relish having to face down a bunch of growling hounds.

He shrugs. "No, but you're human, which makes you less of a threat. Wear something of Thorstein's when you go, the sweatier the better, and they won't pay any attention to you. Probably."

"Shit," I say and it's a much milder word than what I *want* to say. Then, "How did you know I was going to go get him out?"

He grins that half-smile and says, "Su would come after me," as if that explains everything. Then he touches my shoulder. "You don't have to do this. You can still walk away, and no one will think less of you."

That's the second time a Thorvaldson brother has said as much to me, so I answer the same way. "*I* would think less of me." What I don't say is that I can't back down now because I'm pretty sure it would not only break Thorstein's heart if I abandoned him, it would break *mine*.

So Tuesday finds me hurrying from work, dragging along a few necessities I packed the night before, and making my way by public transit to a small auto shop in a run-down part of town. It's the sort of place you look at and figure they're either going to rip you off, or they've got the best mechanics in town. Or possibly either one, depending on if they like you or not.

The guy who comes to the front desk when I walk in looks like he could be a distant Thorvaldson cousin. He's somewhere over six feet, with sinewy arms and a beer gut, and has pale blue eyes and hair that could maybe, on a very sunny day, be described as some variety of blond.

"I'm here to pick up a truck for Thorvaldson?" I say, hating how anxiety turns my sentence into a question.

The guy looks me up and down, and when I was younger I might have tried to use his interest as a weapon and turn it against him. But obviously I've changed, because now it just makes me feel gross.

"Name?" he says.

"Raine Chevalier."

"You Thorstein's new chick?" he says. "Or is it Bjarni you're fucking?"

Well, I guess that's one way of asking. I shake off the anxiety and let anger and disgust take its place. Not too obviously, though, because I still don't have the keys and I don't even know which truck it is.

"Let's just say I have self respect," I answer.

He laughs, a wet smoker's rasp, and says, "Thorstein's, then."

He pulls a set of keys off a hook and tosses them to me. Luckily, I've had enough things thrown at me by cousins and siblings over the years that I catch them easily.

"Red Ford 250 in the first row," he says, then walks away, presumably to go back to fixing something.

The truck in question has seen better days – and looks like something with hooves has kicked it more than once – but it's been pretty well cared for otherwise, and the cab is a big two-full-row crew cab and spotlessly clean. It's roomy enough that all four Thorvaldson men (and I'm assuming that Dad is as large as his sons) could fit comfortably inside at once, assuming they'd ever want to all be in the same place at the same time.

I manage not to get lost leaving town, and then I'm on the highway, heading for the Bottomlands and farm country. I've timed it so I'll arrive just before dark, so I can find the place. I'll scope out where I need to turn off, then I'll find somewhere to pull over until full dark. I know Thorstein will already be locked in the basement, though he will hopefully not yet be affected by the moon. The plan, such as it is, is to wait for his father to fall asleep, then sneak Thors out and drive like hell for Wonder Island. That way, we hope, his father won't even realize he's gone until it's too late to stop us.

There's so much that could go wrong with this plan. Starting with the fact that I miss the turn-off to the farm and don't manage to find it until it's completely dark, and then I have to creep along the road and find the driveway that leads to Thorstein's house, where the truck will be out of view of the main farmhouse.

By the time I stop and get the truck turned around and prepared to leave again at a moment's notice, I'm shaking. I take deep breaths and study the house in the dim light. It's a Craftsman, two-story, well-built, and beautifully kept. At least from what I can see in the near-dark. I suddenly want very badly to see inside, to *be* inside with Thorstein, doing ordinary things like making dinner and reading. I want that so badly for him.

And for me.

When I feel steady enough, I feel under the seat and pull out the t-shirt Thorstein said he'd leave for me there, so I'd smell familiar to the farm dogs. It's ridiculously big on me, but it smells like Thorstein and man-sweat, which is weirdly comforting.

I make sure the basement key is in my pocket and get out of the truck. I check the time on my phone. Just after nine. According to Thorstein, his dad is one of those "early to bed, early to rise" types, and should be just about asleep by now.

I look for the path to the main house, and really wish I'd brought a flashlight. I almost use the one on my phone, but then I realize it'll be visible once I get close to the house. I'll just have to hope the almost-full moon clears the trees soon, and that I don't break my ankle in the meantime.

I start at every noise, even though I grew up in the country and know what most of the sounds are. I'm expecting a pack of giant dogs to leap out at me at any moment, but the closest I get is some distant barking.

The main house looks exactly like what you'd expect a farmhouse to look like in Anywhere, North America. White-painted, two-and-a-half story, a big wrap-around porch – complete with a fucking porch swing, no less.

There are no lights on, and I can't tell what color the front door is. Green maybe, or blue. A couple of large potted flowering plants lurk on each side of the front steps, and there's a big bristly mat with "WELCOME" on it in worn block letters, and a boot brush squatting right next to a boot jack.

I realize I'm shaking again, and I can't make myself go any closer. I just stand on the slate-paved walkway and stare at the house. Just three steps up the porch, a door to go through, a hall to the kitchen, and then a lock to open. And I can't move.

"Breathe, Raine," I tell myself. "Just fucking breathe."

I try to do as I say, but it doesn't work; my breath just keeps coming in rapid gasps and I'm starting to feel lightheaded. I haven't had a panic attack since I was twenty-three and had to do a presentation for an art history class at uni.

The dogs I heard earlier bark again, closer.

I have to move.

Then I hear another sound, fainter. A soft, keening sort of howl. It's coming from the house, I think. The basement.

Then the sound turns to a growl, and a roar, and there's a thump, then silence.

"Oh fuck," I whisper. It's Thorstein, and he's already under the influence of the *berserkrgang*. He had thought it would hold off until tomorrow, had hoped it would, anyway. But what else could it be? The thought of him locked in there, alone for three agonizing days makes me want to cry, and it makes me angry.

"I'm coming, Thors," I say under my breath, and finally I *can* breathe.

I take the steps slowly, trying not to make them creak. Then I ease open the front door, slip inside, and close it behind me. I'm about to follow the hall toward where the kitchen should be when I glance up at the stairs to the floor above.

Right into the hard blue eyes of the man coming down them.

<h1 style="text-align:center">Chapter Fourteen</h1>

AGAIN, I CAN'T MOVE.

The man – and who else could he be but Thorstein's father Thorgrim? – stares at me as he comes down the stairs.

He's shorter than Thorstein, maybe six feet, and slighter, but still powerfully built. His dark blond hair is long, with braids at the front, and his substantial beard is braided, too. He looks too much like Thorstein for comfort.

"Who are you?" he says. Demands. His voice is as cold and hard as his eyes and for a fraction of a second, I can't think at all.

"Oh," I say, and force a giggle. "I think I'm in the wrong house." I pretend to sway drunkenly and reach for the door handle. "You're not –" I almost say "Thorstein" but at the last instant manage to blurt out "Bjarni." I hope he doesn't notice the slight hesitation.

"We were supposed to party," I say, adding another giggle. I think my gamble might pay off; Thorgrim Thorvaldson doesn't look suspicious. He looks disgusted.

He reaches the bottom of the stairs and steps closer and it's then I realize he's only wearing boxer shorts, and the moonlight just filtering through the windows picks out every curve of tense, powerful muscle, and every pale line of the scars that cover his body.

I mean, I knew he was a werewolf, too, but I guess I never really thought about what that meant. And I never expected him to look so much like Thorstein. To *move* like Thorstein.

He gets closer, right in my face, and his blue eyes bore into me. I almost breathe a sigh of thanks that they're a shade darker than Thorstein's, and not even a little green.

"Bjarni isn't here," he says finally.

"I see," I say, aiming for drunken confidence. "I'll go look for him." I reach for the door handle again.

His head suddenly snaps up and his eyes shift from mine to somewhere beyond the door. And then I hear it, the clamor of dogs. Then there's a commotion on the steps and the door opens and the hall fills with dogs, sniffing and wagging. One of them thrusts its nose into my hand and I pet it automatically.

"I love dogs," I declare in my drunk bimbo voice, and tear my eyes away from Thorstein's father to look at the animals milling around. It turns out there are only three of them, but they're so big and enthusiastic that it seems like twenty.

Thorgrim barks out a command and all at once the dogs are still, sitting attentively and watching him. Then he says something else – something in a language I don't know – and all three dogs get up again and file out down the hall.

I straighten up, turn back for the door, and there's Bjarni, looking at me with a frown.

His father turns the same cold, disgusted look on him that he earlier used on me. "How many times have I told you not to bring your whores to the farm?"

"Hey!" I say, the objection slipping out before I can stop it.

"Never, actually," Bjarni says. "And she's not a whore, Dad." He steps forward and drapes an arm around me. I want to shove him away, but I'm supposed to be playing a role and if he's going to play along, so much the better. He's my only chance to get out of this, anyway. So I slide my arm around his waist and lean into him, put my lips against his neck, and say, "You promised me a party." I let a bit of whine creep into my voice.

"And I'll give you one, sweetheart," Bjarni says. He looks at his dad.

"You're the one who wants me to get hitched," he says. "You could try to be polite to my date." And he pulls me with him towards the door.

"You could make better choices in *dates*," his father says, and the way he says "dates" creeps me out, like he knows Bjarni doesn't date anyone, he just fucks them, and like he thinks I'm not good enough to even do that.

"I just stopped over to let the dogs in," Bjarni says. "I'm going out again."

"You have work in the morning," his father says.

"And I'll be here, bright eyed and bushy tailed." Bjarni bares his teeth as he talks, and the coldness in his eyes echoes his father's. And I realize that of the three brothers, *he's* the one most like his dad, and that's a bit terrifying since I'm currently relying on him to get me out of this.

"You'd better be."

We make it out to the porch before Thorgrim speaks again. "You might want to wonder why she smells like your brother," he growls.

Because, fuck me, he's a werewolf and can smell Thorstein on his t-shirt as clearly as the dogs could.

Bjarni pauses, looks at me, and says, "She was cold. All I could find in the truck was one of Thorstein's old t-shirts to give her." He shrugs, then turns to his dad and leers. "She'll smell like me soon enough."

His father makes a disgusted sound. And then I hear growling from the basement, low and dangerous, and Thorgrim turns his head sharply.

"Your dogs are fucking scary," I say, drunk giggling again.

"Get her out of here, Bjarni." And he slams the door.

Bjarni keeps his arm around me and pulls me with him along the front walk, then turns away from the path to Thorstein's house along a bark-mulched trail that leads through a copse of trees. I lurch along next to him.

"Don't overdo it," he says. "He's not observant, but he's also not stupid."

"Do you think he's still watching?"

"Probably."

He doesn't let go of me until we're through the trees and approaching another house, smaller and darker than the farmhouse, but with a cheery light on the porch, and another showing through the window. When he does let go, he lets his hand run down my back and over my ass, and it's all

I can do not to smack him.

"We have to go back," I say. "*I* have to go back."

"I don't know what the fuck you thought you were doing, but Thorstein's not in any shape to see you." He walks over to the Mitsubishi Evo parked in the driveway and opens the passenger door. "Get in." And fuck me, all three brothers apparently have decent automotive tastes.

"I know what state Thorstein is in," I say. "That's why I'm here. To get him help. I have to go back, to take him away from here."

He shakes his head. "You can't help him, Raine. It doesn't matter how much you think you love him, no one can help him."

"Have you ever fucking tried?" I yell.

He's fucking fast and is next to me, hand clamped over my mouth, before I can move. He hisses in my ear. "Quiet!" he says. "If you know about Thorstein then you probably know our fucking father is a fucking werewolf and has really fucking good hearing."

I'm not sure I've ever heard anyone say fuck even more than I do, but I have to admit it's effective.

"Get in the car," he says. "I'll drive you home, and you can explain to me exactly what you think you were going to do."

When he lets me go, I whisper, "I have to go back."

"You can't. Dad might not suspect you, but you just being there is going to mean he'll be extra watchful. Not even a goddamn mouse is going to sneak down those basement stairs tonight."

"Fuck," I say, suddenly feeling completely defeated. I want to cry but there's no way in hell I'll shed a single tear in front of *Bjarni*. So I get in the passenger seat of the shiny black rally car and put on the seatbelt. I stay quiet until we're away from the farm and on the highway.

"Shit," I say. "I left a bag of my things in the truck."

"The farm truck?" he says. "I was wondering why Thorstein didn't ask me to go get it."

I nod, and Bjarni's jaw clenches. "When I get back, I'll put your things in Thorstein's house. You can get them from him next week. Or have him bring your bag next time he stops in for a booty call."

"Fuck you," I say. I shouldn't care what he thinks, but first he says I only *think* I love Thorstein, and now he's saying all we do is fuck. And fine, maybe it's not so far from the truth, but it's not the way things are going to continue.

He sighs, shifts gears, and settles back in his seat. "What were you doing there?" he says. "Sneaking in for a little girl-on-monster action?"

"Fuck you," I say again.

"So? Why were you there? Going to set him free? You know he's fucking dangerous in that state?"

I stare out the window. I do *not* want to reveal anything to Bjarni. But I guess I haven't got much choice.

"He calms down when I'm there," I say. "Or he did that time –" I start to say. "Just like he did –" I snap my mouth shut.

"When you were on a date and got mugged," he says, finishing my first sentence. "And when Magne was a kid." He says it softly, and I look at him carefully.

He meets my eyes for a moment, then looks back at the road.

"Yeah," I say. "We have… we found someone who can help. I just needed to get him there."

"Where?"

I don't answer.

"Where?" he asks again, louder. "I'm not going to run home to Daddy and spill all your secrets," he says. "If that's what you think." His knuckles are white on the steering wheel and his voice is tight with hatred. "It's what everyone else thinks," he says, almost spitting out the words. He hates his father? I thought he was the favored one.

I look back out the window. "Wonder Island."

He laughs. When I look back at him with a glare, the smile vanishes. "You're serious."

"There's someone there who can teach him how to control his… rages. Someone who can teach him things he should have learned when your *father* –" and I practically spit out the word, echoing the way he was just speaking about the man "– first realized what he was."

He flexes his hands, drops one from the wheel to rest on the gearshift.

"I didn't know that was possible."

"Neither did he, until recently."

"So why are *you* helping him?"

"Because I —" But I can't say it. I can't admit I actually *do* love Thorstein to his asshole younger brother before I even say it to *him*.

He slants a sideways glance at me. "Shit," he says. "Katie said you were a slut like her." He grins when he sees my expression. "But you're not, are you? You really do care about him."

"I do," I say. "And that's why I need to get him out of there."

"Hunh," he says. Then, "Where am I taking you?"

I glance up, out the front windshield, and see we're approaching the cluster of off ramps to the various parts of Riverbend. I want to go home, drink something alcoholic, and curl up in bed and cry, but — aside from the fact that I don't want Bjarni to know where I live — I need to talk to Magne, and I don't think I can manage a phone conversation right now.

"Take the riverfront exit," I say, and Bjarni nods and switches lanes. He's choppier with the gearshift than Thorstein, or maybe it's just that a rally car lacks the smooth-as-butter shifting of a BMW.

"Can I ask who you were going to take him to?"

"I don't know," I say. "This was going to be the first meeting. I — Magne and Su were meeting us at the Wonder Island dock and then we were going over together."

"Fucking hell, Raine. You couldn't have warned me? I'm the last fucking person Magne's going to want to see. Like, ever." Because we're on River Road now, and the ferry is visible just ahead, lights blazing, waiting for me — for me and Thorstein — at the dock.

"You can just drop me off and go," I say. "In fact, just drive by and pull over and I'll walk."

"Fuck," he says, and slows to pull the car into the lot, stopping a couple rows away from Magne's truck, even though there are no other cars.

"Thanks," I say, and hop out. "Please don't forget to move my stuff out of the truck for me?"

"Fuck," he says again, and slams his hand on the wheel. Then he turns off the engine with a jerk, and climbs out.

I turn to see Magne stalking across the parking lot, and I do mean *stalking*. He looks predatory. Beautiful. Scary as fuck.

"You brought me the wrong brother," he growls, but he's looking at Bjarni.

"Hey, shit stain," Bjarni says, pasting a cocky grin on his face. "I found her trying to break into Dad's house."

"What happened?" Su says. I didn't even hear – or see – her approach.

"And you just had to interfere?" Magne says, his deep voice lower than I've ever heard it. Lower than Thorstein's even.

"Your dad caught me," I finally manage to say. And I almost burst into tears at the look Magne turns on me. Worry, regret, deep sadness.

"Oh, shit," says Su. "Are you okay?"

"He didn't suspect anything," I say.

"All thanks to yours truly," says Bjarni, cocky grin still in place. "I pretended she was my date and wandered into the wrong house. Got to work in a nice grope while I was at it." I feel Su's hand on my arm, pulling me back a few steps, but I don't see Magne move. I don't realize he *has* moved until Bjarni's on the ground, holding his face, blood seeping between his fingers.

"Holy shit," I say.

"Werewolves like to work out their differences physically," Su says.

Magne stands over his brother, teeth bared, and I swear his canines are bigger than they should be. Way bigger.

"Fuck, Magne," Bjarni says. You broke my nose." There's a crunch as he adjusts his face and then he drops his hands, leans back on them, and looks up at his brother.

The blood has stopped, but he doesn't bother to wipe it away. When he grins again, I can see it staining his teeth. "I guess I deserved that," he says.

"Yes, you fucking deserved that," says Magne. Then he holds out his hand. Wary, Bjarni takes it, but all Magne does is pull him to his feet. "But thank you for getting Raine out of there safely."

"I'm sorry I couldn't get Bear out, too," Bjarni says, and it takes me a second to realize "Bear" is Thorstein. "But I didn't really fancy grievous bodily harm tonight, and if Dad didn't get me, Thorstein would have.

"He never could stand you near when he was…"

"Yeah."

They stare at each other for a moment.

"Now what?" I say. "I couldn't get him out, so what do we do now?

Try again tomorrow? Next month? Or are we too late?"

Magne turns away from his brother, steps closer to me, and grips my shoulders. "We're not giving up," he says. "This isn't a failure, just a delay." He glances over at the ferry, where I can see someone waiting. Crew, maybe. Then he looks back at me. "Go home, get some rest. I'll talk to Wolfram."

Su looks pointedly at Bjarni, then back at me. "Can we count on *his* help?" she says.

"I've never counted on him for anything in my life. Don't see a reason to now." Magne doesn't even look at his brother.

"Werewolf, remember," Bjarni says. "I can *hear* you."

Magne ignores him. "I suspect Wolfram will advise waiting until next full moon. Maybe getting him out *before* the *berserkrgang* hits. But I'll let you know."

Bjarni steps closer, grabs Magne's arm, and jerks him around to meet his eyes. I wince and wait for Magne to hit him again.

But Magne just looks down at Bjarni, using his extra five inches of height to good advantage.

"He's my brother, too," says Bjarni, and when Magne sneers at him, he sneers right back. "Look," he says. "I know you think I'm an asshole. Fuck, I know I *am* an asshole. But he's my brother, and so are you. Let me help."

"You," says Magne, some of the venom going out of his voice, "Were the one always running to Dad to tattle."

"I did not *tattle*," Bjarni says "I was an adult before you were even born. Adults do not fucking tattle."

Magne just raises an eyebrow.

"Fine," says Bjarni. "I used to tell Dad shit. I thought..." He clenches his jaw and flares his nostrils. Then he jerks his head to one side, like he's dragging out a confession he doesn't want to give. "I thought he'd *like* me better. That he'd..."

"Make you his heir," Magne says.

"I never wanted to be his fucking *heir*," Bjarni says, the hatred I heard earlier creeping back into his voice. "I just wanted him to be proud of me for something. To even fucking notice I existed."

"He wasn't proud of any of us," Magne says.

"No," says Bjarni. "Except you."

"He fucking wasn't. He tried to make Thorstein kill me when I was fucking thirteen years old."

Bjarni's grin returns, dimples and all. "He tried to make you *stronger*. You never saw it, Mangy, but he *was* proud of you. Not for the things you *wanted* him to be proud for. Not for being good at drawing, or being kind to animals, or smart as a fucking whip." He pauses and grips the back of Magne's neck, pulls his head down so their foreheads rest together, almost mirror images of each other.

"I saw your art show," he says. "When Raine wasn't there."

"Katie didn't tell me," I say.

"I asked her not to." He sighs. "No, Magne. Dad was proud of how quickly your wolf shape developed, how good a hunter – a killer – you were. How all the girls tried to get your attention from the time you hit puberty."

"What?" Magne says, but his voice is softer. "What the hell are you talking about?"

"You know Dad wanted *you* to be the one to take over from him someday."

"Not until very recently," Magne says. "I still don't get why."

"Everyone else knew," Bjarni says. "And it was because everyone loves you. Everyone in the pack would follow you in a heartbeat. And that's why, when he was finally able to admit you'd never obey him, when he found out you were actually working *against* him – "

"He decided to have Thors deal with me. For good this time."

Bjarni nods. "I didn't realize," he says. "I thought we were just bringing you back to the Elders." He sighs and steps back. "Fuck, Magne, even the Elders would probably have sided with you this time, that's how far Dad's control has slipped."

"That's because wolves don't want a pack leader who controls them. They want one who *protects* them."

"Exactly."

"You didn't know he was going to make Bear kill me?"

"Bjarni shakes his head. "Not until he got back to the truck, so fucking angry he couldn't speak. He was…" He glances at me, then away.

When he picks up the sentence, his voice is quiet, but harsh with anger. "He was fucking brutal to Thorstein when we got home, for not doing what he wanted. For… He said Odin's wolves were there. I'm sorry I missed that."

"Another time," Magne says. "I have shit to do, if we're going to salvage this." He turns away abruptly. "Come on Raine, I'll drive you home."

"I can take her, Magne." Bjarni's voice is tight.

Magne whirls back around. "I don't fucking trust you, Bjarni."

"I know. But let me help."

I'm thinking about what Bjarni might have meant about his father being brutal to Thorstein. Or trying *not* to think about it. But I shake it off enough to say, "It's okay, Magne. Let Bjarni drive me home. He got me this far without stabbing me in the back."

I even manage to make it into my bed – still fully clothed, including Thorstein's sweaty shirt – before breaking down into sobs.

Chapter Fifteen

I CAN'T STAND THE THOUGHT of mooching around home all day, waiting for Magne to text me, so I drag myself out of bed and message Katie that I'm coming in after all, plans fell through and all that.

She takes one look at me when I get in and points to the workroom door. "You, my darling, are not fit to face the public, so go back there and catch up on framing orders."

I nod and head for the back, but as I'm opening the door, I turn and say, "You didn't tell me Bjarni came to see Magne's show."

She blinks at me, so I say, "I ran into him the other day."

"He didn't want Magne to know," she says. "So I figured it was safer not to tell you, either."

"Betrayal," I say, in mock heartbreak, and press the back of my hand to my forehead, pretend to swoon. "So you two are a thing now?"

"Me and Bjarni? Fuck no. He was a nice one-night stand, that's it."

"Not nice enough for a repeat," I tease.

"See, this is exactly why I didn't tell you," she says. "And you know I don't do repeats." She looks thoughtful. "He might be turning out to be something resembling a friend, though. You know, like attracts like. We're both assholes." She grins.

I get through a few jobs before she comes into the back room, her turn to interrogate me.

"So your hunky boyfriend get cold feet?" she says. "In my opinion, getting attached was a mistake in the first place."

"That's not what you told me at the opening. 'Go for it,' you said. And I used to agree."

"But this one's different," she says, skeptically. "So different he promised you a getaway and stood you up."

"He didn't stand me up," I say, sharply, suddenly annoyed at her flippancy. But I immediately smile and apologize. She doesn't know what's been going on, and Katie is Katie; opinions of the male sex aside, her heart's a good one.

"He's sick," I say. And it's not even – entirely – a lie. "Like bedridden, kind of finding death the better option sick."

She looks at me with narrowed eyes. "Then why were you recently bawling your fool eyes out?"

"Because I'm worried," I say, exasperation creeping back into my voice.

"He's *that* sick? Shouldn't he be in the hospital?"

"Yeah, he's that sick, and he doesn't do hospitals," I say, and must look actually worried – I *am* fucking worried, though not for the reason she thinks – because she gives me a hug.

"You just better not be contagious," she says.

By lunchtime I must have checked my phone a hundred times, hoping for something from Magne. Even a "still working on it" would be better than nothing.

Then I look at the last texts Thorstein and I exchanged.

off 2 xile, he'd sent. *wont rly see u til w.i works magic.* Then three red hearts.

I'd replied. *See u on the way to WI. Maybe sooner.* Because, of course, I would have seen him sooner, and he'd have seen me. He just might not have remembered it. Or known me. Or known himself.

I remembered hovering my finger over the heart emoji, not quite able to send it. I wish now I had. I wish I hadn't been so afraid of my own feelings.

I stare at the screen now, the little icon that means he's offline. Then I click away from it, open a new text message and find Bjarni's contact. He insisted on giving it to me when he dropped me off, "just in case."

Now, I'm glad. *Does ur dad read T's msgs?* I type.

There's no immediate answer, so I set my phone aside and try to eat my sandwich. Then I give up on food and go back to work. At least I don't really have to think while I'm working. I'm just wrapping the latest completed order when my phone vibrates. I make myself stick the tape firmly on the paper, attach the work order to the front, and add the piece to the "to be called" shelf before I check my messages.

Bjarni has replied. *T hides phone when locked up.*

A second message comes while I'm reading the first. *Never found where. Dad either.* A brief pause, then, *safe to sext. Or can send nudes to me instead.*

I don't bother to get mad. It's probably the reaction he wants. I just send *thx* and leave it at that. Then I switch back to my messages with Thorstein and resume staring at them.

Finally, I type. Emojis first, because for some reason he loves using them. A kissy face followed by two red hearts. I hesitate, then send them. I hope they'll be the first thing he sees. But then I think about how awful it will be for him to regain his senses fully and realize he's still trapped in the farmhouse basement.

So I type, *I'm so sorry. Hit a snag. Magne's working on a plan B. We *will* figure this out.*

I send and make myself get back to work. It'll suck to read that, but at least he'll have hope.

Finally, late in the afternoon, right before I'm ready to stop for the day, a text from Magne.

Sorry I took so long, he writes. *But we were trying to come up with the best plan.* As usual, texting in full sentences. *Meet at Wonder Island dock?*

When? I reply.

How soon can you get there?

I check the clock. It's almost five and the gallery isn't too far from the waterfront. Maybe fifteen minutes' walk.

25 mins, I say, and get a thumbs up in reply.

As I'm leaving the gallery, Katie says, "Tell hunk o' beefcake I hope he gets better soon." She grins a shit-eating smile at me. "So I can have something more companionable than a zombie working in the gallery with me."

"I'll make sure he knows," I say. Her laugh is much warmer than her words.

"Get some rest," she says.

Magne is alone on the Wonder Island dock, leaning on the railing and staring out over the water. I wonder if he knows how much like his brother he actually is.

As usual, his perfectly-fitting jeans and snug t-shirt leave little to the imagination, and I'm pretty sure ninety-nine percent of the women who walk by – and a fair number of the men – give him a good long ogle as they pass.

Hell, I'm checking him out as I approach, and I've got it bad for his brother.

"Hey," he says and something hurts in my chest. He even sounds like Thorstein.

"Hey," I say. "What's up?"

He grins, and for a second I think he's going to make a crude pun on what I said, but it passes and he just says, "Wolfram thinks we don't need to wait until the next full moon."

"Tonight?" I say, hope and fear battling it out in my gut.

He shakes his head. "Dark moon," he says. "It's the best time for this kind of training, apparently." When I open my mouth to point out the obvious, he holds up a hand.

"I know," he says. "If that's the case, then why were we trying for full moon?"

He leans back against the railing. "The idea," he says, "Was to give him a way to moderate the immediate effects of full moon, to give the *seidhr* priestess a chance to see the worst. After that, training would have switched to the new moon."

"Okay," I say. "So two weeks?"

He nods.

"That's going to feel like two goddam years," I say, and lean next to him.

"I know," he says, and puts an arm around me, giving me a comforting squeeze. For a moment, I let myself relax against him, feel his strength and warmth.

"You would have made a good pack leader," I say. "Not that I know anything about real-life werewolves. Which I'm guessing are not very much like paranormal romance werewolves."

He chuckles. "Maybe not *so* different. But Thorstein will make a better leader, once he's got his *berserkr* nature under control."

"Except for the part about having to talk to people."

He snorts. "Yeah, he's not so good at that."

"He can get Bjarni to handle the peopley stuff."

This time he laughs. "That's something Little Bear would be good at."

I have to look at him then. "Little Bear?"

His grin grows. "He hates that." He looks down at me. "You know Thorstein's full name?"

"Thorstein Bjorn Thorvaldson," I answer.

"Bjorn means 'bear'," he says. "And Bjarni is the diminutive of Bjorn. So 'little bear'."

"Your brothers have the same name? That's kind of mean."

"Worse than naming every eldest son, every generation, something that starts with 'Thor'?" He snorts again. "It's also kind of weird, because our whole family is werewolves, not were-bears. But Dad really liked the name. So Granddad started calling them Big Bear and Little Bear."

"What did he call you?"

"Cub." He smiles.

"And your sister?"

"Princess. Or Goldilocks." When that finally gets a smile out of me, he says, "I hope you get to meet Granddad. Once all this is over. I think he'd like you."

"How come he isn't pack leader?"

"He got old, and Dad took over. Neither of them talks about it."

Then he straightens up from the rail and I realize, all over again, how fucking *tall* he is. And how gigantic that really makes Thorstein.

"I promised Su I'd pick up curry on the way home," he says. "One of these days I'll find a good recipe and make it myself."

"Butter chicken?" I say, thinking that actually sounds pretty good right about now.

"Vindaloo," he answers.

"Ouch."

"Not into spicy?" His smile gets a little cheeky and I'm pretty sure he's making a double entendre, with "spicy" as in "spicy romance."

"Not *that* spicy," I say, and wiggle an eyebrow.

"Want a ride home?" He gestures at his truck. I shake my head.

"I think I'll walk a bit," I say.

He nods and takes a couple of steps. "I'm glad I chose your shop to get my framing done," he says. "That day."

"I thought it was because someone told you we were the best in town," I answer, teasing.

"Well, yeah, but there's a decent shop a lot closer to my apartment."

"Frame Magic?" I say, and he nods. "Yeah, they're good."

"Anyway."

"I'm glad, too."

Then I stare out over the water, take out my phone, and look at my last message to Thorstein.

Dark moon, I type. *That's when Magne says we try again.*

I stare at the water some more, thinking about the quiet and not so quiet noises I heard from the farmhouse basement. Sounds of a creature in distress. Did he know I was there, somehow? I brush away a tear. I'm *not* going to cry again. We have a new plan. It *will* work.

I look back at my phone.

I fucking love you Thorstein, I type and before I have a chance to chicken out, I hit send, put my phone in my pocket, and start walking.

I wake up way too early on Saturday morning to the insistent electrical noise of my apartment's buzzer.

I stumble out of my bedroom to the door and press the button, just to shut it up.

"What?" I say, not even trying to keep the irritation out of my voice.

"Hey." That one soft word in his deep smoky voice. I don't answer, I just press the door switch and hope the ancient electronic lock actually works and then unlock the door and run to the bathroom to brush my teeth.

When I straighten up from the sink and turn around, he's there, and his arms are around me, his mouth on mine. He presses me against the sink and I grab his shoulders, his hair, try to pull him closer when it's impossible to get any closer. I don't want to let him go when he pulls away to look at me.

"I'm so fucking sorry," I whisper.

He shakes his head. "Bjarni told be what happened. I'm just glad you're okay."

I touch his face, study it, trying to find all the ways he *doesn't* look like his father. And then I don't care. Thorstein looks like Thorstein, and he's *mine*.

"I missed you," I say, and for a moment I'm not even sure if sound comes out.

"I missed you, too," he says. "I –" He shakes his head and looks into my eyes. "I think I knew something was missing, that *you* were missing. Even when I didn't remember who I was. Why I was trapped in that basement."

"I love you," I say.

His mouth curls up and I put my fingertips there before he can reply. I'm not done.

"I was afraid of what it meant. To say it, to tell you."

He waits for me to finish, one hand stroking my hair, the other firmly on my hip.

"I never expected to find someone I'd want to… to spend my life with. Shit, I never expected to find someone I'd want to spend more than a few weeks with."

He smiles against my touch. "You might still change your mind," he says, lips brushing my fingers as he speaks. It feels incredibly erotic and suddenly I want him naked, in bed, body pressed down on mine. But I make myself finish what I need to say.

"I thought that, at first." He nods but doesn't interrupt again. "But that night, the thought of you stuck in that basement broke my cold, bitchy heart." He smiles again, lips curling against my fingers.

"And then your asshole brother said that I only thought I was in love with you. *Thought* I was. And I wanted to tell him he was wrong. I didn't *think* anything. I knew."

He kisses my fingertips.

"But I didn't want *him* to be the first person I said that to, so I didn't even tell him off.

He takes my hand in his, moves his mouth to my palm, trails kisses up my arm.

"And okay, I've known you for, what, two months? So maybe I shouldn't be so certain. But I am." I take a deep breath, enough to get out the last of the words I need to say before I give in to the hot, tingling mess he's making of my nerve endings. I pull away, take his face between my hands so he focuses his blue-green gaze on my eyes.

"I love you, Thorstein, and I want a goddamn fucking future with you."

He laughs. "I want a goddamn fucking future with you, too, Raine. So much."

Then I take his hand, pull him out of my tiny bathroom that seems so much smaller with him in it, and lead him to the bedroom. I don't say anything else, *can't* say anything else, I just pull his long-sleeved t-shirt over his head, unbuckle his belt and let his jeans drop to the floor. Then I step back and pull my night shirt off. He reaches out and slides my underwear over my hips, pulls me back to him, presses our skin together.

It amazes me, how well we fit together, even though he's so much taller than me. For a long time, we just stand that way, skin to skin, arms around each other. I feel his breath warm in my hair.

"I couldn't stand the thought of you regaining yourself, only to be still locked in that goddamn basement," I whisper against his chest.

"I've done it more times than I can count. I survived this time, just like every time before."

"I hate it," I say. "I hate *him*. Your father." I turn my head to lay my cheek on his chest, listen to his strong, steady heartbeat.

"Shh…" he says. "It's going to be okay."

I pull back, look up into his face. "It *will* be," I say.

He bends, brushes his lips against mine, and I kiss him back, turn my head to get a better angle, slide my tongue into his mouth. His hands make long strokes down my back, over my ass, back up again. Gentle, firm. Heat spreads everywhere he touches.

He starts to push me back towards the bed, but I anchor my hands on his hips – and holy hell, he's even got sexy *hip* muscles – turn him so I'm backing *him* towards the bed, sitting him on the edge, and climbing into his lap.

"On the bed," I tell him. "Lay down." I get up enough that he can move to the middle of the mattress, lay back against the pillows. Then I climb over him again, let him pull me down on top of him, and kiss his forehead, his nose, his chin, before claiming his mouth again. I can tell he doesn't want me to stop kissing him, but I do, only long enough to trace the line of his neck with my tongue. Then I work my way down, kissing his throat, his collarbone, his pecs.

I slide my hands over him, finding the steel ring piercing his left nipple and tugging it with my finger. He growls, so I move my mouth there, slide the tip of my tongue under the ring, suck until his nipple hardens. Then I move across to the other side, where the scar bisects his other nipple and bite him gently. His hands slide into my hair and his breathing hitches, and I start to work my way lower, tracing the outline of his muscles with my tongue as I go.

Before I can do more than taste his erection, he stops me. "Come here," he says, voice ragged and deep.

I climb back up his body, slide my skin against his. "I need you," he says. "Raine. I need to be inside you."

So I dig a condom out from under the pillow – I do believe in being prepared – open it and roll it onto him, and then he's lifting me, hands on my hips, and I reach down to grasp him, guide him into me, gasp as he lowers me, fills me.

"I need you," he says again, almost whispering.

"You've got me," I say. "Always." And I let him lift and lower me, help him with my legs, with the thrust of my hips, lean over him to get my mouth on his again.

I feel the urgency building in him, feel him thrust into me faster until suddenly, he slows again.

"When I'm done," he says, hoarse. "I want you to sit on my face."

"You what?" I say, clenching my muscles around him, pushing my hips hard against him until he starts to move faster again. With each thrust I feel heat building, tension growing, until his movements grow desperate under me, his hands tighten on my hips, and his back arches and a long groan escapes him.

He strokes his hands up my hips, over my rib cage, and back again. "Here," he says, lifting me off him, moving me forward to sit on his ribs. He tucks his arms under my legs and lifts me again, hands under my butt, to sit on his chest and then I grab for the headboard as he lifts me one more time, wriggles under me to get me positioned exactly where he wants me.

Before he sets me down, he growls, "I want you to fuck my mouth the way you just fucked my cock." And then he lowers me onto his face, onto his mouth, and I cling to the headboard like a lifeline.

All I can hear for several long moments are the wet sounds of his tongue, his lips, probing and sucking, and my own gasps until I can't hold it back anymore and I don't even know what kind of noises come out as I thrust myself against his mouth and experience the most intense fucking orgasm build and break and wash over me.

When the throbbing eases, Thorstein gently lifts me away from his face until I'm sitting on his chest again.

"Holy fuck," I manage to say. I look down at him and his eyes are half-closed, his lips curled in a contented smile, and the entire lower half of his face, his beard, his neck, are slick with my fluids.

"Mmm," he says. "I've wanted to do that for a long time." Then he has to help me lie down because my legs are too wobbly.

Chapter Sixteen

As I predicted, the two weeks between full moon and new seem to drag on forever, and I don't see much of Thorstein. He's busy catching up on farm chores that lapsed while he was locked up, and then with trying to get ahead so everything will go smoothly while he's away at the new moon.

I tell Katie the new dates of our supposed romantic getaway, then work my ass off finishing orders, so we won't get behind.

The only bright spot is when, halfway between full moon and new, Thorstein texts me a photo of a newborn foal, still wet and wobbly on his legs, standing next to a beautiful black mare.

she had a colt, he says.

he's beautiful, I answer.

Half an hour later, I get a message from Bjarni. No text, just a photo that I stare at for a very long time before making it my lock screen image. It's Thorstein, kneeling next to the colt, rubbing the newborn horse dry with a towel. Bjarni caught him in the middle of turning to face the camera – probably unaware the phone was even pointed at him – and the look on his face is such pure joy I have to sit down to catch my breath.

Thank you, I reply. *Maybe you're not such an asshole after all.*

Yeah I am, he answers. *Say hi to Katie for me.*

Do it yourself, I say. He doesn't answer.

Wonder Island is pretty much exactly as it was last time we visited, right down to waiting on the dock while someone fetches Magne. This time, Magne's t-shirt says "Monster Boyfriend" under a picture of a *Creature From the Black Lagoon* style fish man.

Thorstein ruffles Magne's hair, and Magne ducks away and says, "Hey!" and two women passing by slow down to watch.

One of the women says, not very quietly, "I want to see those two put on a sideshow," and her friend answers, "I'd pay a lot of money to see that."

I know they've both heard, because Thorstein blushes and Magne grins and winks at the women, then smacks his brother on the shoulder. I just shake my head.

"If farming doesn't work out for you," Magne says. "The strongmen here are thinking of retiring."

Thorstein just glares back.

"You could wear a little speedo, and really show off your ass… ets." Magne really draws out the space between syllables on that last word.

Thorstein mumbles something about shit-disturbing little brothers, then suddenly grabs Magne around the waist, hoists him up, and Magne's laughing so hard he's almost tearing up as Thorstein raises his brother over his head.

In a smooth, too-quick-to-follow motion, Magne twists, gets his feet on Thorstein's shoulders, and leaps. He does a flip in mid-air and lands on his feet back where he started. He almost botches the landing because he's still laughing.

Thorstein is laughing now, too, and people have stopped to stare, and applaud. So Magne grabs Thorstein's arm, and they bow together.

"I feel like I should pass around a hat," says Su, appearing next to me in that disconcerting way she has.

"You'd probably get at least enough to buy them both lunch," I say, and I realize I'm grinning almost as much as the brothers, and it's such a huge relief to see them happy. I can believe, then, that everything will be okay.

"If you two are done trying to put me out of business," says Wolfram, appearing just as stealthily as Su did. "We have an appointment to keep."

The nervy churning I felt on the boat ride over returns all at once.

As we approach a huge old stone building that forms an L shape with the equally large concrete building where we met last time, Wolfram pauses and turns to face us.

"I'm taking you somewhere very few non-Islanders are ever allowed to go," he says. "I had to present several very long and persuasive arguments to the council to get them to agree, and in the end I suspect they only gave their consent because they knew I would bring you here anyway."

He looks at Thorstein. "Magne has been there. And Su. But they are now as good as Islanders. I'm still not certain I'm doing the right thing in letting you in the House, but I suppose the House itself will decide if I've made a mistake."

I vaguely remember Su and Magne trying to explain how the island has its own kind of sentience, and I suppose this must be similar.

"Unfortunately," he turns to me. "You're going to have to wait outside."

"I'm going with him," I say, and reach for Thorstein's hand.

"The first time I came here," Magne says, "I had to wait outside while my friend went in to face the worst ordeal of his life." He touches my shoulder. "I didn't like it either, but there are some things that have to be faced alone."

I look at Thorstein, search his face.

"I'll be okay," he says. "I want you with me, but if I have to go alone… I'll be okay." He kisses my forehead.

I look at Su and she shrugs.

I bite my lip. I don't want to be left waiting for three days again, not knowing if whatever he's doing is working, or if we're going to face disappointment again. I open my mouth to argue why I should go, too, why *I*, merely a human and insignificant in this world of magical beings, should be allowed to enter what must be a sacred space. But I can't think of any reasons that would sway them. Wolfram is not unsympathetic, if the kind look he's giving me is any indication, but he doesn't look like he's going to change his mind.

"I'll teach you kung fu while you wait," says Su. "It's excellent for taking your mind off all kinds of shit, and good for self-defense in the bargain."

I look around at them again, and god fucking dammit, I'm not going to burst into tears. That's *not* who I am. Finally, I look away, lean my forehead against Thorstein.

"If you're not out in three days, I'm coming to find you, no matter what anyone says."

He strokes my hair. "I don't doubt you will," he says, love and amusement in his voice. "And knowing you're waiting will bring me back from whatever happens next."

"This way, then," says Wolfram. "Just you and me until we meet Syr." He turns and takes a step, and stops. The door into the blank stone wall is open, and a very tall woman stands between it and us.

Surprise appears and vanishes on Wolfram's face so quickly I'm not sure I've actually seen it.

The woman has dark hair in elaborate braids, a simple dark blue dress to her ankles, bare feet, and a blindfold over her eyes. I wonder if she's blind.

"Syr," says Wolfram.

She nods. "You needn't trouble yourself to bring him to me," she says, in a quiet, dry voice like a desert breeze.

"I didn't expect to see you so close to the carnival," Wolfram says.

She turns her head as if she's looking around. "Such a crass and noisy place," she murmurs. "But sometimes it's good to remind oneself why one prefers quiet and solitude."

She turns to face Thorstein, tilting her head like she's listening as much as looking. She must be over six feet tall and even next to Thorstein she looks imposing. She lifts a hand and silver jewelry clanks and rings on her wrist. "This is the boy I'm to train," she says. It's not a question.

"It is," says Wolfram. "Thorstein Thorvaldson."

Syr's lips curl back into something like a snarl or a sneer. "Thorgrim's son," she says. Again, not a question. "I was wondering if he had survived his childhood."

"You know me?" Thorstein says, and her sneer turns to a haughty smile.

"I make it my business to note when new *berserkr* children are born. Had I been allowed, I would have begun training you long ago. Before either you or I came to these shores." She moves her raised hand and lays it on Thorstein's forehead. He jerks slightly, like she's given him an electric shock, but then holds still.

"But not such a boy any longer," she says. "I hope I'm not too late."

Suddenly she turns to me, and I feel like she's looking right into me through that blindfold.

"You love him?" she asks.

"Yes," I say, quietly, unable to force my voice to normal volume. Somehow, whispers feel more appropriate with her.

"Are you willing to learn alongside him?" she says, moving her hand from his forehead to mine.

"I –" I don't know what to say. It's not even something I considered. Be *with* him while he learned, yes. But learn myself? "I'm not an… a pagan," I stumble out. "I don't even know *what* I believe."

"But are you willing?" she says. "Will you have an open mind? Be his anchor? Follow him into darkness if need be?"

"I –" I try again and don't get anything else out.

"It's okay, love," Thorstein says. "Don't do anything you don't want to."

Syr's mouth curls up on one side. "You're an independent one," she says. "That's good. If you had immediately said 'yes' only because *he* needed you, I'd have let you wait out here."

My stomach clenches, thinking about how I very nearly *did* say 'yes,' because I don't want him to have to be alone. I swallow.

"I'm not only asking you to help this boy you love," she says, and I wonder how old *she* is, that Thorstein's one hundred and seven years counts as a boy to her. "I'm also offering you something for yourself. *Seidhr* is not just a path to prophecy, or a way to calm the raging beast inside." She puts her hand on her chest. "It is also a way to access the depths, the source of your own creativity." She tilts her head. "You are an artist." Again, she says it as a statement, not a query.

"Yes," I say. "Not that I practice much, lately."

"But art drives you, no? Creativity is your source of joy?"

"Yes," I say. I glance at Thorstein and he's smiling at me. I smile back.

"Oh, he gives you joy, too, obviously. But one cannot be one's full self without something of one's own, separate from the people one loves."

I nod.

"Good," she says. "Then come with me, Raine Chevalier, Thorstein Thorvaldson. Let us talk further." She leads the way to the door, but before we go inside she pauses and glances back.

"Wolfram," she says. He raises his eyebrows. "I expect you're keeping up with your studies as well?" He nods. She turns to Magne. "And you, young wolf, will need to learn a few of the things I teach soon enough. Maybe even you, fox child," she says to Su. Then she steps through the door and hand-in-hand, Thorstein and I follow.

The door closes on its own, and the lock clicks into place and for a moment, we're enclosed in utter darkness.

Then blue light appears, burning along the outlines of designs carved into the walls. Dragons and other creatures, heroes and gods, entwined lines of Viking knotwork, all slowly limned in glowing blue.

I glance up at Thorstein, enjoying the wonder on his face, and he looks at me and I see my own wonder reflected in his eyes.

"Come, children," Syr says, already several paces ahead down the hall. "The House is not a good place to fall behind in. There's no telling where it might lead you, left to its own devices."

I couldn't even begin to guess how long we follow Syr through the halls of the massive stone building. It doesn't seem long, but the number of intersecting hallways we follow are too many to be a quick journey.

"The House will become less confusing once it accepts you," Syr says, as if in answer to the question I didn't quite dare ask.

But soon, or eventually, she opens a door and sunlight floods through, and we step out into a courtyard. Stone walls all around, another door opposite, windows as blank and opaque as the stone. Moss grows between the paving and there's an old fountain in the middle, cracked and dry, with a statue of a man in the middle, leaning on a staff, glaring out into eternity through one eye – the other is crossed by a jagged scar.

"Allfather Odin," Thorstein says, awe in his voice.

"Are you religious, werewolf?" Syr asks. The curiosity in her voice makes her sound friendlier than she has so far.

"Not really," says Thorstein. "I'm not a god-follower."

"Then what are you?"

"An animist, I suppose," Thorstein says. "I attend the festivals, everyone in the pack does, but I prefer to honor the spirits of the land, day to day."

Syr smiles at that. "The gods do exist," she says. "I can tell you that. But they don't take much interest in this world anymore, if they ever did." She reaches up and removes her blindfold, tucks it in a pocket in her dress. Her eyes are milky and opaque, blind, but it doesn't seem to bother her. "Animism is a much more appropriate faith for a *völva*. Or in your case, a *seidhmathr*."

She sits on the lip of the fountain and gestures for us to sit at her feet. "We pay lip service to Freyja, who taught *seidhr* to the gods, and to Odin, who was her first student. But we honor the spirits of nature most of all."

She turns her blind gaze on Thorstein again. "Does it bother you, that you'll be pursuing a path mostly followed by women? That men who follow this art are considered womanly? Homosexual, even?"

Thorstein laughs. "I read romance novels," he says. "I learned to spin and weave at my mother's knee. I even knit, a little, and embroider. I'm really not concerned with whether or not something makes me manly."

"I think you're pretty manly," I mock-whisper and he puts a hand on my knee.

The smile Syr gives him this time is pure delight. "That you already know how to spin is good," she says. "Spinning is central to *seidhr*. It is a meditation practice and a means of altering consciousness."

Thorstein nods. "When I first found out I was a *berserkr*, I used to carry a drop spindle and a pocket full of wool everywhere with me. It was the easiest way to calm myself. Later, I learned that breathing can work, too."

"But it doesn't work during the full moon?"

"No."

"And now? Do you still spin?"

"When I can," he says. "When I need to find calm, I imagine the feel of the wool and spindle in my hands, make myself breathe consciously. It helps."

Syr claps her hands lightly. "Well," she says. "You have already made the first step. Soon I will teach you to spin flax. It is a rather different fiber, and more loaded with symbolism."

"I've tried," he says. "But I'm not very good at it yet." He looks thoughtful. "I planted flax in the meadow this year. It seemed like the right thing to put there."

"Will I learn to spin?" I say. I've never dabbled in textile arts before, but it's something I've wanted to try for ages.

"You will," she says. "That is your first lesson. Eventually, while you spin, you will be able to enter a meditative state. Thorstein, you will learn that now, so I may read you more deeply, to see what I can do for you in the immediate future."

She pulls two drop spindles out from her deep pockets – and I have no idea how they fit in there – and then two wads of pale gray wool.

"Begin," she says to Thorstein, who takes a spindle and shifts onto his knees to give it more room to drop. He pulls a length of wool free of the ball, leaving it still attached at one end, and twists it between his fingers and ties it onto the shaft of the spindle.

"I'm more used to a bottom-weighted spindle," he says. "But I think I can manage." And then he sets the wooden rod spinning, the designs on the ceramic whorl blending, and begins to draw out a thread. It looks fragile between his big fingers, but his movements are sure and smooth, and the thread doesn't break.

Syr nods, and then has me sit next to her on the edge of the fountain. She demonstrates the park-and-draft technique for me – the easiest way for a beginner to learn, she says. The yarn I make is lumpy and ugly, and I keep breaking the strand and having to attach it back together, but she tells me I'm doing just fine for my first try.

When she turns back to Thorstein, his ball of wool is nearly gone. The yarn wound on his spindle is thin, even, and neat. His fingers move and he's not even looking at what he's doing. His eyes are closed, and though he's not smiling, he looks content. I want to tell him how beautiful he is, but I keep my mouth shut and concentrate on my own yarn.

"Oh, very good," Syr says. She hands him more wool, then stands up and steps closer. "Keep spinning while I read you," she says, and puts her fingertips on Thorstein's temples. She stands that way for a long time, until the second batch of wool runs out and he has to stop.

Then she steps back and sits on the edge of the fountain again.

I hurriedly turn back to my own task, but she doesn't look at me. She seems to be staring into nothingness.

"How strange," she says. "And how infuriating."

Chapter Seventeen

Thorstein winds the last of his perfect, smooth yarn onto the shaft of the spindle, then sits back with it in his lap.

"What did you see?" He speaks softly, like he doesn't want to disturb Syr's thoughts.

I reattach my broken yarn for the umpteenth time, carefully draw out some more wool, set my spindle going again, and let the wool twist between my fingers. When the last of the wool I've drafted is twisted tight, I stop the spindle and clamp it between my knees to pull free more wool. Syr still hasn't spoken, so I glance up. She's frowning. Then she says, "What do you know of the *berserkr* clans?"

"It's said there were three clans," Thorstein says, "Though Dad thought that was nonsense." He holds his spindle gently in his fingers, tracing over the designs incised on the ceramic whorl. Some kind of birds are depicted on mine, but I can't tell from where I'm sitting if his is the same.

"One book I read said *berserkr* refers specifically to bear warriors. Wolf warriors were called *ulfhethnar* and boar warriors were *jöfurr*."

Syr nods. "Most scholars say the *jöfurr* are speculative, and it's true there are no references in the sagas, but that is only because they were very rare. Because while boars are fierce, they are also prey.

"*Ulfhethnar* were more common," she continues. "Though not much remains in the literature. The most common shape-changing warriors followed the bear cult, and it is they who gave their name to the *berserkir.*"

She sighs and reaches out for Thorstein's spindle. He hands it to her, and she examines the yarn, looking at it with unseeing eyes, feeling it with her fingers. She nods and sets it aside. Then she takes mine, uneven and with a tuft of wool still unspun.

"Sorry," I say, and she shakes her head.

"You draw?" she asks. "Paint?"

"A little of both," I say.

"And was your first painting good?"

"Fuck, no."

"Precisely," she says, and sets my work aside, too. "If you stay on this path, you will improve."

Then she looks at Thorstein again. "You already have the tools you need to keep the frenzy off you when you are not afflicted by the song the full moon sings to your werewolf nature."

Thorstein opens his mouth, and Syr holds up her hand, so he closes it again.

"Wolfram told me you felt it on you when you were attacked, and again when you determined how your father controlled you and became angry."

"It was those words," he says.

"'Deal with him'," she says, and I pull in a sharp breath, look at Thorstein, but he is as calm as before.

"Wolfram removed that spell," he says.

"And others, I understand," she replies. "But I would not be surprised if your father still had some hold over you."

She touches the spindle closest to her absently, stroking my lumpy yarn with her fingertips. "Had you been *ulfhethnar* you would likely have had more control at the full moon, but your rages would have been stronger when you unleashed them." She looks up at him, blind eyes seeming to search his face.

"But early training would have been very effective, and even at a young age, the *berserkrgang* would soon only have come when you called it. Wolf and wolf would be in harmony."

She turns her face to the sun. "But your clan is the bear. You are *berserkr*. And the bear clashes with the wolf. Two very different predators war in you."

"Then why have I not… become unstable when I take wolf shape?" Thorstein asks. "It's only at full moon. And before, when I got very angry."

She tilts her head to one side. "I can only speculate, but I believe it is because the *berserkr*, the bear, sleeps when you are content, and rouses only when you are angry, or when the moon sings too loudly in your veins. Then it wakes and the two parts of your nature clash and threaten to destroy the essence of your being. Your mother unknowingly gave you a stronger tool to cope with the mis-fitting of your nature than anything your father did.

"It's a miracle you survived this long without destroying yourself. Your spinning practice saved you."

Then she turns her face back to him. "Did you ever have anyone around whom the bear was calm?"

"Raine," says Thorstein. "The *berserkrgang* was much less when she was there."

"And Magne," I add.

She turns her head to me. "Indeed," she says, then turns back to Thorstein. "He is your younger brother, yes?"

"The baby of the family. He was born when I was sixty-five." There's something about Syr, now that she doesn't seem so cold or haughty, that has made him relax, has made him able to speak to her without being choked by anxiety. "From the time he could walk he would visit me at full moon when I was locked up. He wasn't supposed to be there, but he figured out how to sneak in, and when he was there, I was calm. Sometimes I even remembered who I was."

She smiles. "Sixty-five and more years surviving alone, and then he gave you some reprieve. Some rest."

"*He* saved me," Thorstein says.

But Syr shakes her head. "You had already survived that long, you most likely would have continued. But it's good that he gave you rest. This was from then until now?"

Thorstein shakes his head. "He left home the day he turned eighteen."

"Ah." Syr looks sad. "Still, eighteen years of rest is much."

Again, Thorstein shakes his head. We were… estranged before that. Not long after his thirteenth birthday. I –"

"No," she says. "Wolfram *did* tell me some of this, you needn't relive it." She tilts her head. "You may want to consider that you probably have PTSD."

It's weird, hearing such a modern term from her, who seems so far outside of time, but even Wonder Island has internet and cell service, so I guess it only makes sense that some of its denizens would keep up with modern knowledge.

"I know," he says.

"*Seidhr* training will help you with that, as well," she says.

"So what do I do?"

"For now, we will continue your training from the beginning. Expect to do a lot of spinning, and a lot of meditation."

She drums her fingers on the edge of the fountain. "If we are to deal with your full moon issue fully, however, you must make a choice."

"What are my options?"

"First," and she holds up one hand, palm up, like one half of the scales of Lady Justice. "You could choose the path of the bear, become fully a *berserkr*. And second," she holds up her other hand, forming the other half of the scale, "You could choose the path of the wolf, and become *ulfhethinn*." Then she closes her hands into fists and drops them to her lap.

"Either way," she says, "You remain *berserkr* and *other*, because there is no way to cease being either, your brother's experience aside. And either way, the two parts of your nature are aligned, allowing you to become a whole person, as you probably not have been since you were a small boy, watching his mother spin and asking to learn."

Thorstein stares at his hands as she speaks but looks up sharply at that last sentence. "How did you know I asked my mother to teach me? Why didn't you assume she made me learn in spite of my father's forbidding it?"

She smiles. "I am a *völva*, a seer and a sorceress. I read the past as well as the future." Her smile grows. "And the past is easier because it has already happened, while the future shifts and changes all the time."

Then she laughs. "Besides, you seem like the sort of man who likes to learn things, and as you said, you are not afraid to look unmanly." Then she looks him up and down, or seems to. "Not that anyone would dare suggest such a thing, looking as you do."

Thorstein blushes. "How soon do I need to choose?"

"Soon," she says. "I would like to have your natures aligned before you are trapped under a full moon again."

"Can it happen so quickly?"

"Once you choose, it is a matter of a single night, followed by a lifetime of practice."

"One night is all it takes?" he says. I know he's probably thinking of all the nights he's wasted.

"One night," Syr says. "But it will feel like an eternity. Whichever path you choose, you will be ripping free a part of yourself and shaping it into something else. It will be very difficult, and extremely painful."

"What do I have to do?"

"If you choose the bear, we will bring you a bear man, a bear changer, to make your body anew."

A muscle tenses in Thorstein's jaw. "A were bear will tear me apart and infuse me with a new symbiont?"

"Yes."

"And that would work? It would overwhelm my werewolf symbiont and heal me as a bear changer?"

"There is always the danger it could kill you, but yes."

"And the second option?" I notice he's absently rubbing the scars on one wrist with the other hand. He looks up, sees me watching, and abruptly stops, stuffs both hands under his legs so his wrists are hidden against his thighs. I think maybe Syr notices, too, but she doesn't comment.

"If you choose the wolf, it is not a procedure that will be done to you, it is something you must do to yourself, to make your warrior spirit anew."

"What would I have to do?"

"Wolfram would guide you into a deep meditation, take you journeying beyond your current skill level, into the underworld, the spirit world, have you peel bare the skeleton of your spirit body and remake it into wolf shape in order to match your physical body."

"Why Wolfram and not you?"

"Because he is also *ulfhethnarr*."

"That doesn't sound so bad."

Syr laughs and it is not a happy sound.

"It's sounds like something I read about once," I say. "I think it was Siberian lore, or maybe Inuit. Arctic, anyway, where a potential shaman goes to the otherworld and is devoured by spirits and has to reassemble himself and crawl back up to the mortal world. And if he's still sane after that, he becomes a shaman."

"And if not?" says Thorstein, in a whisper.

"Then he's a madman, I guess," I say.

"The principle is the same," says Syr. "And following this path would have the added benefit of developing an ability to travel to the spirit world. But do not think it the easier path. It is not. You would emerge worse off than before if you fail.

"It is very much the harder path, because you must not only endure a pain as if you were being flayed and defleshed alive, skin and muscle down to a bare skeleton, pain that will feel every bit as real as if it *were* real, but you must inflict it all upon yourself."

"So you advise the path of the bear?" says Thorstein.

"I advise you to spend the rest of the day contemplating your choice, and choose carefully, Thorstein Thorvaldson."

She stands and pulls more wool from her pockets, which I'm pretty sure are like Dungeons & Dragons Pockets of Holding or a portal into a pocket universe, until there's a big pile on the rim of the fountain.

"And you, girl child, keep practicing until you can spin without thought. Do not worry about perfection but concentrate on learning the feel of the spindle and the wool. Once your movements are smooth, then work on consistency of thickness."

She takes a few steps towards the door. "I will return later to take you back to the carnival where you'll be given lodgings in the main building."

"Tomorrow," she says, "We continue your training."

Then she leaves us alone. I get up from the fountain and stretch. The pile of wool she's left me is a lot bigger than the one I spent all morning making into lumpy yarn. "How did she fit that in her pockets?" I say.

"What?" says Thorstein, and I realize he's been lost in his own thoughts. He looks at the pile of wool and smiles. "By the time you're done that, you'll be a pro," he says.

"I doubt that," I say. "But I'll settle for not broken and relatively smooth." I step close and he puts his arms around my legs, rests his face on my thighs. I feel the heat of his breath through my thin linen trousers. I stroke both hands over his hair, smooth the braids down and feel how silky it is in my fingers.

He looks up at me. "Do you see me as a bear or as a wolf?" he says, offering a lopsided smile.

"Would you rather have a bear tear you apart, or do it yourself?" His smile grows a little. "I'll love you either way," I say. "I'll support you, whatever you choose."

"My siblings are all werewolves," he says. "My cousins and aunts and uncles. My whole family."

"Your family hasn't been all that good to you," I remind him.

He sighs and pulls me down to him, into his lap, and I rest my head on his chest.

"Think it through," I say. "You don't have to decide this instant."

"Fuck," he says, resting his head on top of mine.

I wish we could just sit that way for the rest of the afternoon, but there's a big pile of pale gray wool waiting for me to spin it into lumpy yarn.

When the afternoon does end, I swear I can hear my stomach rumbles echoing off the courtyard walls. I've made my way through the whole endless-seeming pile of wool and by the time I get through the last of it, my yarn is pretty consistent in thickness, even if it still is on the chunky side – the *very* chunky side – compared to Thorstein's.

He spends his time sitting against the wall, or pacing, or leaning over the edge of the fountain, staring at where there would once have been a pool of water. He hardly speaks the whole time, and his eyes are far away, and I don't want to disturb his thoughts with questions.

The sun is dipping over the tallest trees to the west, though it will still be light for a few hours yet, when Syr comes back through the door. She smiles when she notices the big ball of yarn I've made.

"Excellent," she says. "Tomorrow, you will work on making it thinner."

"I've decided," says Thorstein, but she holds up a hand.

"No," she says. "Wait until morning. See how you dream. As you will soon learn, dreams can be very important to *seidhr*, especially once you have learned proper technique."

He sighs, and nods, and follows when Syr leads us back through the stone building – the House – and out to the carnival again. The shift from the silence of the courtyard and the stone walls to the bustle and blare of the midway is unpleasant, and I usually *like* bright lights and cheerful noise.

I wonder if practicing *seidhr* will make me a hermit, and then I glance at the man I'd be spending my hermitage with, and I don't think I'd mind.

Wolfram is waiting, like he knew to expect us, and he leads us into the concrete building where we had our meeting before the disastrous full moon attempt, and upstairs to the staff cafeteria.

The food is good, and filling, but I'm ready to curl up with a book and my sweetheart, and I couldn't tell you what I ate even five minutes after we were done.

I think Wolfram senses that Thorstein doesn't want to talk – not that he ever does, really – and that I don't have a whole lot to say, for once. I mean, shit, I spent the whole day trying to turn wool into yarn and mostly succeeding, but it doesn't make for the most riveting story.

Finally, we're alone again, in an open-plan guest room that's as big as my apartment, except here only the bathroom is a separate room. Thorstein collapses on the couch and stares at the wall. I sit next to him, touch his shoulder, and he sighs, looks at me, and smiles. No dimple, though. He puts his arms around me and pulls me close.

"Do you want to know what I've decided?" he says.

"If you want to tell me," I say. "But aren't you going to wait until morning, to see if you dream anything significant?"

He shrugs, and I see resignation in his blue-green eyes, written on his strong jaw. "I'm going to choose the bear," he says.

"Yeah," I say. "How come?" I keep my voice carefully neutral. I'm not really sure what I think of either choice, but I don't want to influence his decision with anything that might seem like a positive or negative reaction.

"Because it's what I *should* have been," he says. "I was a *berserkr* first, of the bear clan, and a werewolf later. And being a werewolf isn't genetic, so it's not like I was born that way." He runs a finger along my jaw, presses a brief kiss to my lips.

"I was meant to be a bear," he says. "It's even in my name. Thorstein Bjorn. It's who I should have been." He puts one foot up on the coffee table. "And I know what to expect, I know what to do, with being made a were. I've done it before. It hurts like hell, but it's over relatively quickly. I know I'll survive intact."

I don't want to point out that he can't know that, because part of being a were-anything is almost dying, of being so close to death that the symbiont in the blood can take over. But he knows that better than I ever could. Because he *has* done it before. And if he survived when he was sixteen, he can survive now, when he's so much stronger.

"So what you're saying," I say, making my voice light, "Is that in a few days' time, I'm going to be fucking a b-movie bear shifter instead of a b-movie werewolf."

He laughs, and growls, and pulls me onto his lap, where he pretends to bite my neck and savage my jugular. Then he *does* bite my neck, but gently, and kisses it and kisses that spot beneath my ear that gets me wet almost instantly.

I pull away long enough to look into his eyes again, give him a cheeky grin. "I'm so glad your manly manhood isn't threatened by doing girly things," I tease.

"I'll show you my manly manhood," he says, letting his voice go deep and rumbly, and he scoops me up and carries me to the bed, where he spends the next while demonstrating exactly how manly he is.

Chapter Eighteen

I CAN'T SAY I SLEEP WELL exactly, because Thorstein is restless, and I'm pretty sure he hardly sleeps at all. When we crawl out of bed way too early, he's got dark shadows under his eyes, and he looks older than usual. Not every year of his one hundred and seven, but definitely every one of the equivalent-to-forty-five human years.

He makes coffee in the guest room's kitchen area and finally, when we're sitting on the couch drinking it, he says, "I dreamed last night."

"I wasn't sure you even *slept* last night," I say.

"Did I keep you awake?" He strokes the side of my face and gently touches the spot under one of my eyes that looked bruised from lack of sleep when I looked in the bathroom mirror while brushing my teeth.

I shrug. "I don't think I could have slept much, anyway."

"I'm sorry, love." He leans over and kisses each of my eyelids, and his lips are hot from the coffee. It feels unbelievably good on my tired eyes.

"What did you dream?" I ask.

"Odin's wolves came like they did when… when they were protecting Magne from me."

"And?"

"That's it. Every time I dozed off, they were there, watching me, blocking my path. I think they were telling me that way is not for me."

"Which path were they blocking, though?"

"Theirs."

You're sure? They weren't waiting for you to follow?"

He shrugs one shoulder and sets his coffee aside, only half-finished. "I never stayed asleep long enough to find out."

He turns slightly, so he's facing me on the couch. "You don't have to be there, to watch."

"Be where?" I say, and set my cup aside, too, so I can concentrate on him.

"When the bear re-makes me."

"Of course I'll be there."

"He's going to literally rip me apart, injure me badly enough to bleed out, so when he infuses me with his blood, there won't be enough left of the wolf to resist."

"I'm not letting you almost die alone."

"I won't be alone."

"You know what I mean. You're not going to stop me from being there, so don't even try."

A soft tap on the door stops whatever response he might have had.

It's Wolfram. "Syr is waiting at the House door," he says. "But first I need to know your decision, so I can prepare for tonight."

Thorstein nods. He hesitates a moment, and then just says, "Bear."

Wolfram gives him a sharp look, but asks, "Have you eaten breakfast?"

"No."

"Good. Don't. Fasting will make the process go faster. Afterwards, we'll stuff you with rare steaks."

Thorstein smiles at that, but it's a cautious expression. "Tonight?" he asks.

"Tonight," says Wolfram. "For now, go to Syr, let her help you prepare your mind. When it gets dark, I'll bring you a friend of mine to help you evict your wolf symbiont and make you a bear instead."

He shakes his head as he turns to go. "I'm not sure Magne will be happy with your decision." Something tells me Wolfram might not be overjoyed about it himself, but I don't say anything.

"It was my decision to make."

"Of course. And he'll respect that. But he won't be happy."

"So don't tell him until it's too late."

Wolfram smiles. "And have him angry at me? That boy's anger takes years to die down. Besides, it might be good to have him there."

"Why?"

"When you were made a werewolf, they left you alone to survive or not, correct?"

Thorstein nods.

"I believe in having people near who love you. People who can lend you strength when you think you have no more." And with that, he leaves.

"This is going to be a long day," I say, as we follow more slowly after, down the stairs and outside. As we turn to head through the market to the House, Thorstein takes my arm and stops me.

"What?" I say, when he doesn't do anything but look at me.

"I'm just so glad I met you," he says. "Thank you. Thank you for loving me, despite what I am. I –"

I stop him by grabbing his hair and dragging him down to my level so I can kiss him.

"I'm glad I met you," I say. "I'm glad you even wanted to go on a date with me, knowing I was a total slut who just wanted to jump your bones and never see you again."

He grins, and his big teeth show. "Maybe I thought *I* wanted to fuck once and forget," he says, voice low. "Maybe I didn't care if I'd ever see you again, as long as I felt *something* for once." He takes my hand, and we weave our way through the carnival folk setting up the market.

"How long was it since you'd last gone on a date? Fucked someone and never saw them again?" I say, trying not to sound jealous.

"Years," he says.

"Why?"

"I didn't think I deserved happiness. Even as brief and fleeting as a quick orgasm with someone who only wanted the same thing from me."

"You deserve so much more than that," I say. "And I'm going to make sure you get it. *All* of it."

"All of it?" he repeats.

"Yes," I say, and we proceed to our long day of learning how to use spinning with a drop spindle as a means of shifting our consciousness from the everyday to the spiritual.

By the time darkness falls and we put away our spindles, I'm pretty sure the lightheadedness from hunger is helping a great deal with the ease with which I manage to shift my consciousness.

Because I was expecting to spend the day making thinner and more consistent yarn, but instead I've learned to find stillness, to find the dark inside my head, and I've learned to look for the deep green spark that is Thorstein, just below the surface of what is, how to reach out with my own light to touch his. I seem to shift between blue and yellow, never quite settling on green – Syr says forest green shows Thorstein is a werewolf, while my blue-and-yellow marks me as something more airy, less directly connected to nature. Because I'm human, she says, my light is more about communication and less about communion.

When it does get dark, Wolfram arrives with Magne and another man, the were-bear, presumably. They set lanterns around the courtyard – one next to each of the four walls – that cast just enough light to keep us from tripping over each other. Though I suppose for everyone but me, their non-human vision doesn't need much illumination.

Magne grips Thorstein's forearm and says, "You're sure?"

Thorstein nods and draws his brother into a hug.

Then Wolfram introduces the other man, Cliff. He's shorter than I was expecting, for a bear, but easily as muscular as Thorstein. His hair is dark – brown, I think – though it's hard to tell in the uncertain lamplight.

"So let's do this," Cliff says.

"So quick?" says Magne.

"Sooner we start, sooner it's done," replies Cliff.

Thorstein nods. "Tell me what you need me to do."

"If you don't want your clothes ruined, take them off," Cliff says.

"The rest of you," says Wolfram, "Stay near, but not too close. He may lash out. He *will* lash out, once the symbiont starts its work."

Everyone except me turns away while Thorstein undresses, though he doesn't seem at all self-conscious, except where it comes to baring his scarred wrists. In fact, he almost seems more confident naked, here, than he usually seems fully clothed out in the regular world.

I'm not ashamed to say I watch his every move, drink in the sight of him as he bares himself to the lantern light. He meets my eyes as he sets the last piece of clothing aside and smiles gently.

"You don't have to watch," he says.

"I like watching," I say.

"I didn't mean me getting naked."

"I know," I say. "I don't want to watch you being hurt, but I'm not leaving."

"Okay," says Cliff, touching my arm to steer me father away. He looks up at Thorstein, "You're too fucking tall," he says. "Kneel down."

So Thorstein gets on his knees in the middle of the dark courtyard and bares his throat to the other were. And before I can say anything else, before anyone can react, Cliff's face erupts in a long snout, huge with teeth, and his hands sprout six-inch claws, and he roars and sinks his teeth into Thorstein's neck.

Thorstein doesn't flinch, doesn't make a sound, but I see his hands clench into fists, start to change into claws, but he forces them back, forces his body to relax, even as Cliff backs away, retracts his teeth, and blood gushes from Thorstein's jugular.

"Make it quick, bear man," Thorstein growls. So Cliff slashes out with his claws, opens up Thorstein's thigh to the bone, and he topples backwards. I only just manage to fling myself to my knees and catch his head before it hits the stone.

Then everyone waits. Waits while Thorstein's blood pumps out, spurts and splashes on the stone, pools under him. So much blood.

"You should stay back, love," he says, his voice thin and pained. "I could hurt you by accident."

I bend over him, kiss his forehead, and say, "I love you."

"Love you," he says softly, his eyes fluttering closed.

I look up at Cliff, and he's watching Thorstein carefully as the blood flow becomes sluggish and Thorstein's breathing goes shallow.

"Finish it," snarls Magne.

"In its time," says Cliff, but he steps forward, rolls up his sleeve and makes a long, deep cut in his forearm. He kneels and presses the wound to Thorstein's neck, waits while his blood flows into the wound, then withdraws, cuts his other arm, and lets the blood run into the gaping thigh wound. Then he pulls bandages out of his pocket, wraps his arms, and steps away.

"You'll want to get back, woman," he says to me. "He's going to thrash around a bit as his body tries to fight the new symbiont."

I ignore him, and keep Thorstein's head cradled in my lap, watch his face. For a long time he seems too still and only the faint movement of his chest tells me he's still alive, still with me. Then his eyes roll beneath his lids, and he groans.

He flings his head back, or tries to, grinding the back of his cranium into my thighs. It hurts, but I won't move.

"This isn't right," says Magne.

I glance up to see Wolfram looking at Magne in concern. "You were made a werewolf in utero, would you even know what a change should look like?"

"I've seen a few," Magne says. "When a young wolf is made, often the whole pack is there. We all give blood to the process. Thorstein should be healing by now."

A soft keening noise starts, and I realize it's Thorstein just as it erupts into a roar and his body arches on the ground. He grabs my arm and I feel his fingers dig in.

"There," says Cliff. "The bear is taking over now. This isn't the same as making a human into a were. The struggle is worse."

"Raine, get back," says Magne, but Thorstein has my upper arm in a death grip, and I can't move. Every thrash and spasm twists his fingers harder into my arm until my hand goes numb.

"Talk to him," says Syr. "See if you can calm him." So I do. I babble meaningless words at him, hardly even knowing what I'm saying. I tell him I love him, that I can hardly wait to have a normal, ordinary life with him. I tell him we're all here for him, that he's strong, that he will not only survive, but thrive. That maybe someday when he's ready, when I'm ready, we'll have children.

At first, it seems to work. His body relaxes, he lies still on the stones, head in my lap, hand still on my arm, but no longer bruising. Blood still seeps sluggishly from his wounds.

"Should he still be bleeding?" says Magne, turning to Cliff. "Shouldn't the symbiont at least be stopping the bleeding?"

Cliff shakes his head, uncertain. "I don't know."

Then Thorstein's eyes snap open and he stares around him. "Raine?" he says.

"I'm here, love."

He strains to look up at me. "It burns," he says.

I stroke his face. "Just hang on, love," I say.

"It burns," he says again. "I can feel it. I can feel my wolf symbiont fighting the bear, and it burns."

I look up, meet Magne's worried eyes, and as one we look at Wolfram. The small man is holding out one hand towards Thorstein, eyes closed. He shakes his head.

"I can't be certain," he says, "But I think Thorstein's wolf is fighting off the bear. Even weakened by blood loss, his wolf symbiont is incredibly strong."

"Can we induce the *berserkrgang*, to give more strength to the bear?" Magne asks.

"He's so strong," whispers Wolfram. "I didn't realize how strong he was as a werewolf." He looks at Magne, horror growing in his eyes. "I think we may have made a terrible mistake."

"He chose the bear," I say. "Maybe it was a mistake, but he chose it."

"Fuck," says Magne, kneeling next to his brother, grasping his hand. "Can we stop this?"

"We can only give him the strength to survive it," says Syr suddenly, stepping out from where she was waiting in the shadows.

Then Thorstein screams. I want to cover my ears, but one arm is trapped by Thorstein's grip, and covering only one ear does nothing to block out the terrible sound.

"Hold him down," says Wolfram suddenly, and Magne flings himself across Thorstein's body, trying to pin him to the ground, just as Thorstein starts thrashing.

The scream becomes a roar and subsides to a growl, and I watch as

Thorstein's big teeth descend, as his face tries to form into a muzzle, seems to falter between wolf and bear, and then his claws emerge, one hand slashing across Magne's arm and the other digging into mine, piercing my skin and suddenly tearing free to claw at the stones he's lying on.

He fights. I don't know what he's fighting, but his body twists and writhes and spasms, and Magne tries in vain to keep him pinned. Magne is crazy strong, but Thorstein is bigger, and even depleted of blood he can't be held still.

I just do all I can to keep his head from hitting the cobbles. I don't even notice the blood running down my arm until Thorstein finally goes still. And even then, I only hiss, glance at it absently, and focus on Thorstein, on trying to find a pulse in his neck.

Magne sits up, he's bleeding, too, but his arm scabs over even as I look at it.

"Is he breathing?" I say.

No one answers.

"Is he breathing?" I say, louder, not caring that my voice sounds panicky. "Magne?"

Magne puts a hand on his brother's chest, then leans over and presses his ear there. He sits up again. "He's alive," he says. "He's weak, but he's alive." He looks at Wolfram, then suddenly seems to make a decision, pulls a knife from his pocket and holds out his bare forearm.

I don't even see Wolfram move until he's gripping the hand in which Magne holds the knife. "It won't work, son," he says gently.

"I've done it before," Magne says. "I saved Tyler. My symbiont will strengthen Thorstein's."

Wolfram shakes his head. "Even if you were still a werewolf, you have your mother's symbiont only. Thorstein had only your father's."

"He had the whole pack's," Magne says.

"No," says Wolfram. "He was made in the Old Country. And your father did it alone." He looks sternly at Magne. "And you are *not* a werewolf. Not anymore."

A muscle in Magne's jaw jumps as he clenches his teeth.

"The Island took your symbiont from you, son, remember. And it made you something else."

"Fuck," says Magne, relaxing his arm and putting the knife away when Wolfram releases him. "Fuck!"

"I won't let him die," I say. "There must be something we can do."

Wolfram sighs. "We can try to give him strength, and hope he pulls through."

Then Magne says, "Bjarni," and pulls out his phone.

"It's at least a half hour to your farm," says Wolfram. "Another fifteen or twenty minutes on the ferry. He'll never get here in time."

Magne ignores him, fingers flying as he types out a text. "Come on, asshole," he mutters. His phone vibrates and he looks at the screen, hisses in annoyance, and pokes more buttons. Then he holds the phone to his ear.

"Answer you fucking waste of oxygen," he growls. Then, "Get your ass to the Wonder Island ferry dock." His voice is clipped and terse, the smoky smoothness ripped away by grief and worry. He listens to the answer on the other end of the line, growls out, "I'm not asking you to help me, I'm asking you to help Bear. Thorstein *needs* you, Bjarni." A pause. "Because he's going to fucking die if you don't."

That last sentence leaves me cold, and it feels like everyone listening holds their breath. Except Wolfram, who's jabbing out a text on his own phone.

Finally, Magne hangs up. "He's coming. He'll be at the dock in fifteen minutes."

"How?" I say.

"He had a date. She lives nearby." He smiles, but it's all teeth and anger.

"They're holding the ferry for you," Wolfram says, looking up from his phone. "And there will be a speedboat waiting at the rental place to bring you back."

Magne hesitates, looking at Thorstein, who is not moving, only his chest barely rising and falling. His eyelids twitch. He's so pale.

"Go, Magne," says Wolfram.

"Fuck," says Magne. "Hang on, Thors."

"Go!" And Magne goes, running full tilt and slamming out the door.

Chapter Nineteen

As soon as the door slams behind Magne, it seems like everyone starts talking, but it's just a babble of sound to me, until Wolfram says, "Quiet."

The silence is absolute, as if even the wind doesn't dare make a sound.

Then he says, "Thank you, Cliff, my old friend ,for your help, little good though it did." And, "Syr, please take our guest back to the carnival, and see that he's fed and compensated." She hesitates, glancing at me, but then links her arm through Cliff's.

To me, he says, "Raine, child, you must anchor him. Remind him of what he will lose if he leaves this world. Keep him from crossing as long as you can."

Something clenches tight in my guts. I can't be the one they're depending on to keep Thorstein alive, because then it will be *me* that lets him die. "I don't know how," I say.

Syr pauses with her hand on the door. "You do, girl. You could see his light. All you need do else is make him aware you are with him, talk to him, lend him your strength."

"And I will be here with you," Wolfram says. "You won't be alone, but I can't anchor him here and also do what I need to do." He looks at Syr and she nods and leads Cliff out the door. It closes, and Wolfram turns back to me.

"Go on. Enter your trance. Find his light. Talk to him. You keep his spirit wanting to stay with you, and I will buy his body some time."

So I do as I'm told. I imagine the spindle in my fingers, spinning, twisting the world and drawing me down, in like a spiral until it's as dark as the inside of my head. At first, I don't see anything else except the dark, and my own blue-yellow glow, flickering rapidly with the frantic pulse-beat of my worry. I'm so afraid I'll pull myself out of the trance that seemed so easy to slip into with Thorstein right beside me and Syr whispering words in a language I don't understand.

But I hear Wolfram then, his voice deep and gravelly and gentle. "Stay calm, Raine. Find your center and then find him. I'm right here with you."

And then I see Wolfram, so bright that for a moment I can't look at him, not even with the eyes of my spirit-self. But then his light dims as he says something that sounds like "Halt!" only with an accent. And everything slows down.

Thorstein's heartbeat under my hand slows so much I can barely feel it, and I panic, start to pull myself out of the trance. But then Wolfram's hand is on mine, and I feel normality return. As if being in a trance inside my own head can be called "normal."

"I'm stopping time for him," Wolfram says. "For us three. If I can keep time at bay long enough for Magne to return, we have a chance of saving him. But he is tired, Raine. He is in pain, and he is on the verge of giving up. Now find him and remind him that he is loved."

So I look around again. In my body, I can feel his hair under my fingers, his faint pulse in his temples, hear each slow, ragged draw of breath. But in my spirit self, I can't find him.

"Thors?" I say, and I don't know if my physical self makes sound or not, but I hear it echo in the darkness behind my eyelids, just beneath the surface of the here-and-now, and I see a faint glow and walk towards it. As I get closer, I see it isn't the deep forest green spark that see I Thorstein as in this state of consciousness. It's a door.

I step through into a forest, green and growing, a river rushing by so close I almost step into it. And he's there, crouched on the river back, naked, staring at his arms.

Where in the here-and-now his arms are deeply scarred, in this place the wounds are fresh and ugly. They start to close as I watch, and he draws the claws of one hand over the other wrist, opening up his inner arm again. Then he does the same to the other wrist.

"Thors," I say, and he looks up. He's half-changed, his mouth projecting in an almost-muzzle, his teeth too big. His blue-green eyes are wild with grief.

He's trapped by the memory of almost killing – of thinking he *had* killed – Magne.

"Raine," he says, my name slurred through his too-stretched lips. He sounds confused.

I crouch in front of him, put my hands over his torn inner forearms. "I'm here," I say, and the gouges heal, the blood vanishes. "I love you."

"Raine," he says again, his face re-forming to something more human, but still with the wild, fearsome look of the wolf. "I'm so tired," he says. He looks at the river, and there's a bridge now where there was none before. It leads into a welcoming darkness, and I think I see a vague figure on the other side, just within the shadows.

"I know, love," I say. "But I need you to stay with me. Just a little longer, and then you can rest."

"I killed Magne," he says, looking at his arms. I keep my hands there, wrapping my fingers around them, willing him to feel the warmth of my touch.

"No," I say. "You didn't. He lived. He's alive."

He shakes his head, confusion on his face again, trying to fight his way free of the memory. "He hates me."

"He loves you," I say, moving one hand from his arm to brush his hair away from his face. He leans his cheek against my palm. "He's so proud of you, sweetheart."

"Why would he be proud of me?" His voice becomes a growl, and he surges to his feet. I stand with him, keep one hand on his arm and one on his face. He takes a step towards the bridge and the figure on the other side takes a step closer, edging out of the shadows. It's a woman, thin and frail, so blonde her hair looks silver as it catches the light.

He wants to go to her.

I want to ask who she was, what she meant to him, but I push down my sudden jealousy and say, "He's proud of you because you survived. Because you keep fighting. Because you wanted to be better than your father let you be."

He looks down at me then, shakes his head. "Magne was always the best of us."

"He looked up to you, Thors. He *still* looks up to you."

"Only because I'm taller," he says, and surprises me into a laugh. Surprises *himself* into a laugh. It only lasts a moment, but it gives me hope. Then the woman on the bridge takes a step nearer, holds out a hand, and I feel him wanting to go, to leave me. She takes another step, and the shadows fall away, turn her hair to a blaze of light, and illuminate her eyes, the exact blue-green of Thorstein's.

"Your mother wouldn't want you to give up," I say, and he whips his head back around to look at me.

"*I* don't want you to give up," I say. "And Magne and Bjarni are on their way to help you." I put my other hand on his face, tilt his chin down, and stand on tiptoes to kiss him, just lightly. "Your brothers are coming to help you, sweetheart, and I need you to hang on just a little bit longer."

He stares at me and doesn't look away when the woman steps back into the gloom, and the bridge shivers and disappears.

"I'm so tired, Raine. And everything hurts."

"I know," I say. "I know. And you can rest soon, I promise."

He steps closer to me then, closer again, until I'm pressed against him, and he curls his arms around me. He takes a deep breath, and I feel his body breathe deep in the outside world.

"I love you," he says, crushing me to him. "I'll stay for you."

I want to tell him to stay for himself, to stay for all of us, but right now, as long as he's staying at all, I don't care why.

Then he leans back to look into my eyes. "If I live," he says, and I start to protest. He presses his lips on mine to stop me, then pulls back again. "If I live, marry me. Please."

I've never wanted to be married. Not to anyone. Not even to some abstract idea of the future perfect love. I've spent my life wanting to be very much *not* married. But then I never wanted to fall in love, either. I never expected to find someone I wanted to spend my life with.

"Raine?" he says, doubt creeping into his voice, and it feels like he's drifting apart in my arms.

"I love you, Thors," I say. "Of course, I'll marry you." I say it to keep him from leaving, but when the words come out, I'm surprised to realize that I mean it. I *do* want to marry him. Fuck me. I'm getting married.

The smile he gives me is so full of happiness, of hope, of joy, that I start to tear up. I wonder if I'm crying in the here-and-now, too.

"The monster gets his happily ever after," I say, and his smile grows so much that his dimple appears.

I'm aware, on some level, when Magne returns, bursting through the door with Bjarni right behind him.

"Jesus fucking Christ and Odin on the fucking World Tree," Bjarni says. "What the fuck did you do to him?"

"I told you," Magne says. "Just help him."

"Why didn't you help him?" Bjarni says, but he pulls a knife out of his pocket, flicks it open, and drops to his knees next to Thorstein, opposite where Wolfram kneels.

Wolfram, sounding as tired as Thorstein now, says, "Raine, I have to return time to its normal course. Hold him tight while the symbiont regains a hold." And then it feels like the world crashes down.

The forest vanishes, and the river, but the bridge reappears, looking like the only solid footing. Thorstein moves towards it, pulling me with him.

"No," I say. "Sweetheart, stay."

"It's safe there," he says, taking another step, and another.

"If you cross that bridge," I say. "I can't follow you."

He pauses, looks into my face. "What?" he says.

"That's the way to the other side," I say. "To the afterlife. If you go there, you'll die. I'll lose you." I tangle my hands in his hair, grip them into fists. "I don't want to lose you when I've only just found you."

"Don't you fucking die, you fucking asshole," I hear Bjarni say in the here-and-now, where he bleeds from a cut on his arm onto the ragged bite on Thorstein's neck, cuts open his other arm to bleed on Thorstein's leg. "Why don't *you* help him?" Bjarni says again, accusing, and I know he's glaring at Magne, even as he tries to give his older brother enough of his own blood-symbiont to heal.

"I wanted to, Little Bear, but I can't. I'm not a werewolf anymore."

"What the fuck are you talking about?"

"I told you. No symbiont, no werewolf. Can I explain this later?"

"You fucking better." Bjarni presses one wrist to Thorstein's mouth and I feel Thors flinch away, both in real life and in this place a half-step away. "Fucking drink it," Bjarni says, squeezing his hand into a fist so his blood drips between Thorstein's teeth. "Make him swallow." He reaches out suddenly, grips my arm, and I wince as he presses on the cuts there. I'm vaguely aware that he leaves a bloody handprint on my already bloody arm.

And I'm aware of Magne massaging Thorstein's throat in the waking world, while here in the dark, I say, "Swallow, my love. Let Bjarni's symbiont put you back together from the inside and the outside." And Thorstein swallows, and makes a face, and pulls us both back into the here-and-now.

"That's fucking disgusting, Little Bear," he says, his voice a whisper. Then he's pulled out of my arms, off of my lap, as both of his brothers wrap their arms around him, both of them saying "fucking hell" so much I can't tell them apart.

"Be gentle," says Wolfram. "He has a lot of healing to do and not a lot of time to do it. I think we all need food and rest."

"Raine?" says Thorstein, voice muffled by his brothers.

"I'm here," I say.

Bjarni and Magne lower him back onto my lap, and Wolfram produces a blanket from somewhere and drapes it over him.

Thorstein looks up at me, raises one hand, weak but determined, to touch my face. "Thank you," he says. "For reminding me what I would be leaving behind."

"I'm too selfish to let you go," I say, and he smiles.

Then he blinks and focusses sharply on my eyes. "Did I propose to you?" he says. "By the bridge, in the… on the other side?"

"I believe you did," I say.

"I guess we're getting married, then," he says, relaxing into my lap and closing his eyes.

"You're assuming I said yes," I say, letting my lips twitch with a smile. It feels so good to smile.

His eyes snap open. "Didn't you?"

"Of course she did," says Bjarni, giving me a cheeky grin and a wink. "What woman could resist a big, smelly blond dude covered in blood?"

"He wasn't covered in blood over there. In the in-between." I stick my tongue out at Bjarni. "He *was* naked, though."

"Well, that explains it," says Magne. "She was overwhelmed by his sheer manliness."

I stick my tongue out at Magne, too.

"Food and rest," says Wolfram. "For all of us." I finally look at him, ready to thank him for keeping me from panicking right when it would have been worst, but I can't say anything. He looks like hell. Worn tired and squinting against the flickering lamplight as if it hurts.

"Are you okay?" I say.

"I will be."

"Headache?" says Magne, and Wolfram nods.

"Like you wouldn't believe. I'll get something from Bethy to blunt the worst of it." He gets to his feet, slowly, like more hurts than just his head.

"Can you carry him to the guest suite?" he says, and Magne nods and scoops Thorstein up in his arms like he's carrying a child.

"I'll carry her," Bjarni says with a leer.

"Only if you want to be the next one of your brothers that I have to drag from the brink of death," I say.

"If I get you naked in the otherworld, it might be worth it."

"I didn't say *I* was naked, I said Thorstein was naked."

"If you try to get her naked anywhere," says Thorstein, voice echoing in the stone halls as we make our way through the House, "I will rip your balls off and you can spend the rest of your life regrowing them."

WE END UP SEATED AROUND the big bed, Thorstein tucked under the covers with a tray on his lap, refusing to let anyone help him eat.

Bjarni shovels steak into his mouth like a starving man, which I guess he is, since he just gave a lot of his blood to his brother.

Magne looks around and grimaces. "Last time I was in this room, I was the one sick in bed and everyone was making an ungodly fuss over me. Only I didn't get any steak."

"Want to trade places?" says Thorstein.

"No, thanks," says Magne. Then he adds, "I ended up losing my werewolf symbiont."

"And gaining something new," says Wolfram. "I hope that was some compensation."

"Some," says Magne. Then, "I'm getting used to it. And at least I never have to remember where I left my clothes." Then he sighs. "Let's leave him to rest," he says, and gets up, gripping Bjarni's shoulder.

Wolfram gets up, too. "I'll let you know if anything changes."

When Magne and Bjarni are gone and the dishes cleared away, Wolfram comes back and sits on the edge of the bed.

"How are you son, really?" he says.

Thorstein looks away, studies his hands. "Not great," he says. "Disappointed. Feeling like a huge fucking failure."

Wolfram grips his shoulder and Thorstein looks up, pale blue-green eyes meeting Wolfram's clear gray. "Not succeeding isn't the same as failure. It was the wrong path, but we do have another."

Thorstein looks away again. "That path terrifies me." He looks at me, flinches when I meet his eyes, but I try to fill my look with nothing but love, and he relaxes, even smiles a small, grim, smile.

"What about the path of the wolf terrifies you?" Wolfram asks, no judgement in his voice, only curiosity.

"I want it too much," Thorstein says. "And everything I've ever wanted has been taken from me."

"I'm still here," I say.

He turns back to me, tucks a strand of stray hair behind my ear, and kisses my cheek. "And every day, I'm terrified you'll be snatched away. Driven off by my father, or just… decide you don't…" He closes his eyes. "You don't need me anymore."

I let out an exasperated breath and Thorstein's eyes open. Even Wolfram looks at me.

"I *don't* need you Thors. I've never *needed* anyone, least of all a man."

He looks wounded and I shake my head. "I don't need you, but I do *want* you. Desperately. With everything that I am. And —" I poke his shoulder, careful not to get too close to the bandage that swathes his neck "— I seem to recall you asking me to marry you. And I seem to recall I said yes."

"I thought that was to keep me from giving up."

"I can't lie to you," I say. "You're a werewolf."

His smile is tentative, but it's there.

"So, there's one thing that's very unlikely to be taken from you," says Wolfram. "And I can't say that the path of the wolf will be easy. It won't. But you won't be alone. I'll be there." He slants a glance at me, seems to be making his mind up about something, and says, "And Geri and Freki will be there."

Thorstein's eyes widen, but he only turns slowly to look at Wolfram. "How?"

"They're…" Wolfram hesitates, as if unsure how to explain, or even *if* to explain. "They're here, on the Island," he finally says. "And sometimes, they condescend to do what I ask."

"What *are* you?" Thorstein says, awe creeping into his voice. "*Who* are you?"

Wolfram's mouth quirks up on one side. "A question best left for another time, perhaps. Right now, I need to know, will you follow the path of the wolf? Will you face your fear, and then face it again once you descend into the spirit world?"

Thorstein jerks his chin up at the challenge implicit in Wolfram's tone. "I will," he says.

"Good," says Wolfram. "I had hoped you'd have chosen it first, but I would never have asked."

"Why?"

"We *ulfhethnarr* are rare, and it gets lonely, having no one who understands."

"You?" Thorstein says, forgetting maybe, that Syr had said as much yesterday. or maybe he hadn't believed her.

"Yes, me."

Thorstein bites his lip, frowning, and stares at his hands. I know he wants to ask something but can't get the words out.

When Wolfram gets up to go, and Thorstein still hasn't spoken, I say, "What is it, love?"

Both men look at me.

"Is it… passed on to children?" says Thorstein, asking the question to his hands, clenched around the blankets in his lap.

"It could be, I suppose," says Wolfram. "None of my children lived long enough to find out."

Thorstein does look up at that, sadness on his face as he looks at the older man. Wolfram's expression holds sadness, too, but it's old sorrow.

"I'm sorry," says Thorstein, and something in his voice makes me look at him closely. And I realize he really does want children. He told me he wouldn't have any, in case he passed on the *berserkr* nature. But he wants them, so badly I can hear it in his voice.

Wolfram shakes his head. "It was lifetimes ago." He moves for the door again, hesitates, and turns back. "But Magne has become the son of my spirit." And he watches, *I* watch, as different emotions chase one another across Thorstein's face. Then Thorstein nods.

"I'm glad," he says.

"Prepare yourself for tomorrow night," Wolfram says. "Rest, meditate, pray. Whatever you need. If you thought tonight was difficult, tomorrow will be much, much worse."

"Will it be worth it?"

"You'll be free to call the *berserkrgang* or to dismiss it. Your spirit will match your body. You will have gained a considerable amount of spiritual strength." Wolfram's smile is a feral grin. "I'd say it will be worth it."

Chapter Twenty

Bethy, Wonder Island's herbalist and doctor, arrives early the next morning with a basket over her arm and a tray balanced in her free hand.

She knocks and walks in without waiting for a response, sets the tray on the coffee table, and the basket on the nightstand. Under the clean bandages it holds, I see pale gray wool, and two drop spindles stick out of the top.

Thorstein reluctantly uncurls his body from around me so Bethy can examine his wounds. She peels the tape slowly from his back to examine his neck, then he flinches and yelps as she yanks the bandage the rest of the way off.

His rubs a hand over his chest. "I think I've got a bald patch now," he says.

"It will grow back," she replies mildly, leaning closer to peer at his neck. "The bear man was not fooling around when he bit you," she says. "I think he meant to leave a scar to mark your new status."

Thorstein grunts and tries to look. She swats him on the chin.

"Don't do that," she says. "You'll re-open it, and it will scar for sure."

She makes a satisfied noise, rubs some salve into the bite, and tapes down a new, smaller, bandage.

"Lie down," she says, "And move these blankets out of the way." She starts to pull the covers away from his thigh, and he clutches them close to his lap, which I find extremely amusing since he wasn't bothered about being naked with other people around last night.

"Oh, stop it," she says, straightening up with her hands on her hips. "You don't have anything I'm interested in seeing."

He blushes and pulls the blankets away from his leg, but keeps his groin covered. Bethy snickers and reaches for the bandage. It's dark red where blood has seeped through and she clicks her tongue.

"He wasn't gentle with the claws, either," she remarks as she grips the edge of the bandage and tears.

"Fucking hell!" yelps Thorstein as the bandage comes free. "I think you got some pubic hairs that time. I need those." His cheeks are pink.

Bethy glances at the bandage and smirks. There are, indeed, some longer, curlier, darker blond hairs stuck to the tape.

"Do you want me to re-implant them?" she says, one eyebrow raised and a smirk threatening to take over her face.

"No, thank you. I'll wait for them to re-grow."

She pokes at the four jagged tears in Thorstein's thigh and clicks her tongue again. "They're healing," she says. "Not as fast as I'd like, but it'll have to do."

She re-bandages his leg, then steps back and fixes Thorstein with a stern look. "Are you ready for another taxing night?" she says. "If you don't feel strong enough, I can tell Wolfram it will have to wait."

"I'm ready," Thorstein says, and I remember last night and how difficult it had been for him to admit to Wolfram that he was afraid.

Bethy sighs and nods. She points to the basket. "Syr tells me that's your task for today. Both of you. But first –" she points to the tray on the table "– eat."

"No fasting this time?" Thorstein says. His stomach growls and I stifle a laugh.

"Your body needs food," she says. Then she heads for the door. "And Raine," she says, as she steps through. "*Don't* tire him out. He'll need all his strength."

"I –" I don't even know what I intended to say in protest, but the door closes behind her and it doesn't matter.

So we eat, and shower, and as the hot water cascades over us – lucky for Thorstein this bathroom was constructed to accommodate people of a wide variety of heights – he lets me wash him, bending so I can work shampoo into his hair, and sighing as I slide soapy hands over every inch of his body.

When he gets out, he's trembling, and I don't know if it's from weariness or from the same thing that's giving him a raging hard on.

I rub the towel over him, and he growls softly, pulls me closer so we're pressed together.

"I'm not supposed to tire you," I say, but I open my lips to him when he kisses me, slide my tongue alongside his.

"It's going to take more energy to fight this off than to give in and pleasure you," he says. He lifts me, and turns, sets me on the bathroom counter and pushes my knees apart with his hips to stand between them.

"Is your leg okay?" I say, trailing my fingers down his chest and pausing at his belly button. "You could go lie on the bed and let me take care of you." I reach lower, slide the palm of my hand against his hardness, feel it jump at my touch.

He doesn't answer, he just pulls me closer and buries his face in my neck, nibbles and kisses and licks until I want to melt into him. He lifts my hips and I feel his cock press closer to me.

He moves back to my lips, then says softly, "Are you on birth control?"

"Of course I am," I say. "Why?" Then, "Ohhhhh."

"If you're going to marry me," he says. "Then maybe we don't need condoms anymore?" He holds very still, waiting for my answer, giving the choice to me.

"We don't need condoms anymore," I say, and some of the tension goes out of his shoulders. "I want you bare," I say, and he groans.

He still doesn't push inside me, but takes hold of himself, and rubs his tip between my folds, until I growl, "Fuck me already," and pull him sharply closer with my legs. He spears into me, and I arch my back, trying to get him closer, to make him fill me completely.

He thrusts into me, once, twice, then suddenly lifts me up so I wrap my arms and legs around him, cling to him as he carries me back to the bed. I feel the unsteadiness of his leg, the sigh of relief as he climbs onto the bed with me under him and takes most of the weight off.

Then he lifts himself up onto his knees, slings one of my legs over his shoulder, and looks down at me as he thrusts into me again and again.

"Thors," I say, and it comes out mostly moan. He pauses, licks his thumb, and rests his hand on my hip, his thumb resting right on my center, rubbing me every time he plunges into me.

I want this to last forever, but I can't hold the orgasm back, can't keep in my cries of pleasure, or stop my body from arching against his, my nether muscles from pulsing as I pass my climax.

When I look at Thorstein again, his eyes are half-closed but burning blue-green, and he leans back over me, pressing my knee into my shoulder, to capture my mouth with his as the movement of his hips grows more desperate, until he's the one crying out into my mouth, his body arching and throbbing.

I move my legs into a more comfortable position, pull him firmly against me, and feel him relax. He rolls to one side but keeps me pressed against him, so we lie on our sides, face to face, him still inside me, slowly going soft. I can feel him trembling again, his thigh especially.

"You pushed too hard, love," I say.

"Did I hurt you?" He touches my face, looks closely into my eyes.

I can't help smiling. "No," I say. "You didn't hurt me. But I think you hurt yourself."

"I'll live," he says.

"You better," I say. "I don't want to be a widow before I'm even married."

He settles his bent arm under his head and strokes my cheekbone with his free hand, pushes wet hair back off my face. "You really want to be my…" He falters, uncertain, anxious.

"Your wife?" I say, letting my smile grow. "I never in a million years thought I'd ever say this to anyone, but yes, Thorstein Bjorn Thorvaldson, I very much want to be your wife." I tap the end of his perfect nose. "I'm keeping my name, though."

His lips quirk. "I can live with that."

I consider him, his strong jaw, sharp cheekbones, beautiful eyes. Then

I think, what the hell, in for a penny and all that.

"There's something else I want that I never thought I would," I say.

"Mmm? What's that?" He strokes his hand down my side and lets it rest on my hip.

I bite my lip. Am I really going to do this? To say this? Fuck yes, I am.

"I want to move in with you."

He grins. "I *was* hoping I wouldn't have to keep a separate house from my wife," he says.

"Right away," I say.

A little frown line appears between his eyebrows. "On the farm? With my fucking asshole father right next door?"

Okay, I hadn't really thought of *that*. Or the part where his dad thinks I'm fucking Bjarni. But that's not going to be any different if we wait, anyway.

So, "Yes," I say.

WOLFRAM DOESN'T COMMENT on the mess the bedclothes are in, or the fact that Thorstein is perhaps a little more tired than he should be. He just says," Are you ready?" He glances at the two spindles, both full of yarn, and the empty plates in the sink.

"As ready as I'm going to be," Thorstein says.

We're both dressed and sitting side-by-side on the couch, and I refuse to be embarrassed at how much it smells like sex in here. And if I, with my mere human nose, can smell it, how much stronger must it be for Wolfram?

"On the roof," I think," says Wolfram. "Under the stars. We won't be able to see the dark moon, of course, but we'll feel her singing to us as we enter the spirit realm." We follow him up and out and settle with Thorstein stretched out on his back, a blanket tucked over him, and his head cradled in my lap again. I'm cross-legged on a cushion, as comfortable as I can be, because we could literally be here all night.

Wolfram sits on Thorstein's left side, away from the wounds on his neck and thigh, and grips one of Thorstein's hands, arm-wrestling fashion. He puts his free hand on Thorstein's shoulder.

"You'll be his anchor again," Wolfram says, and I nod, already imagining the spinning of my drop spindle, only the feel of the wool is the silk of Thorstein's hair, and Wolfram recedes into the background as I slip into the darkness behind my eyes, and then into the in-between. There is Wolfram's white spark, banked and dimmed, deliberately I think, so I won't be overwhelmed. And there is Thorstein's deep green glow, strong and steady now, with only an erratic crackle of red to show his nature is not properly aligned, that an alien predator shares his spirit.

I'm aware of Wolfram speaking, something in German, I think. Then Thorstein says, "I don't understand."

"Of course," Wolfram says. "My apologies." Then he switches to another language, something I realize I've heard before, when Thorstein spoke to his brothers, just the odd word or phrase here and there. Norwegian? I don't understand the words, but I listen anyway, watching Thorstein's glow begin to pulse with the rhythm of the words, then fade as he beings to descend deeper into the otherworld, following Wolfram.

I reach out with my own glow, brush against Thorstein's, and a thin bright thread spins out, a lifeline of brilliant green between me, waiting in the shallows of the spirit world, and Thorstein, as he descends deeper.

Wolfram's words run together into a river of sound and he and Thorstein slip away in it, only that green thread left to show where they've gone.

Then the thread suddenly snaps taut, and I try to hold on but I can't. And suddenly I'm falling, pulled deeper in with Thorstein, and deeper still and for a moment everything goes black.

I come to on a springy green surface. Moss. A voice, a harsh but liquid sound, is speaking to me.

I sit up, groggy, and say, "I don't understand."

"She only knows the New Anglo-Saxon," says another voice, like the first, but higher.

"They call it English, now," says the first voice.

"Wake up, girl," says the higher voice.

"I'm awake," I say. "Where am I?"

"You followed him," says one voice.

"He pulled you in," says the other. I twist around to see who's speaking and snap my mouth shut with a click when I see them.

Two ravens, deep inky black, flickers of blue light outlining their feathers, each one the size of an eagle. Bigger.

They look at me, dark eyes bright and curious.

"You're…" I say. How do I even finish that sentence?

"Huginn," says one.

"Muninn," says the other.

"Odin's ravens," I say, remembering the Wikipedia article I read last night, trying to figure out who Geri and Freki were.

"Thought," says the first bird.

"Memory," says the second.

"Where's Thorstein?" I say. "And Wolfram?"

"The werewolf prepares for his trial," says Huginn. I *think* it's Huginn.

"Odinson keeps watch and tells him what he must do."

Odinson? Do they mean Wolfram? Who else could they mean? Does that mean –? What *does* that mean? I shove the thought aside. Right now, I need to figure out what the hell to do about being here, when I'm supposed to be waiting, to be anchoring Thorstein, much closer to the here-and-now, the mortal realm.

"We'll show you," says Muninn.

"Or you could follow that," says Huginn, pointing with its – his? – beak at the bright green thread that extends from my belly button out into the distance.

There's not much else to do but follow, so I follow. It takes forever and no time at all before something appears nearby, seeming to erupt slowly out of the moss as much as it gets closer. A mound, green and grassy, with huge stones all around its base, a stone walkway leading up to an entrance. A dim light flickers from deep inside.

The green glowing thread leads right into the doorway, between two massive stones and under a third, each carved with layers of designs and symbols. I recognize prehistoric triple spirals and stylized animals in a Celtic or Viking style. With a start, I realize they match the tattoos on Wolfram's arms. The two birds on the lintel stone are ravens, and the four-legged fanged beasts on the pillar stones are wolves.

"They won't be able to see you," says one of the birds, the higher voiced one. I've got them mixed up again.

"But *he* will now you're there. Odinson."

"Your wolf will not know. Geri and Freki will see to it."

"Why? Why can't Thorstein know I'm here?" I step towards the mound, the doorway with its flickering light.

"Because," says one raven. "He needs to believe you cannot see him."

The other bird says, "If he knew you were watching him do this, he could not bring himself to do it."

"What is he going to do?"

"Did Wolfram not tell you?"

"He said…" Horror grows in me, settles in my belly like a cold, leaden weight. "Oh shit," I say. "He said Thorstein would have to –" I can't say it.

"Flay himself," says one bird.

"Carve away flesh from skeleton," says the other.

"And remake himself."

"I can't watch this," I say.

"You don't have to," say both birds together. "You can wait here."

I stand there for a long time, until a loud noise echoes out of the mound. A roar. I push aside my fear, my abject terror, like I used to push aside anxiety, and step under the stones, follow the passage deeper into the earth than it should go, judging by the size of the mound.

The passage opens out into a chamber, stone-walled and stone-arched. Another huge slab lies flat on the floor, and around it are three wolves. The ones to each side are gray-brown, with shiny black eyes and blue light flickering along their fur.

"Geri," says one raven.

"And Freki," says the other.

"Greedy."

"And Ravenous."

The third wolf faces me from the far end of the stone. I don't think he sees me, but he knows I'm there. He is huge and black, with clear gray eyes.

"Wolfram," I whisper. The wolf dips his head.

On the stone, stretched out flat, a long cruel-looking knife in his hand, is Thorstein. Only it's not Thorstein like I've ever seen him. He's half-changed, but not into the werewolf shape I saw him in on our first date. No, this is more bear-like, round head, six-inch claws, long snout, and teeth even bigger than his wolf-shape had.

He doesn't see me. He can't see me, and I'm glad.

He roars again.

"His *berserkr* self," says one of the ravens, a mere whisper of sound.

The black wolf, Wolfram, says something in that other language, only somehow I understand it this time. "You will feel pain unlike anything you have ever felt," he says. "It will feel very real, but know it is not. It is not physical pain, but spiritual pain. The pain of tearing free a part of yourself so that you may remake it."

Thorstein is panting now, one hand gripping the edge of the stone, digging in, the other hand holding the knife up. His eyes are closed.

"You will want to stop," says Wolfram. "But once you begin, you must not cease cutting until the flesh is cleaned from the bone. If you stop, you will be lost. Do you understand?"

"Yes." Thorstein gasps out the word.

"Then begin," says Thorstein.

I close my eyes, try not to hear the wet sounds, the panting breaths, the screams through teeth clenched so tight I can hear them grind together.

"I can't do this," I whisper.

"You can wait outside," says one of the ravens.

"You don't need to witness this," says the other.

"Yes, I do," I say, and open my eyes. And almost pass out.

I thought there was a lot of blood last night, but that was nothing compared to now. Thorstein is covered in it, it spurts from his cut flesh, pools under him on the stone, runs from the sides of the slab to gather, slick and dark, on the floor.

Now he makes no sound aside from his panting breath, as he draws the knife across his body with one hand and rips free chunks of skin and muscle with the other.

I want to throw up, to scream, to run, but I make myself stand still, watch as the man I love defleshes himself, strips off skin and muscle until only white bone remains, impossibly clean and gleaming.

Somehow, Thorstein's chest, his empty ribcage, still moves, still seems to pull breaths in and out.

"Are you still with me?" says Wolfram?

"Yes." The voice is Thorstein's, ragged and hoarse, like he's been screaming this whole time, even though his mouth was clamped shut. It's raw, but still strong, deep, rumbly. Still the voice I swore, the first time I heard it, could bring me to orgasm just by talking to me.

"Geri," says Wolfram. "Freki."

The two spectral wolves open their mouths, pink tongues lolling, and then begin to eat Thorstein's discarded flesh, wolfing it down in huge bites, licking the blood from the stone until there is only the skeleton left.

The knife falls from Thorstein's hand with a clatter.

"Thorstein?" Wolfram's voice holds a command in it.

"Yes?" Thorstein's voice is fainter. I clasp my hands together so hard the bones ache.

"Oh dear," says one raven.

"He's fading," says the other.

I look down at the green thread that binds me to Thorstein, watch it grow thin. I look up to where it ends in a green glow, nestled in the bony cage of Thorstein's ribs. It pulses and dims.

"No," I whisper.

I grasp at the light thread, feel it tingle against my palm, and then it falls apart, drifts to the floor like sparks that wink out when they hit cold stone.

Chapter Twenty-One

No!" I YELL AND LEAP forward, but what can I do? Thorstein's empty skeleton lies prone on the slab, a bare flicker of weak green light caged in his ribs.

"He's not entirely lost," Wolfram says. He's suddenly human-shaped again, holding his hands above the skeleton's ribs, feeding his own white light into Thorstein's green. "I need your help," he says.

"What do I do?"

"Remake the thread that bound him so he can find his way home."

I have no idea what that means, but I can't stand here and do nothing. I imagine my spindle and suddenly it's there in my hand, and I pull some of my own blue-and-yellow glow, spin it like I spun the soft gray wool, draft out my own essence and spin until my two colors blend into green, a living green that seems to recognize the faint glow in Thorstein's chest that Wolfram is keeping alive.

I keep spinning and the thread winds onto the spindle but somehow the other end, the end that should be tied to the spindle shaft, has floated free and stretches out, touches Thorstein's faint light, and is absorbed.

"Good," says Wolfram. "Slowly, now. Don't give him all of yourself, just let him use it to come back to us." All around us now, green sparks emerge from the stone, flickering like fireflies, and land on the big skeleton. They coat it like glow-in-the-dark paint, seep into it until there's a rich, pulsing ball of green filling his chest cavity.

"There," says Wolfram, stepping back. "Stop spinning your own light now."

I let go of the spindle, and it vanishes. The wound-up ball of green thread-light spools out on the floor, then slides, some absorbed into Thorstein, and some into me, until it's stretched, firm but not tight, between us.

And still the green sparks filter out of the stone, drift through the air, and land on the skeleton, covering it in green like moss, only glowing.

"What's happening?" I say, softly.

"All the parts he's lost of himself are finding their way back," Wolfram says. His voice holds awe. "He lost so much more than I thought, over the years. I don't know how he was able to keep existing."

"This is all him?"

"Every part of his spirit that he pushed aside, had torn away, or kept hidden, yes. All called home to help him remake himself."

We're speaking in whispers, like we might interrupt something sacred.

"Huginn and Muninn said you couldn't see me."

"I can't."

"But –"

"Oh, I probably could if I looked hard enough, but I feel you there. I hear you."

"Thorstein doesn't know I'm here."

"No."

"Don't tell him," I say. "He needs to believe he did this all on his own. He doesn't believe he's strong. He needs to *know* he is."

Wolfram nods. "I don't like keeping things from him, but I believe you're right."

"I don't like keeping things from him, either."

Then we just watch as the green light sinks into the skeleton, covers it, turns deep red and white and pink and all the colors of organs and muscle and connective tissue, and finally the pale pink-beige freckled with gold of Thorstein's fair skin.

He groans. "Am I still alive?" His voice doesn't sound raw anymore, but he sounds exhausted.

"You are," says Wolfram. "It was close, but you did it. Now try out the new shape of your spirit."

"How?"

"Think yourself a wolf." There's a hint of laughter in Wolfram's voice.

Thorstein pushes himself up from the stone, swings his legs around to sit on it. The scars on his arms are still there, and the faint lines from being made a werewolf. The bear bite and gash are healed, pink scars. For some reason, I thought all those scars would be gone – not from his flesh-and-blood body, but from this spiritual one. But I suppose they're too much a part of who he is, part of his essence.

"Like this," Wolfram says, and Thorstein watches as the small man's human shape vanishes, to be replaced by the huge black wolf.

Thorstein frowns. Then he grins and his human shape, too, is replaced by an even larger wolf, so pale a blond that he's almost white. His spirit body in wolf shape looks nothing like his physical werewolf shape. This wolf looks like a natural wolf, but gigantic, while his werewolf shape looks like a human body put together the wrong way, with added fur, like the werewolf in that old movie *An American Werewolf in London*.

But all of his shapes are beautiful, just different. I want very badly to go to him, to bury my hands in his fur, and tell him how lovely he is. Except I don't want him to know I saw him at his most vulnerable. I don't want him to know I saw him almost die. Again.

So I turn and walk out of the mound and the green thread stretches behind me. Huginn and Muninn follow and as soon as we're outside, they leap into the air, swoop around me, dip their wings, and call out, "Follow us!"

"How?" I say, running to keep up.

"Use your wings, sister," they say.

"I don't have wings." But suddenly I do, feathery appendages sprouting from my shoulders, lifting me into the black, up from wherever in the otherworld we are, and back to that place just beneath the surface of the here-and-now.

My wings disappear as if they were never there, but the green thread is strong, and I feel it hum and vibrate as Thorstein and Wolfram come closer, finding their own way back to the surface.

For a moment, we're three glowing things in the dark space behind my eyes, and then we're all on the roof, stretching and yawning. The stars are fading, and the sky is getting light in the east.

"My feet are asleep," I say.

"My *ass* is asleep," says Thorstein. For a long moment he looks up at me and I look down at him, neither of us moving, just *looking*. Then he smiles.

"I did it," he says.

"Yes, you did."

"It's still going to take work to keep the *berserkrgang* at bay," Wolfram says. "But your father will never be able to use it, or you, again."

Thorstein sits up, rubs his face with both hands.

"I feel like I was hit by a truck," he says. "But I also feel so fucking *alive*."

"You're whole again," I say.

He turns to me, smiles, flashing his dimple at me. "That was really fucking awful," he says. "But this might be one of the best days of my life."

"Yeah?" I say, attempting to stand on tingling feet.

"Yeah," he says, when I fail and stumble, and land in his lap. "I'm free, and the most amazing woman I've ever met actually wants to be mine."

"That does sound pretty good."

Thorstein has to go back to the farm, of course, because there's always too much to do on a farm, and he won't let his animals or even his crops suffer because he's got other things on his mind.

And I have a job, and an apartment to pack, if I'm really going to do this crazy thing and move in with my giant Viking wolf.

"So," I say to Katie when I get to work the next morning. "What if I moved in with a guy?"

She stares at me in horror. "Like as in live together?" She puts a hand over her heart like she's having palpitations. "At least tell me this isn't a *different* guy. Like you haven't lost your mind over two different guys in a row."

"No, it's not a different guy," I say, sorting through work orders and filing them alphabetically in a file box so we can find them later if we need to. One day, we'll set up a proper system on a computer, with a database and everything, but today is not that day. "The same guy."

"Well, at least the view would be nice," she says.

"Yeah, the Bottomlands are pretty," I say. "Especially in the spring and fall."

She snorts. "The only *bottom* I'm talking about is that fine ass he carries around behind him. Tell me it's just as nice naked as it is in jeans."

"Pretty sure you already asked me that."

"And what did you already say?"

"It's not as nice," I reply, trying to hide my grin.

"Pity," she says.

"It's much *much* nicer."

She throws a dust cloth at me.

Later, in my apartment, I look around and realize I don't really have that much I want to take. Clothes, of course, the art on the walls, a few favorite blankets and pillows. My books will be the bulk of it. My furniture and kitchen stuff is all either utilitarian or I got it free. I'm not attached to any of it.

I'll have to get more boxes for the books – a *lot* more boxes – but everything else only takes a few hours to assemble into containers and bags.

All day, I've been getting little red heart emojis texted to me, and all day I've been texting them back.

Now, it's a long string of them, followed by *hot bath wish u wr hre 2*

Bubble bath? I reply.

He sends back a photo of a thick layer of white bubbles with his feet sticking out, far enough from the camera to be blurry.

You have pretty feet, I reply, followed by a staring face emoji.

foot fetish? he says.

For you, maybe.

There's a long pause, then, *I love you.*

I love you, I reply, then we spend way too long texting back and forth random animal emojis before finally saying goodnight.

In the morning, there are more heart emojis, and later in the day, when I'm taking a break at work – catching up on orders on a Sunday – he sends *I told Dad ur moving in.*

And?

Not happy.

You want to wait? We don't have to do this right away. I pause, then type, *I'm not going anywhere.*

A few seconds later, my phone rings. He hates talking on the phone. *I* hate talking on the phone. I answer because he'd only phone if it was important.

"I don't want to wait," he says, when I pick up. His voice is rough. "But I'm worried he'll be shitty. Try to drive you away. Especially once he realizes you're the same woman who accidentally ended up in his house."

"What do you want to do?"

He takes a deep, frustrated breath. I can picture him rubbing a hand over his face, tugging his fingers through his hair. "I don't know." I can hear gravel crunching, like he's pacing in his driveway. "I don't fucking know. I want you here, but I want you safe."

"How about tonight I just come for dinner? We won't start moving any of my stuff in, we'll just have a meal, you give me a tour of the farm, and he can start to get used to the idea."

He snorts out a long breath. "Yeah," he says. "Okay. I just… I don't want to wait anymore. I'm tired of having my life on hold."

Even though he seems as calm as always, I can feel Thorstein's anxiety. It's in the way he glances in the mirrors more often, in how the shift from fifth to sixth on the highway has just a slight hitch in it. It's in the way he breathes, like he's forcing each breath to be the precise same length as every other one. And it spreads to me, makes me fidget with my seatbelt.

Normally, silence doesn't bother me, especially Thorstein's silence, but right now, the quiet amplifies the nervous tension we're both feeling until I can't stand it.

"What's for dinner?" I ask.

He glances at me, smiles, then checks the mirrors. Again.

"Roast duck," he says. "Wild rice, steamed asparagus." Another smile gets through the nervous stillness. "Homemade rose petal ice cream for dessert."

"Rose petal?"

"We have wild roses in the wood lot. It's an unusual flavor, but it's very nice."

"And homemade?"

"Mm."

"By you?"

His smile grows a tiny bit. "I've had a long time to learn how to do things,'" he says. "Not much of a social life. Mostly confined to the farm." He frowns.

"So you cook?"

"I cook." He looks at me from the corners of his eyes, like he's suddenly worried I'll find him off-putting. Like a man who can cook could ever be unattractive for that fact alone.

"The more I learn about you," I say, moving my hand from fiddling with the strap of my bag to stroking his thigh. "The more I'm convinced I won the fucking jackpot."

"I think you might like my house," he says. Then he looks worried again. "I mean, I know Craftsman, Arts and Crafts… I know it's not exactly contemporary, but…?"

"You have a Craftsman house?" I mean I knew that, but I've only seen the outside, in the dark, so it could well be that it was only *formerly* Craftsman.

"Yes. Granddad built it. When he decided he wanted to live in the woods I helped him build his cabin, and he gave me his house."

"Does it have those mica-shaded lamps? Built in cabinets and bookcases? All that luscious quarter-sawn oak?"

"Yes, yes, and yes." The corners of his mouth twitch and he starts to smile again.

"I think I'll marry you just for the house."

He laughs, and a lot of the anxiety that was building up, in both of us, dissipates.

And his house is fucking gorgeous. Even the furniture is mostly Craftsman, some of it well-made repro, but I'm pretty sure a lot of it is original. The fabrics are lush greens and blues and rusts, some in simple blocks of color, and some in ornate William Morris patterns.

The whole downstairs smells like roast duck and suddenly I'm ravenous. I peer into the oven, but it's hard to see much in there. "Did you grow this duck?" I say. "Please tell me it didn't have a name."

He comes up behind me, slides his hands over my hips, and pulls me close. "It probably had a name among its own kind," he says. "And it was one of Hilde's flock."

"Your sister raises ducks?"

"Ducks, chickens, geese, turkeys, quail. She likes birds."

We're interrupted by a sharp knock on the door, and someone walks in without waiting for an answer. I can't see who it is from where we're standing, but Thorstein doesn't seem bothered.

"You get dirt on my floor, you're going to be cleaning it," he calls.

"Yes, mother," comes the mocking reply. Bjarni. "Dad wants you in the sheep barn."

"Tell him I have company."

Bjarni's head pokes around the kitchen door and smirks when he sees us, pressed together. "He knows you have company." His mouth slides into a leer. "I can keep her busy while you see what he wants."

"I thought you liked having testicles," says Thorstein, mildly.

"Fine," says Bjarni. "But if you bring Raine, he's going to clue in that something was up last full moon."

Thorstein looks down at me. "Do you want to wait here?"

"No," I say. "I'm going to have to meet him eventually. Might as well get it over with."

He nods and checks his watch, then punches some buttons on the range's control panel. "That'll shut off the oven if we're not back in half an hour."

The sheep barn isn't far, but it gives me time to stare around me at the parts of the farm I can see. Everything is well-kept, tidy, and flourishing. I hear a neigh from a ways off, followed by another.

"I'll go feed the horses," Bjarni grumbles, like he really wanted to be there when I met his father. Officially.

"Thank you," says Thorstein, not even glancing his way as Bjarni strides away.

When we reach the barn, painted a stereotypical brick red with white trim, Thorstein pauses in the doorway. He laces his fingers through mine, looks at me to see if I'm ready, and then steps inside.

And stops dead. There, in one of the stalls, is a sheep with fleece so thick I have no idea how it can be standing up.

"What the fuck?" Thorstein says.

"Watch your language, boy." Thorstein's father – Thorgrim – turns slowly from where he was leaning on the stall's top rail. His cold eyes flicker over Thorstein, note our joined hands, then settle on me. I resist the urge to shiver.

In daylight, he looks a little less like Thorstein, but just as intimidating. It does help that Thorstein is nearly a foot taller than his dad, but the older man is still terrifying. I make myself stand still, when really I desperately want to hide behind Thorstein.

"Dad, this is Raine," Thorstein says. His father looks at me, and I don't see any recognition in his eyes beyond a faint flicker that might mean he's wondering if he's seen me somewhere before.

"My son cannot give you what you want," he says. He has an accent, like someone who learned English in England, but who wasn't from there.

I find my own voice somehow. "You don't know what I want," I say, and okay maybe they're not strong, or even certain, but at least words come out.

"It doesn't matter what you want," he says, and turns away from me, to point at the sheep.

"Harkett had him. I told him I'd revoke the lease on his garage if I ever found him neglecting an animal again."

"I don't really need another ram," Thorstein says. "But I'll shear him. If he's healthy, he can go in the next auction."

"Good enough," Thorgrim says in a way that makes me think nothing anyone ever does is good enough. He turns to walk past us but pauses to look at me again. "What is your family name?" he suddenly says.

Startled, I automatically blurt out, "Chevalier."

Thorstein's lips twitch, but his father's back is to him. "Knightsbrige Quarter Horses," he says, and his father's nostrils flare.

"Is that so?"

"My dad's Brent Chevalier," I say.

"You're a half-breed," he says.

"I'm a what?"

"Your mother came off the reservation."

"My mother grew up off-rez," I say. "But so what if she had?" I feel anger building in my gut, almost enough to overwhelm the fear, and when I look at Thorstein, his eyes are narrowed in disgust. Not for me; for his father. And I realize it doesn't matter what the older man thinks of me.

"Merely an observation." Then he walks away, out the door, and he's gone.

Thorstein takes a step after him, like he's going to follow, say something he might regret, and I put a hand on his arm.

"It doesn't matter," I say. "You already knew he was a racist prick, among other things. *I* already knew."

He sighs. "I suppose. I just don't like to see him slight you, to talk to you that way." He looks thoughtful. "Though he'd probably have said worse if he wasn't trying to buy a horse from your father."

"Shall I put in a good word for him?" I say, raising an eyebrow.

He laughs. "Fuck yes. A very *good* word."

And then I get to watch as my gorgeous boyfriend strips off his shirt and hefts a large sheep around like it weighs nothing, and shears off several years' worth of dirty fleece with only hand-help clippers – and not the electric kind.

When he's done, the ram looks much smaller, and very startled, and Thorstein is gleaming with sweat. And I think I'm staring with my mouth open. All three of us have forgotten the elder Thorvaldson.

Chapter Twenty-Two

Dinner, of course, is delicious, and Thorstein says, almost shyly, when I ask him why he likes to cook, "I just like making things." He looks at his hands, big, muscular, and calloused. "It feels like my life has been about destroying things, and anything I can create, or grow, or help to be born makes it bearable."

"It'll be different now," I say, curling against him when we sprawl on the couch. Then I poke his belly, wondering if he's as stuffed full of delicious food as I am. "When's dessert?"

He says, "Whenever you like. I think I'll wait a bit to digest first, though." Definitely stuffed full, then.

I trace the outline of his belly muscles through his t-shirt just to feel that rumble he makes in his chest when I touch him. It's like making a cat purr, only sexy.

"Can I eat it off your abs?" I say.

He slides his shirt up to expose the muscles in question.

"On second thought," I say. "They're too bulgy. Ice cream would just slide off the side." I run my finger over the path I imagine said ice cream following. "And your belly button isn't big enough to hold very much."

"Mm," he says, then slides his t-shirt higher. "You could put it right here," and he points to the space between his pecs, where they dip down to join his ribs. There's a hollow there that could hold a scoop or two.

I place a kiss right there, and say, "You'd let me eat ice cream off your body?"

He looks at me, completely serious, and says, "You can do anything you like with my body."

I'm trying to decide whether or not I'm too full to take him up on the offer, when he suddenly sits up and looks towards the door.

"What is it?" I say. I can tell he's heard something, though to me there are just the usual farm-in-evening sounds. I glance at the window and discover that darkness has gathered while we were recovering from our meal and it's later than I thought.

"Dad," he says. "He's angry. But he doesn't usually yell when he's mad." He frowns and gets up. "Stay here, love," then he heads out the door, not even bothering to put shoes on.

I still can't hear anything unusual, but it can't be good if Thorstein had an expression like that on his face.

I wait about two minutes, then follow. Thorstein's nowhere in sight, but I know the way to the farmhouse now, and there's a bit of light from the partial moon. I *do* pause to slip shoes on but move carefully because I don't relish stepping on any of the many things one might encounter in a farmyard. Especially something not easily removed from canvas and rubber.

And then I hear it as I creep out of the trees to the edge of the lawn. Thorstein's dad, voice low and hard. Not loud, but very, very angry.

"Explain, boy," he's saying.

"Explain what?" Thorstein stands on the lawn, arms crossed, watching his father who seems to loom on the porch, the lights of the house casting his shadow in front of him. He looks like the bad guy from a horror movie.

"I thought I'd seen her before," his dad says, taking a step down, then another.

"Seen who, Dad?" Thorstein's voice is calm, but I can hear the edge of tension in it.

"Your whore," his dad says. "She was with Bjarni, and your shit brother admits it." He takes one more step down and faces Thorstein on the lawn. He's got something clenched in his hand, a strap of leather like a leash, like he was about to take one of his giant dogs for a walk when he remembered where he'd seen me. He looks like he might be about to hit Thorstein with it.

"She was in my house," he grinds out. "And she smelled like you."

"Raine is my girlfriend," Thorstein says.

"Yours," his father replies, laughing, a hateful, grating sound. "You have nothing but what I give you." His anger is gone now, replaced by contempt. "I've let you slip your leash these past few months, skip off to the city to fuck yourself silly, because I thought the exercise would do you good. But now it's time to return to your kennel. You are what *I* made you." Something cold settles in my gut at the thought that the elder Thorstein knew when his son was with me, knew what he was doing, even if he didn't realize who I was.

"No, Dad," Thorstein says quietly. "Not anymore."

His father snorts. "Did she creep into my house thinking to rescue you? To save you from the big bad wolf who sired you? Does she know what you are?" He looks up suddenly, eyes finding me in the darkness.

"Does your father know what kind of monster you're fucking?" he says. His voice is so reasonable now, so calm and precise I almost miss the words he's actually used.

"My father knows we're together," I say, though I've only told my parents that I've met someone, not who. I step out onto the lawn, stride forward with way more confidence than I feel, and take Thorstein's hand. I'm terrified, and I know I should have stayed in the house, but this confrontation was probably going to happen sooner or later. Better to get it over with, I guess.

"And I know *exactly* what kind of monster I'm fucking."

Thorstein doesn't look away from his dad, even shifts so he's partly between us, but he strokes my thumb with his, and squeezes my hand gently.

"You should have let your brother keep her," Thorgrim says. "At least he could get a child on her."

Thorstein's chin jerks up at that, and I know his dad has scored a hit. Thorstein won't have children, but he wants them, badly.

"Bjarni never had her," is all he says.

"So that was a lie," his father says. "The little shit dared to lie to me."

"Little Bear's the only one of us who'd try lying to another werewolf," says a voice from the shadow of the trees that separate the farmhouse lawn from Bjarni's house. Magne steps out onto the grass. He's breathing hard and two huge gray wolves slip out of the shadows behind him, one on each side. Flickers of blue light, like the phosphorescence you sometimes see in the wake of a boat on the ocean at night trace the tips of their fur. I recognize Geri and Freki, and seeing them here, in real life, sends a tingle through my nerve endings. Like waking up to something you thought was only a dream is actually real.

What the hell are they doing here? What the hell is *Magne* doing here?

As if to answer my question, Magne says, "Syr had a premonition that I needed to be here tonight. I came as fast as I could."

"How?" Thorstein stares at the spectral wolves, then back at Magne.

"I ran," Magne says, and grins so wide both dimples – and his huge canines – show.

Thorgrim stalks forwards a few paces on the lawn, angling towards Magne. He looks at Geri and Freki, his nostrils flare, and he doesn't get any closer.

"You are banished," he says.

Magne shrugs.

His father whips back around to face Thorstein and me. "Are all my sons conspiring against me? Should I watch for Hilde to brandish a knife in the dark, too?"

"Hilde will always be your princess, Dad," Magne says. "She's the only one of us you ever treated decently."

Thorgrim ignores Magne and stares at Thorstein. Thorstein stares back, which his father seems to find unexpected. I guess he thought Thors would grovel, or at least lower his eyes.

"Kneel, boy, and beg forgiveness. If you're convincing enough, I might not punish you. I might give your woman to Bjarni instead of killing her."

"No, Dad," says Thorstein. "That's never going to happen again."

Thorgrim stares at his oldest son for a long moment. Geri and Freki sit down next to Magne and watch, and Magne crosses his arms and looks like a younger, darker version of his brother.

"You would risk the *berserkr* rage?" Thorgrim finally says, voice gone calm and reasonable again. "You know I'm the only one who can help you control it."

"You never helped me control anything," says Thorstein. "You took control *away* from me. You used me to keep the pack in line, to make them afraid to do anything but what you told them to do."

"And if I did," his father says, voice staying reasonable, almost warm. "It was for your own good. For the good of this family and the good of our pack." He takes a step forward, and another, and Thorstein pushes me behind him as his father puts a hand on his shoulder, slides it to the back of his neck.

"Would you throw that away? Would you endanger your…" He seems to be trying to find a word for me that isn't "whore." "…Lover? Would you risk tearing her apart in your anger just so you can fuck her whenever you want? Would you risk disemboweling her as you once did your beloved baby brother?"

"That was all you, Dad," Magne says.

"I didn't touch you," his father says, turning his head only slightly towards his younger son.

"You didn't have to, when you could use magic to make me do it for you." Thorstein lets go of my hand to push away his father's touch, but before he can, Thorgrim moves his other hand up and flings the leash he was holding, that I'd forgotten he was holding, around Thorstein's neck. It holds.

Thorstein jerks away, pushing me back several more steps. He grabs at the leash, but it's wrapped firmly around his throat, and seems to be getting tighter.

"Kneel," Thorgrim says.

Thorstein kneels.

Magne and I, Geri and Freki, all take a step forward, and the older man snarls, "Come closer and I snap his neck."

We all stop. I hear a whimper and I realize it's me.

"Who put such silly notions in your head, son?" Thorgrim says, voice gentle again. "Who convinced you that you could survive on your own? Have a woman? A life outside this farm?"

Thorstein can't answer. He can barely breathe.

"That's…" I whisper. "The leash. It's magic." The darkness and fear has me half in the in-between, and I don't think Syr would say this was a good development in my skills. But I can see a red crackle, like faint electricity, on the leather strap.

"It *is* magic," says Thorgrim. "And the witch who gave it to me is too long dead to destroy it or to complain about how I use it. Not that she would dare; I gave her what she wanted in return."

Fascinated and horrified, I whisper, "What did she want?"

He sneers at me, like I'm scum who shouldn't even be speaking, but he answers. "What her kind always wants. A girl child to carry on her legacy. Lucky for me, she was an attractive bitch, so the task wasn't all that onerous."

Magne opens his mouth, his face alarmed and oddly fascinated by the revelation. Does this mean their father had another child? That they have another sister somewhere? But Thorgrim silences him with a look.

"Call for your mother, you worthless waste of semen, and your brother suffers."

"He's all the control you have over the pack," Magne says softly. "Kill him and you lose everything."

"Not everything. Bjarni may lie, but he won't dare defy me again after this. He's not entirely useless. Besides, I don't need to kill Thorstein to hurt him. I think I've demonstrated *that* often enough."

I catch faint movement over the older man's shoulder. Has his wife come to see what the commotion is? Will she find out what a monster her husband is after all?

But no. It's Bjarni who stands on the front porch, watching, his face blank and unreadable. He takes a slow, careful step on the old wood planks. He catches my eye and shakes his head slightly.

Bjarni's a liar and an asshole. He's told his father things his brothers wanted kept secret. I can't trust him if his own family doesn't even trust him. But he got me out of his father's house that night, and he came to save Thorstein's life when he was really needed.

So I keep my mouth shut and look away, look at Magne instead. Magne is very deliberately *not* looking in the direction of the farmhouse porch.

Geri and Freki seem to drift over to Thorstein, one on each side, and that weirdness of vision that let me see the magic on the leash shows me that they're lending him their own strength, their blue flicker playing over him, dancing over his green glow like soft lightning.

"Call off your wolves," says Thorgrim. He eyes them, looking from one to the other, like he dares not look away too long.

"They're not mine," says Magne.

Thorstein is still, eyes closed, breathing in quick, pained gasps. His shoulders are tense, his hands clenched around the leash where it twists against his throat.

Bjarni steps down onto the grass, his bare feet making no sound, and moves closer to us, closer to his father. He's just a little shorter, a little leaner, but otherwise he looks like a younger version of Thorgrim – not as exact a match as Thorstein, but in the uncertain moonlight, it looks like the older man is being stalked by his own shadow self.

He bares his teeth, and they flash white in the moonlight.

"Fuck you, Dad," he says softly, and his father starts to turn. He's too slow. Bjarni reaches out with both hands and there's a sudden tension in his upper body, a sudden sickening crunch. Thorgrim's eyes go wide, unbelieving. And then he collapses.

The leash falls away from Thorstein's neck and he falls forward onto his hands, only inches from his father's body.

He looks up and stares at Bjarni. So does Magne. Only Geri and Freki look away, uninterested now that the danger is over.

"Bjarni?" says Thorstein. "Little Bear?"

"Don't call me that, asshole," Bjarni says. Then he seems to realize we're all staring. "What?" he says. "You think you're the only ones he took something from? You two, always wailing about how he took your brother, drove your brother away. Blah, blah, fucking blah." He drags both hands through his hair. "Well, he took both of my brothers from me, okay?" His voice has taken on a desperate edge, and he looks from Thorstein to Magne and back, searching for something in their faces.

Then Thorstein surges to his feet and steps over his father's body to grab Bjarni in a hug. Magne is only a step behind and for a moment the three of them seem to blend together into one big Thorvaldson brother mass.

"It's about fucking time." This new voice is heavily accented and sounds a bit like Thorstein's did when he was trying to talk to me around his werewolf teeth. Like the speaker's lips are pulled too tight and his teeth leave no room for his tongue to shape sounds.

And for the second time this evening – or is it the third? – someone steps out of the shadow of the house into the blend of moon- and porchlight. "I was starting to think I was going to have to put him down myself, and I'm not a big fan of killing my own children."

The speaker is a man, sort of. He's bent, but not with age. Or not *only* with age. He's also more than half-shifted into wolf shape but forcing himself to move upright on two legs.

The brothers break apart and Magne says, "Granddad?" Cautiously.

"You think it's better *we* killed him?" Thorstein says.

"Who's this *we*?" says Bjarni. "I'm not letting any of you take the blame for this."

The werewolf man, their grandfather, moves farther into the light. Though he's bent from age and half-transformation, he doesn't look frail. He appears to be nearly as muscular as his grandsons, and if he were on four legs, he'd probably be just as terrifying – and just as beautiful – in full wolf shape.

He looks at me and smiles, or tries to. It's disconcerting on his b-movie werewolf face, but I've seen Thorstein this way, so it doesn't scare me. Much.

He gestures at himself. "This is what you have to look forward to," he says. "When he gets old."

"If I live that long," I say.

"I smell wolf symbiont on you," he says. And of course he does, because not long ago I was snuggled up close and personal with his grandson. He turns back to the brothers.

"You," he points at Magne. "Are still banished, until your new pack leader says otherwise."

"Granddad," Magne says, but the old werewolf silences him just by raising his eyebrows.

"Go home. No one needs to know you were here tonight."

"And you –" He points at Thorstein. "Go back to your house and enjoy your evening with your lovely date. You were there all night and will know nothing of this until morning."

"And you –." He turns to Bjarni, who flares his nostrils and looks nervous. The older werewolf's stern look softens. "It's about time you took some fucking steps." He grips Bjarni's arm. "What did Thorgrim say when he left the house?"

"That there was something he had to deal with, and he'd be back later."

"Colleen and Hilde didn't react to this?" He gestures vaguely around the yard.

"Hilde's out with one of her boyfriends," Bjarni says. "And Colleen does what she always does and pretended not to hear. She knew Dad was angry, but Thorstein didn't speak loud enough for her to hear his voice."

The old wolf nods. "Poor thing," he says. "So blinded by love she could never see what he was." He lets go of Bjarni's arm. "Go inside. Tell her you saw your dad take off towards the woodlot, pissed off and swearing."

Bjarni nods. "What do I tell her about…?" He gestures around the yard like his granddad did.

"You don't." The old wolf bends, scoops up his son's body, and tosses it over his shoulder, showing exactly how not frail he is. He says, "I'll report to the Elders." A grin that looks an awful lot like Bjarni's crosses his face.

"What will you do with him?" says Thorstein softly.

"Report to the Elders that he finally decided I was too old to live, but he was the one who ended up dead." He smiles sadly. "As for his corpse, it can rot in the woods and be eaten by vultures."

"They won't believe you, Granddad," says Magne.

"They will, because it's true. Even if I wasn't the one who broke his neck. He *did* think I was too old to live. And I was a threat to his hold over the pack, too. They won't look too closely at the evidence, because every one of those Elders fears their own families will decide they've outlived their usefulness, that they're too much of a burden."

Then the old man disappears back into the shadows, carrying his son, as his grandsons watch.

"Fuck, Bjarni," says Magne, finally.

"Tell me you've never thought about it," Bjarni says. His voice is vicious, but his eyes shine wet in the moonlight.

I lean against Thorstein, and he puts an arm around me. "You hated him," I say gently. "All of you. But you're still going to mourn him. He was awful, but he was your dad."

"Fuck him," says Bjarni, and turns away abruptly, heading for the house.

"You're probably right," says Magne. "But so is Bjarni. Fuck him." He grips Thorstein's shoulder, points at the leash still coiled in the grass, and says, "Burn that thing." Then he's a huge brown and gray wolf, loping off into the darkness, flanked by two gray wolves with blue light flickering through their fur.

I take Thorstein home and we eat our ice cream, out of bowls like civilized people, and neither of us says anything.

After we wash up the dishes, Thorstein says, "Should I drive you home?" He doesn't look at me.

"No," I say. "Home is wherever you are."

So he leads me to bed, and I hold him while he cries. His shoulders heave but he makes no sound, and I wipe away tears and snot and it seems to go on for a very long time before he falls asleep. I don't sleep at all, I just watch over him, make sure he feels safe and loved. And when he wakes up as the sun starts to turn the world gray, he says, "Thank you."

I don't say anything. I just kiss him until he falls asleep again.

And the *next* time he wakes up, he pulls me to him, kisses me until my lips feel swollen, and rolls me over to stroke my back, my ribs, slide one hand between me and the mattress to cup my breast.

His mouth on the back of my neck is hot and wet, and I feel every muscle press and slide against my skin, feel him hard against my butt.

I push my hips back against him, curl one arm around to grab his thigh, pull him closer. He rolls on top of me, pinning me to the bed, then lifts himself up on hands and knees and pulls me up with him so my back is pressed against his belly and chest and his erection fits in the crack of my ass.

He slides one hand from my breast down my body, over my belly, and stops. He nips the back of my neck and I tilt my head so he can reach that spot under my ear.

"Touch me," I say, my voice coming out hoarse.

His hand slides between my legs, fingers spreading me open. Then he withdraws his hand and I say, more moan than word, "No."

He chuckles against my neck and I feel his hand near my ass, shifting his cock from my butt crack to between my legs so his length slides deliciously against my wetness.

"Better?" he says, voice all rumbly.

I can only gasp as he pushes against me, but I grab his ass and pull him closer again.

His free hand strokes my skin, my thigh, my ribs, my belly, cups my breast again and massages my nipple until I'm pushing myself desperately against him, making his hardness slide over me again and again.

"Fuck," he says, all breath. "You feel so good." And then he shifts his hips, and his hand is gone again from my skin, his cock from between my legs. And I feel the tip of him against my entrance and I don't wait any more for him to move, I just shove myself back, feel him push inside me. Then pull out, then shove back in.

"Fuck," he says again, then both his hands are on me, pulling me up against him as he shifts his weight entirely to his knees, holding himself upright on the bed, holding me against him as he moves inside me. His mouth burns on my neck and one hand burns on my chest, his fingers rolling my nipple between them until the sensation shoots down between my legs.

Then his other hand follows where that sensation went, finds my wetness, teases until I'm moaning and shoving back against him as hard as I can, and *he's* moaning now, our voices blending together until we're both gasping, both throbbing.

And after that, we lie quietly in bed together, until Bjarni knocks on the door with the "bad news" we already know.

Chapter Twenty-Three

WHEN EVERYONE IS FINALLY gone, the Elders' questions answered – and Thorstein's granddad was right, they're not too thorough in their inquiries – we sit on the farmhouse porch swing.

Even I, with my merely human ears, can hear Magne's mother sobbing, her daughter trying valiantly to stay calm and soothe her, but crying herself, and Bjarni clattering about making tea so he won't feel useless.

"He's gone," says Thorstein, a strange mix of grief and relief in his voice. And guilt. "It's finally over."

I lean on his shoulder and rub absently at my arm. The scratches Thorstein left there during the failed attempt to become a bear-changer have scabbed over and they're itchy. It's funny how they seemed so much deeper at the time. Shock, I guess.

Thorstein looks down at me, watches me dig at the bandages with my fingernails, then gently takes my hand and pulls it away from my arm.

"What happened?" he says, leaning over to look, though he can't see anything with my sleeve pulled down.

"You don't remember?" I say. "No. of course you don't. You were… when the wolf symbiont was fighting the bear…" I pause. I don't really want to tell him he hurt me. He's been forced to hurt enough people he cares about. But I don't have to say any more, because he figures it out.

"I did this?" His fingers are gentle as he pulls up the sleeve of my t-shirt and unwinds the bandage. When he peels back the gauze Bethy taped on, he frowns. "It looks like it might scar," he says. "But it's nearly healed."

I frown, too, and crane my neck to look. "I guess it wasn't as deep as I thought it was."

He runs his fingers softly over the scabs, which have already begun to flake off, leaving three long, thin, pink lines on my arm. His frown deepens.

"It itches," I say.

"Tell me exactly what happened," he says, keeping his voice very low and calm. Like he's trying not to make me nervous, but it *does* make me nervous, because his very calm reasonableness means he's worried.

"You were thrashing, and clipped my arm because I didn't stay back like I was supposed to. But look, it's not bad at all."

"But you thought it was bad at the time."

"It hurt like hell. I'd have sworn you hit bone." Then I snap my mouth shut. I didn't mean to say that part out loud.

His fingers are still gentle as he strokes my cheek. "And then what?"

I shrug. "Everything sort of happened at once. You almost died. Bjarni saved you."

"Was there blood on your arm?"

"The cuts were bleeding, sure," I say.

"My blood?"

"I don't think so."

"Think, love, please. Did you, did anyone get blood on your arm that wasn't yours? The bear-man? Cliff?"

And now he's *really* making me nervous. It's just a cut that's healed well. And so what if it scars? It'll be one hell of a cool scar.

I shake my head. "I don't think anyone got blood on me." But then I remember Bjarni telling me I had to get Thorstein to swallow, how he grabbed my arm and I flinched because it hurt, because he grabbed me right where the cuts were. And how he left a bloody handprint on my already-bloody sleeve.

I look up into Thorstein's eyes, finally realizing what he's really asking.

"Bjarni," I say.

"What did Bjarni do?" he says, his voice gone even softer, but with a dangerous edge.

"He had blood on his hands," I say. "*His* blood, I think, or maybe yours. From trying to save you." I touch his face, try to soothe whatever hard emotion is lurking behind his eyes.

"He needed to get my attention," I say. "So he grabbed my arm." I put my own hand right where Bjarni's had been, right over the three claw-cuts.

Thorstein closes his eyes and rests his forehead on mine. "Bloody hell," he says, but his voice is relaxed, the edge gone.

"What?" I say. I think I know, but I need him to say it out loud.

"You had deep cuts," he says.

"No, but –"

"You had deep cuts," he repeats. "Bjarni touched them with bloody hands, and whether it was his blood or mine, it was full of werewolf symbiont. Now your cuts are almost healed, only days later."

Everything seems to stop. "What?" I say.

"He infected you," he says. "You're becoming a werewolf." And there it is. "That's what Granddad meant when he said he smelled werewolf symbiont on you." He laughs. "I thought he meant he smelled *me* on you."

"Oh." I don't know how to feel about that. I mean, fuck, at least I won't have to worry about getting old while my gorgeous soon-to-be-husband stays young.

"I'm sorry," he says.

"But I haven't sprouted fangs or anything," I say.

"It's a slow process, and that's when there's a lot more blood involved. With so little blood, I don't know how long it could take."

He looks at me again, strokes my cheek.

"I'm sorry," he repeats.

"Tell me what to expect," I say. The world has slowly returned to its normal pace, and I can't say I'm even upset. Not really. Not when I've seen Thorstein's face when he talks about running in the dark forest in wolf shape.

"The symbiont has to overcome your immune system, first," he says. "And since you healed so quickly, I'd say that's well underway. But it will mean you'll be very susceptible to getting sick."

"Is that normal?"

He shakes his head. "The way werewolves are usually made, the symbiont takes over all at once. There's so much blood loss, and new blood spilled on the wounds, that the body's defenses never have time to kick in, let alone fail to fight off sickness." He tilts my head so I have to look into his eyes. "You should think about taking a leave from work, to avoid being around a lot of people."

"Shit," I say. "I like my job. I like people."

He kisses the top of my head. "If everything goes well, you'll begin to feel the moon singing in your blood when she's full. And gradually, you'll be able to change shape. First teeth, then claws, then paws, then you'll be able to run on four legs. You can join the pack after that, to run and hunt under the full moon."

He sighs. "It's not a terrible thing," he says. "I love being a werewolf. I wouldn't want to be anything else."

"You chose to become a bear, instead," I say. "And it almost killed you."

"I didn't really want it, so maybe that's why my body rejected it."

"You wanted to stay a werewolf."

"Yes."

"Thorstein?" He pulls back to study my face again. "What happens if it doesn't go well?"

"Mm?"

"You said, 'if everything goes well,' but what happens if it *doesn't* go well?"

He settles me against his chest.

"Thorstein." He twitches. "What happens if it doesn't go well?"

"If the symbiont overwhelms your immune system to the point it can't recover, you spend the rest of your life having to be very careful not to get sick."

"I'd be a bubble girl." I want to make him laugh, but it doesn't work. Maybe because I don't find it funny, either. "Okay, what if it doesn't overwhelm my immune system at all?"

"You could recover."

"Could?"

"Or it could kill you."

"Could kill me or would kill me?"

"I don't know," he says, sighing. "I've never known someone who was changed this way."

"Fuck," I say.

"It's not likely it would kill you," he says. "It's most likely you'll just be vulnerable until the symbiont asserts dominance and begins to work with your immune system instead of against it. And then you'll become a werewolf, just like any other newly-changed wolf." He strokes my hair, presses his forehead into my temple, like he's willing everything to go well.

"Are you mad?" he says.

"Why would I be mad? It's not like someone did this deliberately against my will. It was an accident."

"You didn't choose this."

"I'm always up for a new experience," I say, forcing my voice to be light. I know he can see right through the attempt. It's very hard to lie to a werewolf. "Just one thing," I say.

"Anything," he says.

"Do you still want to marry me?"

He blinks at me, and then relief floods his expression. "That will never change," he says. "Even if you become a bear shifter." He ducks when I swat at his head.

HEART of OUTCASTS

read on for a preview of the next *Wolves of Autumn* book

Chapter One

IT WAS PROBABLY A MISTAKE, to go for a run in the woods by myself.

I mean, you always hear stories of lone joggers being abducted, or mugged, or otherwise fucked up, but that's usually in urban parks, not out in the middle of nowhere. You know, where it's quiet and out of sight, but there are actually a lot of people nearby. A lot of potential victims to choose from.

And it's usually women who get attacked, not thirty-three-year-old men who look like they know where they're going. Of course, where I was really going was just *away*. And it's not like I'm totally built or anything, but I'm in decent enough shape I usually get left alone. As long as I don't go running somewhere full of frat boys while looking too gay.

And since I seem to have spent my whole life running away, going for a nice long sprint in the woods along the river seemed like a good idea at the time, when everything else in my life was going to shit.

Maybe I should have seen it coming, should have paid more attention when my path took me past a clearing overlooking the river, littered with empty beer cans. Maybe I should have realized something wasn't right when the birds stopped singing and I heard a growl. But there aren't any wolves left in the Bottomlands, are there?

But no, I ignored it all, just listened to my own pounding feet, my own heavy breaths – getting tired now, time to turn back soon – and tried to forget I have no job to go back to, and probably won't have an apartment much longer, either.

And finally I can't ignore it anymore, because it hits me from behind like a freight train, if trains growl and sweat and have breath that smells like old meat and cheap beer. There's a sharp, searing pain as my ankle twists under me and I fall. And more pain as teeth sink into my neck and claws slash across my back.

I hit the ground yelling, find a rock with one hand, and manage to twist around, to hit back. But my eyes are full of dirt and leaf litter and all I know is that I hit something, something that bleeds all over me and then the weight is gone but I'm still falling. Right into the black inside my head.

"Hey, kid." The voice is deep and smoky, very male, with an undertone I recognize from my own voice, sometimes: self-mocking.

I open my eyes and immediately close them again. The light is too bright, and my head is pounding. Everything hurts, and there's a blank in my memory that I don't want to look at too closely.

"Kid," the voice says again, and now I feel a hand on my shoulder, shaking me gently.

"Go away," I say.

There's a laugh. "Not gonna happen until you sit up and convince me you're okay."

I crack my eyes open again, and it's not bright out at all. In fact, it's not even daylight. There's a big moon overhead, visible between the thick tree branches. Just past full.

And there's a guy crouched next to me, bending over me. A naked guy.

"What the fuck?" I scramble backwards until a tree stops me from going farther.

"Yeah, sorry," he says. "My clothes are about six miles away and you looked hurt."

"Your clothes…" I stop, confused. "What… what happened?" And I don't mean to his clothes. I look at my hands. They're dirty. Filthy, actually, but just normal, human hands. Weren't they…? A flash of memory or hallucination and I see my hands, my fingers curling into claws, my vision going grey, the moon singing to me.

"I was hoping you could tell me," the guy says. He doesn't seem to be the least bit concerned by the fact that he's crouching in front of me completely naked. Like maybe he walks around naked all the time. Is he a nudist?

"I'm Bjarni," he says – like *Barney* but with an extra "y" sound after the "b" that doesn't quite work in English, and pronounced with an accent I can't figure out. "My brother's pack leader in the Bottomlands and the River District."

"He's what?"

He cocks his head at me, sending his dark blond hair sliding across his shoulders. His eyes are pale blue and his skin almost glows in the moonlight. He's the kind of good-looking guy I'd have watched secretly in a bar, but never approached. Too aware of his own good looks. And probably straight anyway.

"You *do* know you're a werewolf?" he says, and I guess I look confused or freaked out, but really I think he's a crazy person, probably escaped from an asylum, running around naked in the woods and howling at the moon. "You *don't* know you're a werewolf," he says. "Fucking hell."

"What do you want?" I push myself more upright, sit against the tree, and glance around for a way out. And I notice my shoes are gone and my bare feet are covered in blood. Dried blood and old cuts, pink and sore, but nearly healed.

I can't breathe right. Another memory or hallucination. Running. But then I'm always running. No shoes and the forest floor feels amazing on my bare feet, even when it hurts. The moon sings to me and I howl back at her. I can't catch my breath.

"Hey, kid. It's okay. You're safe now. Breathe." And the man – Bjarni – is next to me, arm around my shoulders, and how did he move without me seeing? I try not to flinch away, but he must notice my slight movement because he lets go, and instead pushes my head between my drawn-up knees. "Breathe. You're okay."

"What the fuck?" I gasp out.

"Breathe," he says again and there's something almost hypnotic about his voice, something that makes me listen, makes me relax.

When the panic subsides and I can feel air moving in and out of my lungs the way it should, I sit up.

He moves a few steps away and sits down right in a patch of moonlight. He's not super tall, definitely taller than me but then I'm short for a guy at only five seven. But he's totally built. Like every muscle looks sculpted, and it looks like he actually uses them, not like they're just there for show. His torso is sprinkled with freckles, concentrated where the sun would hit him most, and thin pale scars crisscross him like a map. His forearms are covered in tattoos, like some kind of Viking designs, and there are runes across his knuckles. He's got dark blond hair across his chest, thicker down his belly and –

I drag my eyes away from where I was about to look and glance back at his face to find amusement there. He smiles a grin with too many teeth, and fear clutches at my belly. Except the smile creates two dimples, one on each side of his mouth.

"You don't look like a werewolf," I say, because it's the first thing that comes out of my stupid mouth. Because of course he's not a fucking werewolf. I'm not in a horror movie, no matter how shitty I feel.

He laughs. "What does a werewolf look like?"

I shrug and look away, glance down at the holes in the knees of my track pants. I don't remember there being holes. My t-shirt looks even worse, slashed and bloodstained, covered in dirt and who knows what else.

"What the fuck happened to me?" I whisper.

"If I had to guess," Bjarni says. "You went for a run, and someone jumped you. How long have you been out here?"

"I –" I look at my hands, at my wrist. My smartwatch is still there, at least, but it won't turn on when I tap the face. The battery is dead.

"It's Saturday," he says. "When did you go running?"

I think back, try to push past the yawning black that threatens to pull me back in again, into a confusion of running, of hot meat-and-beer breath, of sudden pain. Then I look at him. "It was Wednesday," I say. "Wednesday afternoon."

"Full moon day one," he says. "I think someone decided they wanted to make a new wolf. Thorstein's not going to be fucking happy."

I shake my head. "I was out here three days?" I say. "How? Why don't I remember?"

Bjarni has gotten to his feet and is pacing. He doesn't seem to notice he's barefoot. Or naked. I wonder how it feels to be so confident with your own body. And *I* notice. Or try not to. He's exactly the kind of guy I'd fantasize about, but never go out with. As if a guy that looked like him would even want to go out with me. As if a guy like me would ever have a chance.

"Fuck," he says. Then he turns back to me. "What's your name?"

"I –" It takes me a moment to get my thoughts straight again. "I don't even know you, and you're running around naked in the woods pretending werewolves exist and –"

As I talk, he rolls his eyes, and then suddenly he's *changing*. Like his joints creak and snap and bend wrong and I can only stare as he drops to all fours, sprouts extra hair and a tail, his hands and feet rearrange themselves into paws tipped in dark claws, and his face pushes out into a muzzle full of teeth.

And I fight to keep control of my bladder.

"Let's try this again," he says, words slurring around too many teeth. "My name is Bjarni Thorvaldson, and I'm a werewolf for really, really real. What's your name?"

And the black rushes in to hide the monsters again.

This time I wake up with my head in his lap, and the moon is gone but I don't think we're in the same place. He's human again.

"You're heavier than you look," he says.

I scramble to sit up, trying not to think about the way he smells: musky, warm, wild, very very male. I wish I had something more concealing than track pants on. I'm terrified and turned on at the same time.

He doesn't move, he just watches me with that mocking half-smile on his too-perfect face.

"Where did you park?" he says.

"What?"

"I assume you didn't run all the way from Great Valley, or Riverbend, or wherever you came from."

"Great Valley," I say, without thinking. I clamp my mouth shut.

"Look," he says. "This is all weird and fucked up and your sense of reality has just been seriously shaken. I get that. And I'm sorry. If I could send you back in time to before some shit-stain attacked you, I would."

I stare at him for as long as I can face his intense blue eyes – which turns out to be not very long – then I look down at my hands.

"Justin," I say.

"Come again?"

"My name is Justin. Justin Leyendecker." I look up at him again, and the mocking expression is gone. He looks – almost – kind.

"I came to run out here because… because getting lost in the woods seemed better than facing the complete shit show I've made of my life."

"Getting lost? Were you hoping to die of exposure?" I can't read his voice, but he sounds almost like the idea of just giving up on life isn't entirely foreign.

I shrug. "I don't think I was really thinking at all." I look away again, and realize how dark it is, and how well I can still see.

"I parked by the salmon hatchery," I say.

"Fuck," he says. "There weren't any cars there but mine this afternoon."

I laugh, and it sounds lost and broken, even to my own ears. "So they towed my car," I say. "It was a piece of shit anyway. I'm surprised it stayed running long enough to get me there."

He frowns at me. "You got a place to stay if I drive you back to Great Valley?"

I stare at him. "You don't even have clothes on."

He smirks. "My clothes are in my car. Which is parked by the hatchery, where your car is not. Do you have anywhere to stay?"

I look back at my hands, pick at a loose thread hanging from the shredded knee of my pants. I shake my head. "I imagine my landlord has changed the locks on my apartment by now. He really wants his back rent."

"No family?"

"None that I want anything to do with."

"I get that," he says, and I snap my gaze back up.

"I thought your brother was the, what? Alpha of your pack?"

He snickers. "This isn't a romance novel, sweetheart. He's just the pack leader."

"So *you* have family."

"Some. The worst ones are dead."

"Lucky," I say and he laughs again, but this time it's sharp like broken glass.

"Luck had nothing to do with it," he says, and I shiver at the coldness in his voice.

"Why do you even care?" I say.

"Why do I care about what?" He gets up and starts to walk, and there's not much else I can do but follow him. And try not to stare at the stylized bull tattoo on his back. Or his spectacular naked ass.

"What happens to me?" I say.

He stops and turns and suddenly he's too close, so close I can feel his body heat, the tickle of his breath.

He touches one of the rips in my t-shirt, pushes his finger through until it meets my skin, and I flinch like he's cut me.

"Somebody hurt you," he says. "Somebody made you into a werewolf without asking you, without telling you what it would mean." He stares into my eyes and his are angry, but not at me.

Then as suddenly as he stopped, he's walking again. "I might only be our pack leader's disgraced younger brother, but that shit is *not* okay."

I scramble to catch up, my bare feet seeming to find every broken branch and stone on the forest floor.

"Why can't I remember?" I say. I mean, I really want to keep saying he's crazy and I'm not a werewolf, but I did see him change shape. Unless *I'm* crazy, which would also explain why I hit black whenever I try to think about what happened yesterday, or the day before. Or any time between Wednesday afternoon and an hour ago.

"It's pretty normal," he says. "You'll spend your first few full moons, maybe as long as a year's worth, not remembering much after." He glances back at me. "You'll start to remember more once you develop the beginnings of your wolf shape."

"But I remember… I mean, it's just flashes, but I had claws. Paws. I was running, I was a wolf." I have to trot to catch up again, but the effort helps push back the blackness lurking at the edges of my vision when I think about being a wolf. I'm relieved when we come out of the woods onto a path.

He glances at me again, grins. "Those early months you'll be absolutely convinced you're a full-on wolf," he says. "When you're not busy not forgetting everything."

"So I didn't have claws?"

"Not unless you're a fucking prodigy."

"But you –"

He stops again and I almost walk into him. He steadies me with a hand on each shoulder. "I'm old," he says, then flashes that toothy smile. "Not old in werewolf terms, not really, but I've been a werewolf for eighty-two years, so I've had plenty of time to develop my wolf shape."

"Eighty-two isn't old?" I say. I resist the urge to look him up and down. "You're not that old."

He drops his hands from my shoulders and resumes walking. "I will turn exactly one hundred years old in October," he says. "I've been a werewolf since I was eighteen." He slants a look at me from the corners of his eyes. "Once we become wolves, we also age more slowly."

"So in human terms?"

"Are you sure you want to know all this shit at once? It's a lot to take in."

"How old are you in human terms?" I don't even know why I want to know so badly. It's not like he'd ever go on a date with me.

He shrugs. "Thirty-five. Forty. Something like that. It's not an exact correlation."

"Fuck," I say.

He snorts. We come out of the trees into the parking lot, and sure enough, my car is gone. I mean, I already knew it would be, but actually seeing the parking lot without my shitty little Hyundai in it makes it all more real somehow.

I don't realize I'm falling until Bjarni catches me. He holds me upright, arms strong around me, until I feel steady again.

"When was the last time you ate?" he says, walking me over to lean on the very shiny black Mitsubishi Evo that's the only vehicle in the lot. He fishes under the bumper, comes up with a key fob, then opens the door and starts to put on the clothes waiting on the passenger seat.

I feel oddly sad to see him cover all that beautiful skin and muscle. But wearing clothes, it turns out, doesn't make him any less fine to look at, because his jeans and t-shirt are snug and conform to the shape of his body.

It takes me a while to remember he's asked me a question. "I don't know."

"Here," he says, handing me a granola bar and a bottle of water. "Drink first, then eat. Digesting takes fluids and you don't need to be any more dehydrated than you already are."

Vaguely, I wonder if that's why I didn't piss myself in fear when he turned into a werewolf. Because I didn't have any piss left in me.

He stares at me, one eyebrow raised, until I drink half the bottle of car-warm water and start to peel open the granola bar. Then he points at the passenger door.

"Get in."

"Where are you taking me?" I say, once I'm settled, seat belt strapped across me. And I wonder why I didn't think to ask *before* I got into a stranger's car.

He starts the car, and it gives a well-tuned rumble. He looks over at me. "You really have no one to stay with?"

I shake my head.

He sighs. "Well, Thorstein will want to talk to you, anyway. About whoever attacked you."

"I don't remember who attacked me." I feel cold suddenly, light-headed, and the blackness gathers at the edge of my vision.

And then Bjarni's hand is on the back of my neck, warm and real, and the black fades away.

"It's okay," he says. "You don't have to remember. You just have to tell my brother whatever you can."

I nod. "Is he as scary as you?" I don't know why I say it; it just comes out. I sound like a child, and I definitely don't want to sound like a child in front of Bjarni.

He snorts. "Am I scary?"

I look at the empty granola bar wrapper in my hand so I don't have to look at him. He moves his hand away and my neck feels suddenly cold. Then he puts the car in gear and we're pulling out of the lot.

"A bit," I say. *A lot,* I think.

He bares his teeth at me in a mock snarl and it startles a laugh out of me. "That's better," he says. "And no, Thorstein isn't scary. Most of the time." He shifts gears smoothly and I do *not* look at the muscles sliding across his forearm. "He's a fucking giant, but he's also a marshmallow."

I look back at his face.

"I mean, he *can* be scary," he says. "But mostly he's just too fucking *nice.*"

About the Author

NICO SILVER LIVES like a hermit on the edge of the woods, but haunts used bookstores like a wraith. They fully expected to be found someday as a mummified old corpse crushed under a toppled to-be-read pile, but the rise of e-books has made that somewhat less likely, though the books will always outnumber even the dustbunnies. Nico will read just about anything, including the instructions on the back of medicine bottles, but has a particular fondness for good stories with a hint of magic. They write dark, sexy urban fantasy, and sometimes dream in black and white.